Call of the Sandpiper

Also by Kathryn Haydon

Making the Difference 2017 (Mezzanotte) 978-1544250090
Prognosis Guarded 2018 (Mezzanotte) 978-1720729204

Call of the Sandpiper

Kathryn Haydon

Blue Poppy Publishing

Design and layout by Oliver Tooley

Published by Blue Poppy Publishing,
87 High Street, Ilfracombe, Devon EX34 9HG

ISBN: 978-1-83778-055-6

CHAPTER ONE

His first coffee of the day, hot and strong, exactly as he liked it. Sam tipped back his head and drained his mug with a grunt of satisfaction; just the kick start he needed. Right now, things were shaping up nicely. A new post in rugged North Devon, the lease of an old fisherman's cottage and the sea on his doorstep. What more did he want, apart from maybe someone to share it with? He was in no hurry, though. True, the current gap between girlfriends had been longer than usual, but sooner or later he'd meet someone who took his fancy. He always did. Sam grinned. He liked women and enjoyed their company. The fact he'd not had a relationship that he'd been tempted to make permanent yet was neither here nor there.

Sam dropped his mug in the sink and took the narrow, wooden stairs two at a time, keen to finish sorting out his new abode. A glance from the bedroom window picked up a lone runner. He noted her steady rhythm as she headed towards the wide sweep of beach that was Woolacombe Sands. Hair caught up in a ponytail, her long legs flying, she reminded him of a young gazelle. His eyes followed her slim form appreciatively. An attractive girl, Sam thought idly, and like him, an early riser. The day was young, the morning sky still awash with muted shades of pink and gold – and fresh with promise.

Sam turned from the window and grimaced as he stretched muscles stiff from his recent move. If he hadn't been up until all hours last night, unpacking boxes, running was what he would be doing now. But he'd blithely declined offers of help, managing to relocate from Bristol to Woolacombe single handedly. Stupid, with hindsight. No opportunity to take things easy today, either. He'd agreed to drop in at the surgery later and say hi to a few new colleagues, a promise he regretted. A call to the letting agent's office first, though, to enquire if Rowan Cottage was likely to come on the market anytime soon. He'd felt settled from the moment he stepped over the threshold. The place had what his sister would call a good aura.

Sam chuckled. He didn't know much about auras, but he recognised a welcoming feel that whispered home. After five years of moving from one medical post to another to gain experience, Rowan Cottage felt like the perfect place to put down roots. If there was a chance to purchase the property at the end of his six-month lease period, he was keen to know.

Sam frowned as he headed for the shower. This was the one down-side to the place. For a tall guy, it took a bit of manoeuvring to fit into the shower cubicle. An idea struck; why not enquire after the next-door property whilst he was at it. By the look of the board still up, that cottage was tenanted, too. If by some fluke he could purchase that one, as well, there'd be scope to knock through and join both cottages together - subject to the required planning permission being granted, of course. If not, with some clever reconfiguring, he guessed the bathroom could be enlarged, although it would mean taking a chunk off the second bedroom. Not ideal. He flicked a switch on the stereo and grabbed a towel. Then hastily lowered the volume as the old stone walls reverberated to the heady beat of rock music.

The sea shimmered in the sunlight, looking as smooth as a mill pond. It was an ebb tide, and the waves rippled gently as the water receded. Poppy ran by the shoreline, taking lungfuls of the fresh, salty air, glad she'd made the effort to rise early. Her trainer clad feet drummed a rhythm as she quickly found her stride. The beach was hers this morning, and she revelled in the flat, wide-open space. Her only companions were the gulls that swooped and soared overhead. At length, she circled and retraced her steps on the hard packed, damp sand. Already she felt better, even if there wasn't enough time to go far. Thankfully, the fatigue that once dogged her was becoming a distant memory. If only she had realised earlier that something was amiss. Fine nurse she was!

Yet, in fairness, her symptoms had been subtle to begin with, only too easy to ignore. No wonder her diagnosis had taken a while.

Back in Lantern Lane once more, Poppy slowed her pace to stare at the neat, white-washed cottage that never failed to draw her eye. The jaunty, burnt orange blinds were drawn at the upstairs windows today, meaning only one thing. Another tenant must have moved in. Only a few days ago the cottage had stood empty, she was sure of it. Gracious, she passed the place often enough to notice any changes. Poppy sighed, wondering if she would ever achieve her long-held dream of buying Rowan Cottage. Apart from doing well in her profession, this was her one ambition. She had such precious memories of childhood holidays spent under its eaves with her beloved gran.

Acutely conscious of her gran's anguish when age and failing health forced a move closer to family in Exeter, Poppy's memories were bitter sweet. The little stone cottage had been sold to fund the purchase of a soulless, modern flat. Her gran had never really settled there. Aged twelve, Poppy had promised to buy back the quirky North Devon cottage 'as soon as she was grown up and had saved enough money.' Well, she was all grown up now, even if not much money had been saved. However, if the bank granted her a mortgage, hopefully she could scrape together a small deposit. Her first proper home, and here in her favourite place, Woolacombe! A fizz of excitement rippled down her spine.

Her euphoria short lived, Poppy sighed again. Life had had its challenges over the past few years. The ugly break-up that had followed two miscarriages were big events in anyone's book. The loss of her mum when she was barely twenty had been the catalyst that made her rush headlong into an unsuitable relationship, Poppy saw with hindsight. Mark was a smooth-talking charmer who'd hidden his playboy side well.

She brushed away a tear. Oh, she'd been so naïve back then. However, those times were best not dwelt on – even if they did come back to haunt her on occasion. Cheers to the lucky break she'd had about four months ago, after spotting an advert for the post of practice nurse at Bramblewood Surgery in Woolacombe. Appointed swiftly, Poppy had been delighted to relocate from Bristol to North Devon.

To date, she loved her new post, and was living her best life here in Woolacombe. However, if she was able to buy Rowan Cottage in the near future it would make things perfect. Rumour had it among the locals that the owner wanted to sell. Nothing was confirmed and no sale board up yet, but it wouldn't hurt to make enquiries with the letting agent. At the very least she could state her interest. Regrettably, a long-term lease wasn't an option, the rent was too high. Poppy had explored that possibility already. But summer was in its first flush. Whoever had moved in was likely to be just another holiday maker, gone in a week or two and no threat to her long-term plans. She studied the front and wondered, not for the first time, what the old place looked like inside these days.

Poppy heard sounds. She listened, detecting the muffled beat of rock music. Nice! In the right mood she didn't mind a bit of rock herself. Instinctively, she let her body sway to the rhythm. Suddenly one of the upstairs blinds shot up to reveal a toned, male torso, navy bath towel wound tightly round his waist. The man's lightly tanned skin gleamed as he threw open the window, his short dark hair sticking up in spikes, obviously wet from a shower. The low sills exposed the jut of his hips. Yikes, he was looking straight at her! Poppy swallowed. She felt her face heat and it was nothing to do with running. Quickly, she reminded herself of all the reasons why men were off the agenda, even handsome dudes like this one. Valid reasons, each and every one of them.

Hastily, Poppy averted her gaze and ran on, not wishing to be caught staring. She increased her pace and soon she had left Lantern Lane behind. She continued Continuing to push herself, navigating Woolacombe' s winding streets and back roads until she reached her apartment block. She let herself into the entrance hall and stood for a moment, panting hard as she leant against the banister rail for support.

Once she had her breath back, Poppy mounted the three flights of linoleum covered stairs to her attic flat. Situated at the top of the tall building, the only real plus point was the view. Hidden away in a narrow side alley it had been all she could find at short notice in an area within walking distance of Bramblewood Surgery. The poky flat was only a stop gap, though; functional and cheap until she could afford to move again. It hardly mattered that the place wasn't very homey, especially if the next move took her to Rowan Cottage. She unlaced her trainers, peeled off her running gear and jumped into the shower. And tried to block out images of a fit, dark-haired guy staring straight at her from the cottage window!

It was later than she had realised. No time to linger under jets of warm water and day dream, merely a quick soap, rinse and out. Due to hold a diabetic clinic that morning, Poppy knew she needed to be focussed. Yesterday, when she had checked her patient list, the session promised to be a busy one. All appointment slots had been taken. However, busy was the way she liked things. It was her preferred state with no time to dwell on the past. These days love didn't feature in her life. She was a career girl now. Heavens, she'd tried romance once and look how badly that had turned out. How many times was a girl supposed to let her heart get broken? Quite simply, she wasn't a good picker of men. Lessons had been learnt and Poppy Lambert didn't intend to fall in love with a guy ever again. The pain when things fell apart was not worth it.

Dry now, Poppy pulled on a pair of comfy, denim jeans and a floral, cotton top. Then, she twisted her hair into a neat coil and applied a light spritz of body spray, followed by a dab of lip gloss. Done! Neatly ironed, her navy nurse's uniform lay folded and ready to slip into her bag. Julia, the Practice Manager preferred the nursing staff to change into uniform at work – which was fine by Poppy. After a drink of orange juice, she was ready to go. Poppy grabbed a banana to eat en route, humming as she reached for her bag. Belatedly, she realised she was picking up on the beat she'd heard emanating from Rowan Cottage.

From Bramblewood Surgery it was an easy stroll to the town centre. Heading off En route to work, a short detour brought Poppy to the letting agent's office. Dimly, she recollected the place had earlier opening hours mid-week. All was quiet inside, and the lighting appeared dim, not switched on fully. Had she made a mistake? There was only one way to find out. She pushed resolutely on the door.

The door stuck at first. She redoubled her efforts, with the result that it suddenly gave way. Almost catapulted into the room, Poppy found herself face to face with the senior agent, Mr Kerslake. A man she guessed to be in his sixties, he peered at her disapprovingly over the top of a pair of horn-rimmed spectacles. The scrutiny made her feel nervous. After a brief good morning, Poppy went straight to the point, querying the rumour about the owner of Rowan Cottage being poised to put the property on the market. There was a brief silence during which she mentally crossed her fingers while awaiting his reply.

"I don't know, young lady." Mr Kerslake cleared his throat. "We haven't heard anything concrete. I'll make enquiries, but the landlord is away at present. Might take a while to get hold of him. As it happens, you're not the first person to show an interest in the property."

"Oh?" Poppy's heart skipped a beat. "Who else is interested?"

"Obviously, I can't divulge that information," the agent pursed his lips, "but I will say it's a cash buyer. You're aware, I suppose, that Rowan Cottage – pretty enough from the road, I grant you - would need money spent on it after purchase? If, indeed, it does come up for sale. A full structural survey would be advised in view of the property's age."

"Oh." Poppy said again, feeling her cheeks flame, "Well, yes, of course."

Infuriating man! How dare he make assumptions about her financial status. It wasn't his business what she may or may not be able to afford.

If truth be told, Poppy hadn't factored in the cost of upgrading the cottage after purchase. Ditto, buying furniture: but she wasn't going to admit that to Mr Kerslake. Surely the place couldn't be too badly in need of attention. After all, it was rented, and there were rules and regulations that landlords had to comply with. The agent declined her offer to leave a contact number, and advised her to drop by 'in a week or two when he may have heard something.' Crestfallen, Poppy had no option but to nod politely and leave.

She tried not to feel too dejected as she walked away. It seemed the purchase of Rowan Cottage may not be as straightforward as she had hoped. Perhaps she'd been naïve to imagine otherwise. There was more to buying a property than saving enough money and waiting for the current owner to be ready to sell. Certainly, Poppy hadn't factored in another interested buyer. That was a blow. 'I'm trying, Gran. Honestly, I'm trying,' she whispered to herself. 'I'll get your cottage back, you'll see.' However, her gran would never know, one way or the other. The elderly lady had died only eighteen months after a reluctant move to Exeter. Died from a broken heart, her mum used to say. A wash of loneliness hit Poppy as she reached the surgery premises. Granny Flo had been her ally during hard times, and she still missed her.

Poppy threw herself into work with the result that the morning session sped by. Dietary advice, taking routine bloods and blood pressure, checking patients' feet for any signs of diabetic neuropathy, etc., all took time. She thrived on the buzz it gave her. People varied with regards to how they coped with long term, chronic disease. Younger patients were never very good at following rules. It was the nature of youth. They tended to be less compliant, more likely to rail against the fates – resulting in more crises until they realised quality of life really was better if they heeded medical advice. Poppy acknowledged that, when it came to living a normal life, dietary constraints were hard for everyone. These days she could empathise with her patients better than they realised.

Lunchtime arrived, a welcome respite. She reached for her bag, ready to nip out and grab a soup from a nearby café she'd discovered. Today she fancied a change from her usual cheese and tomato sandwiches, so hadn't brought a packed lunch with her. If the soup happened to be carrot and coriander, her favourite, that would be a bonus. The view outside Poppy's window was inviting. She looked forward to a stroll in the fresh air.

As Poppy headed towards the main entrance she felt a tap on the shoulder from Julia, the Practice Manager. Could she please join everyone in the staff room to meet the new doctor. Had his arrival been mentioned before? Julia was meticulous, so the likelihood was yes. No doubt there'd been a 'round robin' email to inform everyone. However, Poppy's morning session had been far too busy to catch up on her latest messages. Ah well, that was one memo she could delete. Soon she would meet the man himself.

Poppy gave a tut of irritation on hearing Julia announce gaily that no one need worry about missing lunch, there were sandwiches and nibbles aplenty laid out. It would be a miracle if there was much on offer that she'd be able to eat!

Hopefully, the rather battered apple she kept forgetting about was still rolling around in her locker. That would have to suffice. Otherwise, she would have to go hungry. It was a timely reminder that she really must stock up on snacks.

"Ah Poppy, wait a sec." Julia beamed as she shepherded her into the staff room. "Before you grab a plate and get yourself some food, let me introduce Dr Sam Brocklehurst. Sam – Poppy. You'll be working together a lot, I imagine."

A tall man to Julia's left stepped forward, hand outstretched. Heavens, the guy was a hunk! Despite being off men, a girl would have to be anaesthetised not to react to a drop-dead gorgeous specimen like this one. Poppy returned his grin with a tentative smile.

"Hello there, Poppy, pleased to meet you." Her hand firmly grasped Poppy had to crane her neck to look up at him. Wow, the guy must be well over six foot tall! Warm brown eyes twinkled down at her. "You must be one of our practice nurses, right?"

"Right." Despite herself, Poppy's smile widened. She'd always been a sucker for a pair of twinkly brown eyes and crinkly, dark hair. Not that it had ever got her anywhere, she reminded herself hastily. "I only started at Bramblewood a couple of months ago myself."

"Great, we're in it together, then." Sam chuckled as he released her hand. "I like that, another newbie. And I hope everyone likes these," he indicated a laden plate being brought in by one of the medical secretaries, "Danish pastries, my treat!" His gaze swung back to Poppy. "Please go first, Poppy."

This was awkward. She would have to refuse. The question was, refuse and explain or refuse and let this new doc draw his own conclusions? Poppy eyed the plate wistfully. For a moment she nearly took a pastry, regardless. They certainly looked tempting.

There was always the option to wrap it in a napkin, ready to ditch later if she couldn't find anyone to pass it onto. Then common sense prevailed. Heck, she was done with feeling embarrassed. No, it had to be a straight refusal. Folk declined cake for all sorts of reasons. Let him think it was because she was figure conscious and forever on a diet. What did she care what conclusion the new doc drew. Besides, what business did he have trying to tempt them all with sweet treats; surely, he could have found healthier titbits to offer.

"Hmm, they do look delicious." She shook her head decisively. "Thanks, but not for me. I'm afraid I don't do cakes."

"No problem." Unperturbed, Sam winked. "All the more for the rest of us."

Someone tapped him on the arm, and he turned, leaving Poppy free to wander across to the buffet table. She eyed the contents warily.

A few of her colleagues looked mildly curious, but no one said anything. There were no 'just one won't hurt' comments, even if they did think she was one of those reed thin control freaks who counted every calorie. Whatever; It had taken strict discipline to get herself this far and she knew that just one would hurt. Yet it was a nuisance having to be constantly on guard where food was concerned. Especially nice food! The Danish pastries had made her mouth water.

Poppy checked out the rest of the spread laid out for the staff to help themselves. As expected, she was faced with the usual array of sandwiches, mini quiches, sausage rolls and little bowls of crisps nestling in between. The crisps had been emptied from their packets which made it impossible to check the list of ingredients. They might be safe for her to eat, but the risk posed was too great if they were not. Frustrated, her spirits plummeted.

This was a medical practice, for heavens' sake. Surely it wasn't beyond the ability of management to cater for staff with special dietary needs, otherwise it was a bit rich to lecture patients about any lack of compliancy on their part. Things needed to change. Poppy debated the wisdom of seeking out Julia for a quiet word later. It had been a steep learning curve when she went gluten free. Although her confidence had grown it still felt like a big deal explaining what being gluten intolerant meant to people.

She shook her head, and politely declined the plate of sausage rolls someone waived in her direction. Wait, though – Eureka! She spied a dish of grapes and melon slices. Poppy slid the fruit onto her plate, found a spare seat and tried to ignore her stomach rumbling. This was another uncomfortable reminder to carry a few gluten-free nibbles in her bag.

Sam took a seat himself and addressed the assembled group.

"Thanks for giving up your lunchtime today, folks. I know time is tight," his voice was deep and authoritative as he glanced around the room, "so, I'll keep it brief."

"It's great to meet everyone, at least, those of you here now. And I look forward to meeting the others in due course. OK, I've been invited to drop in and share a bit about myself and what brought me to North Devon. So, here it is, a potted history. As you'll glean, I've been something of a rolling stone – though I plan to change all that."

A hush fell on the room. Poppy realised what a wealth of experience Sam brought as she listened to him detail his professional journey. He certainly hadn't been idle in the preceding years, including an eighteen-month stint spent overseas with an emergency medical aid organisation. On return to the UK, he'd built on this experience and taken several hospital posts, moving regularly as opportunities arose to further his career.

He claimed to enjoy both A&E and surgery, initially unsure which specialty to opt for.

Sam spoke eloquently. Self-assured, he held the room. A glance was enough to tell Poppy that all the females present were smitten. Despite his relaxed posture, Poppy detected a restless energy about him as though he disliked being confined. Dr Sam Brocklehurst reminded her of a caged tiger with a huge zest for life. She listened, hearing how he had been poised for a hospital career when a chance locum post led him to trial general practice – and realise he had found his niche.

"I like the patient interaction and continuity afforded by general practice. It's good to get to know families. Much as I enjoyed surgery, I decided I preferred my patients awake rather than asleep." His brown eyes twinkled. "I guess I found my calling, primary care, and I look forward to joining the team at Bramblewood."

There was a general murmur of approval. Poppy's attention drifted to Sam's darkly handsome profile. He had the sort of looks that were referred to as rugged, like the wild North Devon coastline. Her lip curled; wearing hip hugging denims and a plain, open-necked rugby shirt, he certainly hadn't dressed up to meet them today. Then she took a closer look. There was something familiar about the set of his jaw and that coal black hair ...

Poppy wondered where she had seen him before. Dr Sam Brocklehurst was not the kind of guy a girl easily forgot. However hard she wracked her brains she couldn't think where it might have been. A dig in the ribs from her colleague, Laura, helped to refocus Poppy's attention. Sam had paused, and thrown open the floor for questions.

"Do you have an area of special interest, Dr Brocklehurst?" Laura's hesitant voice broke the silence. "I mean, some of the other docs here do and I wondered if …"

"Ah, good question – Laura, isn't it?" He smiled encouragingly. "And, by the way, it's Sam, everyone. I don't stand on formality. Yes, I have a special interest in chronic disease. As I'm sure you're all aware, chronic disease has a big impact on quality of life. I'm a firm believer in preventative medicine, keeping the herd healthy, if you like." He frowned. "With NHS resources ever more stretched, we face challenging times. We must educate our patients, not simply be content to diagnose and prescribe."

Ah, so he'd remembered Laura's name. Proof she wasn't merely another nurse to him, but a person he had taken notice of. Poppy was impressed. Unbidden, she wondered if he would remember her name without a prompt. Not, of course, that it mattered either way, she reasoned swiftly. Poppy felt her cheeks grow hot, thankful that the new doc wasn't a mind reader. At least, she certainly hoped he wasn't as his laser-like gaze swept over her. Yet he'd offered them all doughnuts – how health conscious was that! Although, judging by his physique, sweet treats were not his regular diet.

Hastily, Poppy tried to focus on the content of Sam's talk rather than the toned muscles of his body. She must stop wondering what he would look like in a suit or, indeed, if he ever wore one. Perhaps, like some modern medics, he didn't. Today he had dropped in to say hi, so casual dress was fine.

Sam wasn't giving anything away on the personal front, she noted. Was he single? He hadn't mentioned a partner, but a good-looking guy like Dr Sam Brocklehurst had to be either married or have a string of lovelies in tow. Probably the last, Poppy reckoned, pursing her lips. She knew his type and they were best avoided.

"Sam has agreed to be our doctor representative for future PPG meetings." Julia broke in, beaming. "As some of you know, Andrew is stepping down. Early days but, unlike some practices, our Patient Participation Group is thriving."

There were nods of approval.

"At any rate," Julia continued, "the educational talks we put on have been well attended. Poppy, you've volunteered as well. Thank you, both. I'm usually present, too. It's easier if I bring you both up to speed with all PPG related things then. The next scheduled meeting is Wednesday week at 7pm, if this isn't too short notice."

Poppy gaped. True, she had volunteered to step in and relieve Laura, who had young children and didn't find it easy to stay on in the evening after a working day. Although the PPG only met once every couple of months, it was an extra commitment outside of normal surgery hours. Poppy's offer had been made when she thought the PPG would continue to be led by Bramblewood's senior medical partner, the gruff Dr Andrew Doyle. She would have thought twice had she realised a sexy, new doc would be taking his place.

"Excellent." Sam's dark eyes sought her out across the room, sending a delicious tingle down her spine. "I look forward to liaising with you, Poppy. And Wednesday is fine, Julia."

Dr Sam Brocklehurst was too charismatic for his own good – and hers, Poppy thought wryly as she stood to fetch a glass of iced water. She realised that Julia was looking at her, waiting for a response regarding next Wednesday evening's meeting. Poppy gave a careful smile. Hopefully, no one else would guess at her inner turmoil.

"Yes, I'll be there." She cleared her throat. "We have a late finishing clinic that day. I guess it'll be easier if I stay on afterwards, instead of going home and coming back again."

"Grand." Julia beamed again. "A sensible idea, Poppy. That's what Laura usually did, too, didn't you, Laura."

Sam grinned, too. Steadfastly, Poppy tried to ignore him.

CHAPTER TWO

Sam had seen Poppy before, he was certain of it. He never forgot a face. The question was where. Sam had no idea. But the moment he'd been introduced to the slim, young nurse with the light brown hair and long lashed, luminous grey eyes there'd been a jolt of recognition. A pleasurable one. The practice nurse was beautiful in an ethereal kind of way, though he would bet money on the fact that she wasn't aware of it. Maybe she hadn't had enough people in her life telling her just how lovely she was, Sam thought, a crime in his book. Whenever he partnered an attractive woman, he made damn sure to compliment her.

Right now, Poppy had the look of a startled fawn in need of protection. Protection from what, Sam couldn't say, yet there was a vulnerability about her. He sensed it. And this air of vulnerability had triggered what an ex-girlfriend had termed his alpha male response, the urge to defend. Sam was well aware that she had been thrown to discover they would be working together on the PPG. Anxious rather than displeased, but it concerned him none the less. It could be useful to find out her backstory. Sam wasn't used to colleagues feeling tense around him, especially female ones. The knowledge that Poppy felt unsettled didn't sit well with him. Wherever he worked, he liked a happy team.

He noticed Poppy wasn't eating much, having ignored everything bar the fruit on offer. What was that all about? In his experience, staff were only too pleased to have grub laid on at lunchtime meetings; being fed at work events definitely wasn't a given. He knew Poppy had been tempted by the Danish pastries, so why hadn't she taken one – unless she couldn't for some reason? Then why not opt for something else, like a sandwich? Sam narrowed his eyes, remembering how she'd studied everything on the table, then gripped her plate and moved on. This was someone who couldn't eat what was on offer, not wouldn't eat it.

As a doctor it was his job to be observant and her fleeting expression of regret hadn't gone unnoticed when confronted by the plate of Danish pastries. Of course, the answer was obvious. Poppy must have a food intolerance. He'd put money on it being gluten.

Vaguely, Sam was aware of another question being posed by someone who'd just entered the room. Swiftly, he smiled and refocussed. Yes, he would be doing the same hours as his predecessor, plus picking up a regular session or two at the local hospital's A&E department. To keep him on his toes, he added with a grin. A lull followed the responding laughter. No more questions; thankfully, it looked like he was done.

"Thanks for bearing with me, folks." He threw his new colleagues another grin. "I guess that concludes it for this afternoon. I'll leave you to your lunch and look forward to joining you all officially on Monday. Right now, I plan to make the most of this glorious sunshine."

"Thanks for dropping in, Sam." Nick Westcott, the other senior partner, rose to shake his hand. "Welcome aboard! OK, if I'm not mistaken, that's the sound of a trolley on the way with more refreshments. You'll stay for a coffee?"

"Sorry, Nick, love to but I must shoot." The aroma of fresh coffee was inviting but Sam declined.

He felt wired enough. His obligation over, time was tight. As promised, he had dropped into Bramblewood Surgery to meet everyone. Now he felt justified in claiming the rest of the day as his own. The great outdoors beckoned, making Sam impatient to finish sorting Rowan Cottage and don his running gear. He itched for a proper run and the three-mile stretch of Woolacombe Sands was ideal. He wanted to be down there, revelling in the adrenaline surge as, buffeted by the brisk sea breeze, he jogged by the shoreline.

On a whim Sam decided he'd explore the possibility of buying a boat, too. Why not, when you lived by the coast - the perfect location! It had been a while, but he was confident he hadn't lost the knack of sailing. As a lad, he had gone sailing regularly with a curmudgeonly old uncle and loved it. His brothers hadn't been as keen, Sam recalled. Their loss because he and his bachelor uncle had developed quite a rapport.

A glimpse of the sea that morning had whetted Sam's appetite for the nautical life. The water had looked inviting, with enough of a stiff off- shore breeze to catch the sail of a yacht on the horizon, making it billow as it flew along. To be out in the elements, feeling his boat pitch and toss beneath him as it rode the waves, the salty spray on his face – Sam couldn't wait! He paused, standing back as Julia moved ahead to show him out. Not that he needed to be shown out, he could find his own way well enough, but it seemed courteous to let the Practice Manager escort him. He almost bumped into her as she stopped abruptly.

"Oh, I nearly forgot." Julia looked hopeful. "Did I mention our PPG hosts regular educational talks for patients? I did?

Good, because as it happens the next one is scheduled for this Saturday morning, 10.00a.m. until 12noon. A big ask to attend, so don't worry if it's too short notice, Sam. Marvellous if you could look in, though."

"Where do you hold these events?" Sam frowned, mentally reviewing his plans for the weekend. This was one invite he might need to skip. "Who do you have speaking?"

"We use one of the large upstairs rooms of the house opposite, above the dental surgery. In fact, the building belongs to Bramblewood. The Practice rents it out, a beneficial arrangement for all concerned. We have a community dietician booked to give an overview on healthy eating, plus special diets, and allergies, etc. Followed by," she paused, "ah, yes, a word on dairy intolerance from a patient's perspective. We call it the lived experience slot."

"Hmm." Sam liked the sound of that. "Sounds promising. It is short notice, though. I won't commit to anything, Julia, but I'll try and put my nose round the door towards the end. Drop in for the last twenty minutes to say hi. How would that be?"

"Excellent," Julia nodded as she led him towards the main entrance, "that would be very well received. It's Andrew's last session. He'll be able to do an official hand over."

Outside once more, Sam sucked in a lungful of balmy air whilst he stood a moment to survey the scene. Bathed in sunshine, the ivy-clad, red brick building that was Bramblewood looked imposing. Victorian, if he had to guess an era. He could picture it in earlier times, an upstairs, downstairs sort of place, probably the home of some wealthy North Devon family with servants. Whatever its history, the change whenever it had happened was positive. In his opinion, anyway. He was all for echoey old buildings being put to a useful purpose. In its latest incarnation, the large, high-ceilinged, old house lent itself well to a medical practice.

He strolled up the drive to the tarmac parking area behind, catching a glimpse of an overgrown walled garden. Facing south, it had to be a real sun trap. Sam guessed this must belong to the Surgery, too, and made a mental note to enquire. A pity it was so neglected. Spruced up, it would make an ideal spot for staff to sit out with their lunchtime sandwiches. Also, young mums could wander round with fractious toddlers when waiting time for appointments felt overly long. However, apart from a few small fruit trees, plus an attractive creeper of some description, the garden was a tangle of undergrowth. Sam's last post had been in the dust and grime of an inner city, the sort of area where folk were desperate for a green space. To have somewhere like this to enjoy would have been a godsend.

He kicked at a loose stone and grimaced. Perhaps things were viewed differently when you lived in a rural idyll. A prime case of folk not valuing what was under their nose.

It happened often enough. A shame, but there was precious little Sam could do about it. He reached his aged car, zapped the lock and folded his tall frame swiftly into the driver's seat. Time to chill. He would consider the neglected walled garden after he took up post officially. This afternoon there were more pressing matters to attend to.

It was early evening by the time he was ready to dig out his running gear. Rowan Cottage had taken longer than expected to make tidy. Sam set off at a jog. Soon he'd left

Lantern Lane, jogging down the pebble strewn track that was a shortcut to the beach. He sniffed the air, scenting rain on the way. Down on the hard packed sand, he quickly found his stride. There was no cornflower blue sky now. The weather had changed. Low cloud scudded the horizon, dark and threatening, but hopefully it would stay dry for a few hours yet. The water was choppy with quite a swell. Out to sea white horses were visible. Despite a pale sun trying valiantly to shine, the wind had picked up, gusting across the beach.

Several little family groups, holiday makers by the look of it, glanced anxiously at the scudding, grey clouds as they gathered up their belongings. The beach was emptying fast. Only a few hardy surfers in wet suits were in the water now, staying within the green flag area as they paddled to catch the next big roller. And those rollers were getting bigger!

Sam increased his speed as he ran along the shoreline. He kept close but not too close to the water's edge, mindful of the waves' powerful surge. The tide came in swiftly on the flat sands. Suddenly, there ahead of him, he spied a toddler a worrying distance away from his family group. The small boy had wandered dangerously close to the angry, foaming water. Sam shouted a warning, but his voice was drowned out by the roar of the sea and the raucous cry of the gulls. As the inevitable happened Sam felt like he was watching a film in slow motion. Grimly, he raced into the rushing waves.

Bowled over by a large breaker, the child had been dragged under and pulled further out to sea as the wave receded. Although Woolacombe Bay was patrolled regularly by lifeguards, it was past five o'clock and their stand stood empty. Speed was of the essence. It took much less time to drown than most people realised. Sam took a deep breath and dived below the surface, desperate to locate the child. Dimly aware of another runner behind him, also dashing into the shallows, he prayed one of them would get lucky and spot the boy. He surfaced briefly and cast around for any sign of the toddler. Nothing! The boy had gone.

Surely only seconds had elapsed, but each second counted. Damn it, where was the tot? The undertow as the wave pulled back, strong today, could have sucked the little lad out quite a way. What the hell had the parents been thinking of, taking their eyes off a child as young as this one on an open beach! Some folk had no common sense. However, there was no room for emotion; nothing to gain by letting anger get the better of him. Right now, Sam needed all his energy for the rescue. And, dammit, he was going to rescue this boy!

He scanned the surface, and spied a flash of red some distance out. The boy had worn a red jumper! He dived again; swimming underwater, he reached out to grab the flash of red clothing. Then surfaced, pulling the limp little body back towards the shore, careful to lift the child's face clear of the water. There was a blue tinge around the tot's lips and an ominous stillness. Swiftly, Sam tilted the toddler's head, commencing rescue breaths even as he dragged the tot to the shore. There was someone else in the water nearby, a woman. Of course, it must be the other runner keen to assist. Great, a second pair of hands! She called out something as she waded through the surf towards him. Hell, he didn't have time to ask her to repeat it. His whole focus needed to be on the boy.

"Get help." He yelled before resuming the rescue breaths. "Ambulance!"

They were on the beach again now. The female turned away to reach into the pocket of her discarded jacket. Good, Sam thought, as without hesitation she dialled 999. Someone present who was useful. He was aware of her stating their location as she requested the emergency services. Without expert backup, and soon, there was a limit to the success of lone resuscitation measures.

"On its way." Her voice was oddly familiar. "I'll stay on the line to guide the crew in."

Sam lay the toddler flat on the sand, poised to commence full resuscitation. Suddenly there was a choking sound as the little boy gagged and vomited. Sam rolled him expertly onto his side and placed him in the recovery position. A coughing spasm, then a pair of frightened blue eyes flickered open, followed by a frightened wail. Never had the sound of a child's crying been so welcome! It had been a close call and the danger wasn't over yet.

"Hey, little man." Sam grinned with relief. "You gave us quite a scare! But you're going to be fine. Look, here comes your mum."

"Oh, Rupert, Rupert, we told you not to wander off!" Wailing louder than her child, the woman dashed across the sand, pushing at Sam in her desperation to reach her little boy.

"A moment, please." His solid form blocked her. "Your son nearly drowned. I need to finish checking him over."

In her anguish the woman began to pummel Sam's chest.

"It's OK, this man is a doctor. Dr Sam Brocklehurst from Bramblewood Surgery. Please give him space to finish examining your little boy before you hold him." Poppy's voice was calm as she covered Rupert with her discarded jacket. "He won't take a moment, but it's important."

She placed her free arm round the woman's shoulders and continued, "I promise you your son is in safe hands. An ambulance is on its way. See, I'm on the 'phone to them now," she indicated her mobile, "and you'll be able to travel to hospital with him."

Poppy? What was Poppy doing here? Sam swung round to look at her properly, and gaped in astonishment. She looked almost as wet as he was. She must have been the other runner, dashing into the sea behind him. Then it hit him. Of course, she was also the lone runner he had seen from the window of Rowan Cottage that first morning.

"Thought you said he's fine now. Bit of an overkill being carted off in an ambulance then, isn't it?" Jaw thrust forward the burly figure of Rupert's father joined the group. "Why can't you stay put when you're told, you little devil? See all the fuss you've caused."

"Here you are, mum, have a cuddle." Sam scooped up the boy and passed him to his mother. He faced the other man, careful to keep his tone level and not wince at the choice of words used by the boy's father. "Rupert was unconscious when I reached him, sir. He had stopped breathing and needed help to restart." Sam paused to allow the gravity of the situation to sink in. "Yes, he seems recovered, but I'm afraid the risk remains. There's something called secondary drowning that can develop later, affecting the lungs. It's a type of pneumonia and the onset is sudden, the body's reaction to water having been inhaled. Your son needs urgent hospital assessment and observation for a period."

"Well, if you'd explained that in the first place ... " Rupert's father blustered, obviously not prepared to back down easily. However, his tone was slightly less belligerent as he nodded agreement. "OK, Lynne, I suppose you'd better go with him," he addressed his wife, "and I'll follow in the car with the other kids." He uttered an expletive. "Little tyke. Fine start to the holiday this is."

Other kids, what other kids? Sam's head snapped up. What the hell were they up to while all the attention was on their baby brother? Swiftly, he glanced past Rupert's parents. Confronted by two saucer eyed children hovering nearby, he let out a breath and threw them a wink. At least they hadn't become casualties of the sea, as well. It wasn't unknown for such things to happen whilst everyone's attention was on the first victim. Sam grimaced. Thankfully, he could delete the image of a second drama unfolding while the adults were still caught up with the first. He'd heard the parents of young children often say they could do with a sheepdog to keep everyone together. Now he understood the reason why; keeping track of tots, indeed, children in general, must be a veritable nightmare.

"I hear the ambulance." Poppy listened, still holding her mobile. "Yes, that's definitely a siren." She looked at Rupert's father. "We need a bit of help, please. I gave them a detailed description of our whereabouts, but if you could walk on up the beach and wave, please, that would be great. You're taller than me, so they'll spot you better." She pointed to an area on the cliffs where it was just possible to see vehicles parked. "The ambulance will stop up there, I expect. The crew will meet us down on the sand via that rocky cliff path."

Even as they looked the flashing blue lights of an emergency vehicle hove into view.

"Great, let's walk to meet them. Mum, are you OK with Rupert?" Aware that Poppy was trying to make Rupert's father feel more in control of the situation by giving him a task, Sam also knew he didn't want to remain in proximity with this man for much longer.

Damn it, they'd plucked his son from the jaws of an angry sea! How hard was it to grasp the implications? Sam strode ahead as two paramedics arrived at a jog. He gave the crew a concise update, happy to leave Rupert in their care now. He and Poppy had done all they could, it was time to go home. He'd ring the hospital later for news of the lad's progress.

"Cold?" His attention switched to Poppy as he noticed her shiver – whether from shock or the drenching she had taken, he wasn't sure.

Likely to be a bit of both, Sam suspected, hurrying her up the beach. The brisk wind had cooled the June evening by several degrees, and a fine drizzle was beginning to fall. The beach appeared to be deserted. Even the hardy surfers had packed up and gone home now. He remembered that Rupert was still wrapped in Poppy's tracksuit jacket. No one had thought to remove it when the crew proffered blankets. She wore only a skimpy pair of shorts and a vest top, both clinging damply to her svelte body in the cool evening air. Studiously, he averted his eyes from the outline of her pert breasts.

"N – no, I'm f- fine." Despite her best efforts, Poppy couldn't stop her teeth from chattering. There were goose bumps on her bare arms. "Well, a bit c-cold, but I'll be f – fine once I'm home."

Sam uttered an expletive. No way was he going to allow Poppy to walk back alone to where ever she lived.

"I've a better idea." He grabbed her hand to pull her along with him. "You're coming back to my place. It's not far, I'm renting one of those old fishermen's cottages in Lantern Lane. You need dry clothes and a hot drink, stat., no argument."

"Oh, you've no need to w … "

Her protestations ignored Sam led Poppy in the direction of Rowan Cottage. Soon they were at the old, oak front door. He heard a stifled sob as, briefly, he let go of her hand to delve for the key he'd left hidden under a flowerpot. Puzzled, he swung round, alarmed to see that despite their brisk pace back her face was ashen. Hell, what was wrong?

"Hey, come on, it's OK." He propelled her through the door, and steered her towards the warmest room, the kitchen. "Sit there and wait a mo."

He pushed her down in a comfy armchair by the Aga, then flicked a switch on the kettle and went in search of a blanket. On his return Sam found Poppy sobbing in earnest. Clearly, something was amiss, yet he had no idea what. However, the questions could wait awhile. Ten minutes later, both sipping mugs of hot, sweet tea, Sam was relieved to see Poppy's colour return. Bar the odd hiccough, her sobbing had stopped, although she still hadn't said anything apart from a mumbled thanks for the hot drink. The stricken look remained as Sam watched her.

"Poppy," he spoke gently, "what gives? Is it that tot nearly drowning, or something else? And don't tell me nothing because I won't buy it."

She bit her lip, and remained quiet. Sam wondered if she was embarrassed or weighing up how much to say. Perhaps she didn't trust him enough to share deep emotions.

"Listen, you don't have to ... " He leant back to give the impression of affording her space, but found himself interrupted.

"Th– this is where my gran lived." Knuckles white, Poppy gripped her mug. "I spent amazing holidays here as a child. Gran and I were really close. She only moved when she became too frail to stay here on her own. But she hated leaving. Apart from tonight, I've not been back since and," she hesitated, "it threw me. I didn't expect to come to Rowan Cottage tonight, Sam. I didn't even know you were the new tenant."

"I don't follow." Sam frowned, not sure if her comment was a veiled criticism. "Would it have made any difference if you had known?"

"N - no." A delicate blush stained her pale cheeks.

He waited while she struggled to articulate her emotions.

"Sorry." Poppy cleared her throat. "I meant I'd have been better prepared, that's all. After the drama on the beach, I felt ... "she hiccoughed, "a bit overwhelmed."

Instinctively, Sam refrained from saying that he hoped to buy the property. It wasn't the right moment. Could something else be amiss, too, something that she wasn't telling him? Poppy's reaction still seemed a tad extreme. Maybe another, older trauma had been tapped into, it wasn't unheard of. Everyone reacted differently. Then again, he could be reading more into it than was necessary. Perhaps it was simply a case of emotions running high, triggering shakiness after the adrenalin rush caused by events down on the beach. A debrief would be wise if she'd agree to it, though he could tell from Poppy's closed expression that that was unlikely. She had withdrawn again. Sam shrugged. He'd learnt long ago that people couldn't be forced to talk; they shared the big stuff only when they were ready.

"Listen, there's plenty of hot water." He stood. "Why don't you take the first shower, Poppy. I'll leave out something for you to put on afterwards and bung your shorts and top in the washing machine. It's a washer-dryer; your stuff won't take long to be ready to wear again. While we wait, let's share the jacket spud I left baking in the oven. It's huge, far too big for one, before you say anything." He winked. "You'll be doing my waistline a favour."

Was he pushing things? Should he have stopped at the blanket and tea stage, then driven her home? There was silence while Poppy debated her answer. She looked poised to refuse, then capitulated. Her body language told Sam that she was going along with his suggestion only because she didn't have the strength left to put up a fight.

Or, more likely, couldn't think of a counter argument, he guessed. Not much of a coup either way, but whatever! At least she wasn't determined to leave, despite the return of her frightened fawn look. Swiftly, Sam drained his mug of tea and focused on the bathroom, instructing her to hang on while he fished out a clean towel and checked the whereabouts of his bathrobe. He ran up the rickety stairs two at a time. For good measure, he put out one of his T-shirts, too. On Poppy's slight frame it would fit like a mini dress if she felt happier to wear something underneath the bathrobe – and he felt pretty sure that she would. As for toiletries, options were limited. She would have to be content with the basics, plain soap, and shampoo, because that's all that was on offer.

Sam collected Poppy's wet clothes, shoving them into the washing machine as soon as he heard the sound of running water. They hardly knew each other, yet it felt strangely right for her to be here under his roof. However, she was certainly a girl who came with baggage. He could sense it a mile off. Whereas he had always been a straightforward kind of guy who went for a straightforward kind of girl. He resolved to keep this in mind when her presence fanned the flames of desire. It would be sensible to keep a healthy emotional distance.

He emptied a can of baked beans into a saucepan, put them on a low heat and dug out some honey roasted ham. Also, he found a thick slab of cheese to grate. As an afterthought, he opened the 'fridge and pulled out a dish of cherry tomatoes, a head of lettuce and half a cucumber. There was a lemon wedge wrapped in foil, too. That would come in handy for a homemade salad dressing. He seldom bothered to buy the ready-made stuff. A rustic meal, but hopefully it would suffice. Then he'd run her home. Sam frowned, rummaging in the cupboard for olive oil and black pepper. He had unpacked both, but where the hell had he put them?

This was the trouble with a house move, it took ages to locate everything.

"That was great. Thanks, Sam, the shower's all yours. You're right, it's made all the difference." Poppy's voice made him start. "I feel more human now. Sorry about before."

Sam swung round from the cupboard, narrowly missing banging his head on the door. The sound of the washing machine must have masked Poppy's soft tread on the stairs. Lord, but the lady washed up well! Wrapped in his towelling bathrobe, her peachy skin had a rosy glow. Her light brown hair hung in tendrils around her oval shaped face, while her long lashed, clear grey eyes shone like quicksilver. She stood only feet away. His reaction was age old and primal. Steadfastly, he tried to ignore it.

"Fine, I'll follow suit, then." Even to his own ears Sam's voice sounded husky. He cleared his throat and gave her a curt nod. "Sit yourself down by the stove, Poppy. Or grate that cheese if you want a job. I'll be five minutes, max."

Upstairs in the shower, Sam scowled as he turned down the control for the water temperature. Whose idea had it been to invite the lady back to Rowan Cottage, anyway? OK, his, but he must need his head examined. Yet he couldn't have let her go home alone, not the way she'd looked down on the beach. Unfortunately, he'd have to forgo the pleasure of standing under a cascade of hot water after hanging around in his own damp attire. With luck, the cool setting would dampen his libido.

The sight of Poppy wandering into his kitchen had taken him by surprise; it seemed prudent to make sure she didn't realise the effect she'd had on him. There was only so long a bloke could stand under a cold shower without his brain freezing. Other parts of his anatomy, too, Sam thought wryly. However, it had had the desired effect. His libido under control, he towelled himself dry.

Attracted to her or not, Poppy needn't worry. He wasn't about to jump her bones, delectable as those bones undoubtedly were. Sam scowled again. Hell, he should get out more. It went against his nature to live like a monk.

Clad in an ancient tracksuit, he ran downstairs, grateful to enter the warmth of the kitchen. The scene that greeted him indicated that Poppy hadn't been idle. A dish of grated cheese sat in the centre of the pine table. She'd prepared a salad, too, and even found a pair of salad tongs he'd forgotten about, a Christmas present from one of his sisters-in-law. Packed in haste, the tongs must have been rammed down at the bottom of the cutlery box. Luckily, he travelled light. He didn't want to move again in a hurry, that was for sure.

"Great stuff!" Sam threw her a grin. "I see you've had a root around and found everything. OK, let's eat. I'm famished!"

He liked the shy smile Poppy gave at his nod of approval. He strode across the flagstone floor, opened the oven and fished out a large baking potato. Then he sliced it down the middle and, with a flourish, placed half on each plate. The spud was done to perfection, crispy on the outside, soft on the inside. Sam heard his stomach rumble.

"Dig in." He pulled out his own chair, motioning for Poppy to sit down, too. "Oh, hang on, butter!" Sam swung round and went to peer in the 'fridge. "Yep, I thought I had a new tub. Want some? I'll put a couple of pats on a saucer."

He grinned. "Afraid I don't bother with social niceties when it's just me, but for guests – the works."

He grabbed a knife, cut into the soft yellow block, and offered her the saucer. Briefly, his fingers brushed hers. Their gaze met and Sam saw Poppy's grey eyes become smoky and her pupils dilate. Her cheeks had a tinge of pink now.

Was she aroused, too? The physical signs told him yes. He turned abruptly, aware that his iron control had begun to slip.

"Coffee?" Sam flicked the switch on the kettle and opened the cupboard to retrieve two clean mugs.

Behind him, he heard Poppy request tea instead.

"No problem." He grabbed the caddy and fished out a tea bag. "Don't you drink coffee, Poppy?"

"Occasionally." She smiled. "I prefer tea, though."

"Each to their own." Sam threw her a wink, conscious of the struggle to act nonchalantly. "Do start, Poppy. It won't take me long to make a mug of tea."

She sat quietly, toying with her knife and fork, watching him with her beautiful grey eyes. He wondered what was on her mind.

"It's hot." She said by way of explanation, indicating the potato.

It wasn't the only thing that was hot, but Sam refrained from making a comment. Upstairs came the unmistakable creak of old floorboards, like footsteps above them. The spirit of the old cottage, he imagined his sister would say.

"Don't worry, it's only the sound of the wood contracting – or is it expanding, I forget which way round it is." Glad of the distraction, Sam chuckled. "It's something that happens in older properties at night. The floorboards heat up and expand during the day, then contract as the temperature drops. That makes the creaking, or cracking noise you just heard." He laughed. "We don't have an intruder – or ghosts."

Poppy opened her mouth as if poised to say something. The silence felt loud. He raised an eyebrow, waiting. But all she said in the end was,

"Oh."

The kitchen felt overly warm, whether from the stove or the summer night, it was hard to tell. While on his feet, Sam decided to open a window. Immediately the scent of lavender drifted in on the evening air, catching the scent of the shrubs beneath the sill.

"Hmm, I remember that smell." Poppy inhaled, closing her eyes, a smile playing round her mouth. "Granny always grew lavender in the garden here."

"There's plenty of the stuff around, that's for sure." Sam chuckled. "It's a wonder the place wasn't named after it."

"There's another Lavender Cottage further along the lane, I think." Poppy laughed. "Though I always thought it didn't have as much lavender as we did." She studied him a moment. "Did you know that lavender is said to have healing properties, Sam – besides being a soporific? It used to be strewn on church floors to avert evil spirits, apparently, as well as used in spells by wise women to sharpen the mind and strengthen pure love."

"Goodness," Sam raised an eyebrow, "and there was I thinking it was only used to make perfume, or lavender bags to make things smell nice. It certainly packs a punch, then."

He glanced at the sky, noting a change in weather. The air was now heavy and humid.

"I wouldn't be surprised if there was a storm tonight. That's why the atmosphere is so charged."

Who was he trying to kid? Poppy was the reason Sam's nerve endings were zinging.

CHAPTER THREE

"Hmm," Poppy licked her lips, "this is delicious! A feast and then some. Thanks for sharing your supper, Sam."

Her portion of the jacket potato tasted heavenly. Sam hadn't exaggerated when he'd described it as huge. Even split in half it was large. The accompaniments were good, too. It had only taken her a second to scan the list of ingredients on the empty tin of beans. No gluten, good; it was safe for her to eat. Ditto, the ham was fine: plain, with no breaded crust. Such a faff, continually having to check everything she put into her mouth – but this was her life now. She was adapting fast, though. It wasn't the end of the world, even if she would much prefer not to have to do it.

"You're welcome." Sam's brown eyes twinkled as he speared a tomato with his fork. "Like I said, this spud is too much for one. We both need to eat; it makes sense to share it. Besides," he threw her a wink so sexy it made her bare toes curl, "now that I'm part of Bramblewood Practice, you could say that I have a vested interest in the welfare of the staff. If you were to tell me that you'd have bothered with a meal like this on your own tonight, Poppy Lambert, quite frankly I wouldn't believe you."

"I might have risen to beans on toast." Poppy shrugged, catching the fresh, lemony tang of his soap. Averting her gaze from the sculpted angles of his face, she added, "Although what makes you so sure I don't have someone back at my flat waiting for me with dinner all ready, wondering where I am, Dr Brocklehurst?"

Gracious, what on earth had made her say that? It sounded like she was flirting.

"Do you?" Sam raised an eyebrow, a teasing note in his voice.

"No," Poppy said, a little devil making her add, "not tonight, anyway."

She wasn't sure why it mattered, but she didn't want to appear too lonesome.

"Good." Unfazed, Sam grinned. "Otherwise, I'd have had to say how remiss of him not to check up on you."

"Some men are remiss." Poppy shrugged, wondering what it would be like to have a man care enough to check up on her, worry if she was late home. Someone strong and dependable whom she could trust. Her heart skipped a beat; someone like Sam.

"Then you've been hanging out with the wrong kind of guy." His reply sharp, the teasing note vanished. "Know your worth, Poppy. Not all men are bastards."

Sam's presence filled the room. He studied her, deep brown eyes thoughtful, and Poppy felt exposed. It wasn't a comfortable sensation.

"In my experience a lot are." She swallowed. "It can be hard to weed out the good guys."

In the silence that ensued Poppy regretted speaking so freely. Sam exuded an animal magnetism, a powerful maleness. A tingle of desire shot down her spine. All at once things felt dangerous. It had been a while since she had been alone with a man like this, someone who oozed sex appeal – and then look what had happened. Nothing good! Hastily, she scooped up a forkful of beans. It was high time to finish her supper and leave the charismatic Dr Brocklehurst. The cottage kitchen was pleasantly warm. She noticed that Sam had left the range on low to dry out her trainers. Heavens, he had even wiped her shoes clean, propping them up by a convenient heat source afterwards. Poppy tried to imagine her ex-partner being as considerate and failed. Mark hadn't done things like that.

Why she had stayed with Mark for so long Poppy really did not know. With hindsight, she saw the relationship had been on shaky ground even before her first miscarriage. The warning signs had been present all along, had she chosen to see them. It was a mistake that wouldn't be repeated, though. What did she really know about Sam – nothing!

"Not for me, thanks." Poppy stood to collect their plates, declining his offer of another hot drink. "Let me wash up, then I'd better be making tracks if my clothes are dry enough to wear now." Even if they were not dry, she decided, heading for the sink.

"OK, while you do that, I'll make a call to the hospital and check on Rupert." Sam looked at her. "Save you from going home and fretting about him on your own."

Poppy smiled. It was true, that's exactly what she'd have done. Sam stepped into the sitting room and she began to tidy the kitchen. It didn't take her long and she was ready first. His absence made her feel restless. Not unduly worried, she glanced around for something else to do. No doubt, he'd had difficulty getting through to the right department. It could take an age if the hospital was busy. She spied the washing machine. It had completed a drying cycle, just as Sam had predicted. In her experience, washer-driers were never terribly efficient. However, shorts, a pair of pants and a vest top should not pose the machine too great a challenge.

She opened the machine, pulled out her clothes and cautiously felt them – yay, dry enough to wear! Poppy felt a surge of relief. About to run upstairs and dress, she heard Sam's approach and glanced up. He stood in front of her, 'phone in hand and he wasn't smiling. Despite the warmth of the kitchen, his grim expression made Poppy go cold.

"Bad news?" She gripped the bundle of clothes. "What is it, Sam? Tell me!"

"Rupert is being monitored overnight in Paediatric Intensive Care." Sam ran a hand through his hair. "I've been speaking with the duty SHO. Apparently, his conscious level dropped off immediately after transfer to the ward for observation, and he started exhibiting signs of marked respiratory distress. They've got him on humidified oxygen and I.V. antibiotics now, of course, and haven't needed to ventilate - yet. But if there had been any delay in admission, any delay at all ... "

His voice tailed off and they both fell silent, only too aware of the consequences. Poppy sucked in a breath. Secondary drowning was a spectre to be feared, yet many people were unaware of the condition. It struck suddenly, anything between one and seventy-two hours after the initial immersion. Only a small amount of water in the lungs was needed to trigger the body's inflammatory response and there was no way of determining who was going to be affected. Therefore, every case of near drowning posed a potential risk.

Poopy blinked back tears, remembering the carefree tot running towards the tumbling breakers, oblivious of the danger ahead. Life was fragile. Things changed in an instant. Then another thought struck. Suppose she had been down on the beach trying to rescue Rupert alone? How much notice would the boy's blustering father have taken of her then? That's if she had managed to drag him from the sea in the first place. It didn't take much imagination to picture the boy's father snatching him and ignoring her plea for an ambulance. That's if she'd had Sam's success with the initial resuscitation, of course. Nothing was a given.

As a nurse she'd been witness to other resuscitation attempts. Assisted at several, too – but only ever in a hospital setting with the 'crash team' involved. It was very different being a first responder at an incident with no hospital backup, or medical equipment to hand. Rupert's life really had hung in the balance.

"I've changed my mind." Shakily, she turned towards the kettle. "Think I will have another hot drink, after all. Can I make one for you, too, Sam? Thank goodness you decided to go running this evening! You saved that little boy's life."

"You'd have coped, Poppy. On your own. I mean," Sam clarified, "your gut instincts are good. I can tell. Damn it, how fast do you run, for heaven's sake? I wasn't aware of anyone else around, then suddenly there you were, right behind me as I went into the water. You shot out of nowhere."

Poppy didn't reply. Sam was being nice, that was all. Heavens, he hardly knew her, so how could he judge her capability in an emergency. She busied herself with brewing the tea. She must have arrived on the beach slightly later than him. Initially, she'd been focussed on her run and hadn't recognised Sam until the last moment, either. Then she supposed they had both acted on instinct. It had been Rupert's lucky day to have Sam there, though.

"Dry now?" He took a gulp from the mug Poppy handed him, nodding at the clothes she had abandoned on the chair back. "Don't feel obliged to rush off if they're not."

"Oh, er – yes, they are, thanks. I'll go upstairs and change." She took a hasty mouthful of tea, hardly tasting it. "Then I must make tracks. But I can easily walk."

All at once came an ominous rumble, followed by a jagged streak of lightning zigzagging across a rapidly darkening sky. Poppy stared at the window, recalling how quickly the weather could change along the Atlantic coast. It often took the unwary by surprise.

"There's a storm about to hit. I'll drive you." Sam's voice brooked no argument. He frowned, glancing towards the stove. "Besides, your trainers must still be damp. They won't be very comfortable to walk far in."

About to desist, Poppy flinched at another rumble of thunder, closer this time. Swiftly, Sam moved to close the kitchen window. It was none too soon. A vivid flash lit up the heavens and fat raindrops began to drum on the windowpane. It was going to be a wild night and, no, she didn't relish being out in it. As much as she valued her independence, she wasn't daft enough to insist on walking home in the middle of an electrical storm.

"Offer accepted, kind sir." She took a breath and smiled. "Thanks again, Sam."

Poppy ditched the remainder of her tea, retrieved her clothes and ran upstairs to dress. After ten minutes the worst of the storm had abated, and they chose to chance it. Quickly, she slid into the passenger seat of Sam's car, parked on a patch of rough ground across the road from the cottage. He folded his tall frame into the driving seat, assuring her that first impressions were deceptive - the battered, blue Volvo ran sweet as a nut. Poppy hoped fervently this was true as he threw her a wink and gunned the engine.

"Hold onto your hat, lady, and tell me where you wanna go." Mimicking a gangster drawl, Sam rammed the vehicle into gear, indicating as he edged out into Lantern Lane.

Poppy giggled, huddled in the sweater he had insisted she borrow. This time her goosebumps were unrelated to the cold. It was as well the journey to her flat took barely five minutes by car; being this close to Sam was doing odd things to her pulse rate.

Her street was narrow, more of an alley than a proper road and cars had to crawl down it in single file. Luckily, Poppy hadn't had many visitors. She fumbled for the key to her apartment block and readied herself to jump out as he slowed by the kerb.

"Don't wait." She smiled her appreciation of the lift. "See, door key! I'll be inside in a jiffy. Heck, there's a car coming in the opposite direction. You'll need to reverse, Sam."

"If you'll only be a jiffy, it won't hurt the other chap to wait a minute." Sam raised an eyebrow. "If I drop a lady home, I wait to see her safely inside her front door. End of."

"Oh," Poppy scrambled out, feeling herself flush, "you really don't need to. I'm fine."

In her haste not to hold him up, she lost her footing on the wet pavement, and only just managed to right herself. Poppy cursed her damp trainers, aware it would have been sensible to accept Sam's offer of socks as well as the sweater. It would be a relief to get inside and pull off the offending footwear. She gripped the key, praying for the lock, which could be temperamental, to open at first try. It did! She heaved a sigh of relief, waved to Sam as she slipped inside, and slammed the door shut again.

Once in the dimly lit hallway Poppy felt a wash of loneliness. She trudged up the communal staircase and entered her small flat, noting the stark difference between it and Rowan Cottage. Despite the changed décor, the cottage had felt welcoming and homely, exactly as it had when her gran lived there. Its old walls must have sustained many occupants over the generations. If only walls could talk, Poppy thought, what tales they would have to tell. Compared with Rowan Cottage, her flat was neat and practical, but soulless. Tonight, she felt unsettled and keen to be gone.

Sam had only rented the cottage. She could have asked him, but it was unlikely he intended to stay there long. Why would he when there were so many other, larger places available? He'd hinted at the bathroom being too poky already. Surely, he'd want to move on at the end of his lease period to something more modern. There was nothing to stop her going ahead with her plan to buy the place – apart from this mysterious 'other interested party,' if indeed they existed. Poppy scowled, wondering if it was a marketing ploy used by Mr Kerslake to bump up the price. Such things happened; she wouldn't put it past him.

With her mind set more positive Poppy began to feel happier again. She focussed on her work the following day and the preparations she needed to make. Not much, apart from ironing a clean uniform and sorting out something suitable for a packed lunch – both tasks easily completed. Her sessions would include a mother and baby clinic in the morning and a contraceptive clinic in the afternoon. Poppy smiled at the irony of the sequence. Life seldom went according to plan, and perhaps things would become boring if it did.

Her thoughts returned to Sam. It had given her a jolt to find him living in what she still considered to be her gran's home. Yet he'd fitted into Rowan Cottage surprisingly well, she mused. Something about him suited the place, despite the constraints of the tiny bathroom – which, with his tall frame, must be a squeeze. Hastily, she banished that train of thought, feeling herself blush. The picture she had in her mind of Sam showering conjured up far too many X-rated images. It seemed that he was single. At least, there had been no evidence of a female around, no feminine items on show – and Dr Sam Brocklehurst was unquestioningly heterosexual, of that Poppy was in no doubt!

Out of habit Poppy switched on the T.V. There was nothing that held her attention, so she switched it off again. Certainly not the late news, she'd had more than enough drama of her own over the last few hours. She stifled a yawn. Events of the day had caught up with her; it was time to clean her teeth and retire to bed. Her head touched the pillow, and within minutes Poppy fell into a deep sleep. Her dreams were jumbled, apart from one where she was a child again. It was the start of a school summer holiday. The sun shone as she raced down Lantern Lane to Rowan Cottage, having broken free of her father's hand. Her beloved gran stood at the door, smiling, waiting to greet them with her usual warm hug. Then the image faded, and Poppy fancied she heard the distant call of a sandpiper.

She woke to find her cheeks wet with tears, a mix of happy and sad.

The day proved busy, and then some. Thursday was the day when the practice nurses ordered fresh supplies, and a weekly stock take had to be undertaken. Poppy moved swiftly through her tasks with hardly a moment to draw breath. However, the fast pace suited her. In truth, she preferred every working day to be like this. The need to remain focussed left no room for anything else, no space for random thoughts to catch her out. She jumped at a tap on her shoulder as she snatched a drink from the water dispenser.

"Did you see the late news last night, Poppy?" Julia winked. "Our new boy, Sam was quite the hero! Made the local headlines. Seems he rescued a toddler from drowning while jogging down on the Sands last evening. I don't know, fancy letting the little lad go off on his own!" She tutted. "Holiday makers can be so stupid when it comes to water safety."

"B-but the beach was pretty near deserted!" Poppy gaped. "How on earth did the incident get reported on?"

"A bystander filmed it on his mobile as folk are wont to do these days. Hmm, you do know about it, then?" There was a definite twinkle in Julia's eye. "Apparently, another person was involved in the rescue. An unnamed young female jogger, fitting your description as it happens, Poppy. Was it you, by any chance?"

"Well, whoever it was could have offered to help instead of just filming. Honestly, people!" Poppy fumed. "Although I never noticed anyone else nearby. The weather had turned, the beach was emptying fast, and ... ." Aware she had given herself away, she stopped. "OK, yes, it was me. By pure chance, though. I often run on the beach after work. My timing happened to coincide with Sam being down there, that's all."

"No explanation necessary, Poppy." Julia's twinkle remained. "Anyway, well done. It sounds like you both did a sterling job. Right, while I see you, a quick reminder about the next PPG event scheduled for this Saturday. I do hope you're free to come along?"

"It's in my diary." Glad of the change of topic, Poppy relaxed. "I look forward to seeing the format of these meetings. We didn't have anything like this set up at my last practice, although there was talk about starting up a PPG. It's a government directive now, isn't it?"

"Yes, although PPGs have been slow to get off the ground in some areas." Julia nodded. "Now, about Saturday's agenda. I'll do the intros, then Kate, our community dietician will start off with a talk and slides on healthy eating, with an overview on allergies and special diets. Finally, before we throw open the floor for questions and discussion, we'll have a talk from a patient's perspective – the Lived Experience. Kate is organising that, I'm waiting for her to confirm the speaker. A simple format works best for these things, I find, whatever the topic. Oh, and for all our PPG events we join forces with another local practice, Coombe Vale. It boosts attendances and makes the effort put in worthwhile."

The rest of the day flew by. By the time Poppy left Bramblewood Surgery, she felt weary, for once glad to be going home. Although the storm had blown itself out overnight, the weather remained capricious. She remembered Sam's borrowed sweater back at her flat as she debated a run. It needed to be returned. If she did go for a run, she could take it with her and ring the doorbell as she passed by Rowan Cottage. There was no guarantee that he would be at home, of course, but there was no harm in trying. She nibbled her lip. She'd wondered if Sam would drop in during surgery hours to seek her out with a further update on Rupert. If honest, Poppy had half expected him to appear. After all, it wasn't every day that a child was plucked from the jaws of an inhospitable sea!

Then another idea struck. She was hungry but cooking after work always felt like a chore. Decision made! Why not go for a short run, hand over Sam's sweater, and make a detour by Ben's Plaice. The clifftop venue did wonderful fish and chips, exactly as the ads claimed. There was even a reasonably sized area kitted out with table and chairs for those who preferred to eat in. More importantly, the chips were gluten free. There was a grilled fish option, too, instead of the gluten free batter that she didn't much enjoy. Nestled on the edge of the coastal path, Ben's Plaice had become one of her favourite haunts.

Poppy stood in front of Rowan Cottage and knocked again, louder this time. There was no response. Sam must be out. Regretfully, she stepped away, planning to stop by on her return. For now, the sweater could be left rolled up safely in her rucksack. Relishing the salty tang of the sea air, Poppy ran further than intended, her mood lifted by the surroundings. There was a distinct dampness in the atmosphere but the clouds were too high for rain. In fact, she thought the evening had brightened. Only a few people were about. Her main companions were seagulls, looking for tasty titbits as they swooped and soared above the wide expanse of beach. The wind whipped her hair, teasing it from the hurriedly made ponytail caught up by her favourite scarlet scrunchy. Resolutely, Poppy emptied her mind, concentrating solely on the feel of the hard packed sand beneath her feet. The pale sun had dipped in a sky ribboned with gold as she circled, and headed towards Ben's Plaice. The gleaming white shack hove into view, its bold sign swinging gently in the off shore breeze. Poppy put on a spurt, breathing hard, aware of the ache in her calf muscles. If she ate her supper on the premises, she could relax and enjoy a panoramic view of the bay.

"One grilled cod and chips, please, Ben. Yes, to eat in." Poppy turned from the counter to find a free table. Her heart skipped a beat as her gaze alighted on the guy in the corner.

CHAPTER FOUR

His long, denim clad legs stretched out, Sam sat only yards away, occupying a small table at the end overlooking the sea. Poppy noted the take-away coffee as he threw her a wave; not planning to stay then, she thought with relief. Darkly handsome, he looked as rugged as the North Devon landscape. He wore hiking boots today, she noted, plus a waterproof jacket and she guessed he must have been out exploring. Poppy wondered which route he'd taken. There were so many picturesque walks in the area. Against her better judgement she hovered, returning his smile of acknowledgement.

"Sam, hi." Poppy hoped she didn't sound too gauche. Already she could feel herself blushing like a schoolgirl. "I see you've found Woolacombe's best chippy."

"Poppy," the timbre of Sam's voice, warm like treacle made her insides do a somersault, "what a surprise! A nice one, of course. No more dramas down on the beach, I hope. I'm guessing that's where you've come from?"

Sam stood and pulled out a chair, leaving Poppy with no option but to accept the tacit invitation to join him. Obviously, he must be waiting for a portion of fish and chips, too, although with the take-away coffee it looked like he planned to bring his supper back to the cottage. She let out a breath; exchanging a few minutes of pleasantries felt safe enough.

"Yep," she laughed, "running on the beach again. And no more dramas, thank goodness. I've had quite enough of those. How about you? Enjoying your last few days of freedom before you're reclaimed by the demands of medicine?"

"Something like that." Sam chuckled, launching into a description of the hike he'd been on.

Poppy listened agog, forgetting her nervousness as Sam detailed his day.

It seemed he'd had a proper tramp, covering a good seven or eight miles by the sound of it - heading towards Baggy Point, separating Croyde Bay and Morte Bay, he'd taken a wide sweep round the headland and returned via the cliff path. And still he seemed to be full of energy. Poppy, who seized any opportunity for a trek along the coastal path, felt a stab of regret at not being there with him. Instinct told her that Sam would make a great walking partner. Apparently, he was a bit of a local history buff, too.

"Did you know there's evidence of human occupation in that area dating back to the Mesolithic era?" Sam remarked. "Amazing, isn't it!"

"Yes." Poppy sighed wistfully. Sam's hike sounded wonderful, and she couldn't help but feel envious. "Wish I'd been there with you. I love it up around Baggy Point."

Hastily, she rushed on, fearful of giving him the wrong signals, "I mean, this area is so beautiful, isn't it, and we've been flat out at the surgery for ages. I haven't had a chance to get out and about as much as I'd like to, yet. That's why I make myself go for a run after work, to get some fresh air. Well, that and I didn't feel like cooking this evening."

Poppy cringed, aware that she was gabbling like a teenage fan girl.

"Ditto, with regards the cooking." Sam gave another throaty chuckle. He nodded a thanks to Ben as his order was placed on the table. "Looks like you're eating in, Poppy, think I'll join you." He undid the wrapping. "I intended to take mine home, but as the winds of fate seem to have blown us together again ... ," he shrugged, "company would be nice. That's if having supper with me two evenings in a row isn't too much, of course?"

"N-no, of course not." Poppy swallowed, feeling her cheeks burn.

Oh heavens, this put a different spin on things. She wasn't fooled for a minute, though. Sam wasn't a man who lacked confidence. The twinkle in his brown eyes told her the comment had been made in jest. She doubted it would ever occur to Dr Sam Brocklehurst that he might be too much for anyone. Anyone female, at least. Did she mind sharing supper with him again? In truth, she wasn't sure. All she knew was that Sam's proximity felt dangerous – like being at the zoo only to discover someone had taken the guard fence away from the big cat enclosure. And a prowling tiger had her in its sights.

She smiled at Ben as he passed her a laden plate, grateful for the distraction. A glance at Sam revealed that he was watching her with an amused lift of his dark eyebrows.

"Sorry, that came out wrong. I mean, no, it's fine." Poppy shrugged, aware of conflicting emotions. "This is a good spot to sit and watch the go down. Really peaceful. And eating in saves the chips from getting cold unless I nibble them on the way. I've a longer walk back than you, remember."

"I remember." Sam studied her, the teasing note gone.

Poppy sucked in a breath. She wondered what else Sam remembered; her taking a shower at Rowan Cottage and emerging in his bathrobe, perhaps? Well, he wasn't the only one with good recall. She remembered things, too. Like the jut of his hips the first time she'd seen him standing at the upstairs window of the cottage, with nothing but a towel slung round his trim waist. Heavens, what an image to conjure up now! She coughed and reached hastily for the cutlery stacked neatly at the side of the table. Sam's side. Her hand accidentally brushed his and sent a frisson of awareness through her body. Impervious to guys or not, she couldn't deny the chemistry. The air fizzed with it.

Her immunity must be low, that was the problem, Poppy decided. She needed a booster injection, stat! Dr Sam Brocklehurst might be sexy as hell, with an attractive undercurrent of danger but she needed to steer clear. She had to avoid spending too much of her off duty time in his presence because that was courting trouble.

The expression in Sam's eyes and her reaction to him scared her. Heavens, they worked together, or would be working together very soon – and lived in the same vicinity, not to mention their shared love of running. They were destined to bump into each other on a regular basis. He might be a great guy, but this simmering attraction would only serve to complicate things. What was Sam's agenda? He wasn't easy to read. Poppy speared a chip and dipped it in tomato sauce, wondering if she needed to be clear from the outset.

Yes, she decided, if Sam did harbour any romantic ideas they were better quashed now. She'd make it plain that the only relationship she was interested in was a harmonious working one. Hopefully, this wouldn't sound too pompous. She took a breath aware she'd feel very silly if the mere mention of a romantic liaison shocked him. Or, worse, made him roar with laughter. However, it was a risk worth taking if she hadn't mistaken the look in those soulful brown eyes. A fleeting look but it had been there all the same.

"Um, Sam." Poppy hesitated, toying with a piece of fish. "I just want to say that, as colleagues, it's best if we ... "

"Wow, will you look at that sunset!" Sam nudged her, and pointed towards the window. "Nature's very own picture show right there in front of us."

Poppy followed his gaze. The sun had chosen that very moment to sink low on the horizon, becoming a crimson ball of fire as its rays reflected across the darkening water.

She gasped, what she had been about to say forgotten in the magic of the moment. The view was spellbinding, holding them both in thrall as the sun dipped below the skyline and disappeared. Then Poppy stilled, realising that Sam had coined a phrase she often used herself: 'nature's very own picture show.' Dr Sam Brocklehurst was on her wavelength, and she didn't know whether to be pleased about that or alarmed.

"Sorry, Poppy, you were saying?" His attention switched back to her. "I'm afraid I interrupted, but that sight was too good to miss."

Sam glanced at her enquiringly as he took another swig of coffee.

Poppy blinked. Yes, she had been about to say something; something important if her memory served her right. The words had been on the tip of her tongue. What was it, though? Oddly, she had forgotten. Ah, a cautionary word about relationships, that was it! Yet the matter didn't feel so urgent anymore. In fact, she rather thought it was premature to mention relationships at all.

"Nothing important." She smiled as she speared another chip and dipped it into tomato sauce. "Like I said, the view over the bay is wonderful from up here."

"Ditto, these fish and chips." Sam attacked his meal with gusto. "Well worth the walk to get them."

The minutes flew by as they ate their supper and shared snippets of their day. Sam was a good raconteur, and Poppy enjoyed hearing further details of his hike. In his turn, he didn't object to listening to her talk shop. After all, Bramblewood Surgery was their common ground, or soon would be. Indeed, he seemed to be interested in anything she could tell him about the Practice. Slowly, she began to relax in his presence.

"So, no regrets about the new job, Poppy?" Sam pushed aside his plate and raised an eyebrow. "You're happy at Bramblewood?"

"Oh yes, it's a great team, "Poppy enthused, "and I'm surrounded by all this." She gestured to the window. "What's to regret. Besides, I always dreamed of settling here in North Devon. Now here I am."

She continued in response to his enquiring look. "As I said the other evening, I visited Woolacombe a lot as a child. Such happy memories, it's lovely to be back."

After a last bite of fish, Poppy set aside her own plate. She felt deliciously full, but it was high time she left now. She rose, attempting nonchalance as she scraped back her chair and made murmurings about the lateness of the evening. There was a split second when she wondered if Sam was about to leave, too. An edge of anxiety crept in as she imagined them strolling down the cliff path together in the fading June light. If Sam reached for her hand, how was she supposed to react? What if he offered to walk her home? Part of her hoped he would, the other, more sensible part really hoped he wouldn't.

"There's a 'phone call I need to make. Think I'll order another coffee and do it here instead of back at the cottage." He rose courteously as Poppy stood, adding, "A boat is up for sale that I fancy taking a closer look at. The Sea Nymph. The owner suggests I pop round on Saturday morning to give her the once over, but I need to confirm a time. Although that means I may struggle to make this PPG event. Listen, if I don't show, perhaps you'd give Julia my apologies."

"Yes, of course." Aware of a stab of disappointment, Poppy nodded. "Bye, Sam. See you on Monday. Good luck with the boat."

"Cheers, Poppy." Sam reached for his mobile.

The Sea Nymph: she liked that name. What sort of boat was it? She imagined Sam at the helm, sure he'd look every inch the rakish sailor as he rode the waves. Poppy sighed as she retraced her steps along the cliff path. Such flights of fantasy were best not entertained. All right, Dr Sam Brocklehurst could be congenial company – when he wanted to be, no doubt - but what did that prove. Nothing! She needed to remind herself that she was done with men, especially charismatic ones.

Relieved when she stepped out into Lantern Lane, Poppy glanced around in the half-light. Funny how she was always drawn to walk past Rowan Cottage. Although her grandmother was long gone, sometimes she could sense the old lady's presence. 'I've come home, Gran,' she whispered, 'just like I said I would. And I haven't forgotten my promise.'

Fatigue washed over her. Tonight, the walk back to her flat seemed longer than usual. Another whisper she chose to ignore said 'you're missing Sam's company.' With a start Poppy realised she still had his sweater tucked up in her rucksack. If she'd had her wits about her, she could have given it to him back at the café. A missed opportunity. Ah well, it was too late to retrace her steps. She'd have to return it another time.

At last, she reached her flat, and checked the communal mailbox more out of habit than any expectation of post. There was indeed a letter for her. Poppy studied the official looking white envelope and frowned. Forwarded to her new address by her Exeter based aunt, the letter had a hospital logo. Tentatively, Poppy ripped open the envelope. Her heart skipped a beat as she scanned the contents: an appointment for a repeat endoscopy. Not unexpected, but not something she was looking forward to, either. She clicked her tongue in disbelief on noting the date – next Friday.

Poppy toyed with the idea of ringing the department to reschedule, but another part of her just wanted the procedure done. Ideally, this appointment would have fallen over a weekend, thus avoiding the need to request time off. She was new in post, after all. Plus, she would need to have someone stay with her overnight after the endoscopy. There was no one locally she could ask at short notice, that was the problem after relocation to a new area. No, she would need to stay overnight in Exeter. That's if her aunt hadn't gone off on holiday already. Poppy tried to recall which week her aunt had mentioned and failed. Then another idea struck. Why not ring her cousin, Maisie; fingers crossed, her cousin wasn't frantically busy and away travelling somewhere in a work capacity.

Hopefully, post-endoscopy, Maisie would be free to collect her, drive her back to North Devon and stay for the weekend. Alternatively, she might have to stay with Maisie on the Friday. Regardless, there was no way Poppy would opt to have that procedure done without sedation, she wasn't brave enough! After sedation, someone to stay with her overnight was mandatory. The rules were clearly stated. Poppy hesitated, then made a decision. if Maisie wasn't available on the date specified, she'd have to alter the appointment.

She fished out her mobile. Maisie answered after the second ring and listened as Poppy explained the situation. She let out a breath on hearing that not only was her cousin free, but she'd been planning a visit to North Devon around that weekend, anyway. Poppy's request had come at a good moment. They could spend a few nice days together .

"You know you're welcome to stay at mine, if that's easier." Maisie said. "But I do fancy a change of scene, and it's time I saw where you've moved to. I can't believe we haven't met up since you left! How are you enjoying it down in Woolacombe?"

They chatted briefly before agreeing on a proper catch up when they saw each other.

"Listen, get the train to Exeter, St. David's and I'll meet you at the station." Maisie instructed. There was a peal of laughter. "I would treat you to breakfast, Pops, but, obviously, you'll be nil by mouth before the 'scope. That's one saving, anyway."

"Oh, ha-ha, very funny!" Poppy retorted, giggling despite herself.

The call ended, she looked around her flat, daunted by the lack of space. She'd have to juggle things to fit in an overnight guest. However, it was only Maisie; they would manage. One of them could use the small sofa, comfy enough with a blanket and pillow. Hopefully, it wouldn't be long before the purchase of Rowan Cottage was underway. While that might not be the largest abode, and a quirky design to boot, it did boast two bedrooms. Plus, a surprisingly roomy kitchen that felt snug no matter how cold the weather outside.

Idly, Poppy thought about décor once Rowan Cottage was hers. She wrinkled her nose, wondering whether to keep or change the blinds at the window. True, they were smart and functional but she rather fancied daisy patterned, primrose yellow curtains. She closed her eyes, picturing them billowing softly in the breeze. Yellow was such a cheerful colour, especially in winter when everywhere tended to look dull.

Poppy wondered about the expense of a refurb. Obviously, there'd be furniture to be bought, too. No matter, she could update the cottage bit by bit. There was no rush to do everything at once. As for any structural defects hinted at by the letting agent, well, the place had been standing for over a century. She'd wager a bet it was stronger than anything built today. A wave of fatigue hit and Poppy stretched. Right now, all she wanted to do was sleep. Only Friday to go then it was the weekend, thank goodness. Swiftly, she cleaned her teeth in the tiny bathroom – described as 'compact' when she'd first viewed the flat - and stifled a yawn. Tonight, she felt ready for bed.

Poppy's last waking thought was of a need to build more rest and relaxation into her working week. Otherwise, no matter how much she loved her job, she risked burnout.

Friday promised to be another full-on day, par for the course in any GP practice as patients sought appointments before close of surgery. The doctors tried to fit in anyone with an ailment that couldn't wait until Monday. Poppy herself had a routine session to begin with: patients booked in for dressing changes, blood pressure checks, blood tests, etcetera. Then, a quick lunch break. In the afternoon she saw that she'd been delegated to assist David Jennings, one of the GPs, in the minor ops' clinic, a task she always enjoyed.

The hours flew past. Poppy felt a warm glow of achievement as she finished her final session and prepared to go off duty. She waved a cheery goodbye to her colleagues.

"Have a good weekend, Laura - Faye." A late thought made her turn to call after Laura. "Oh, by the way, am I supposed to pitch up in uniform for this PPG thingummy? I meant to ask Julia, but I forgot, and she's already left."

"No, it's mufti." Laura smiled. "Smart casual, but remember to pin on your name badge for ID."

"Thanks, Laura."

"No, thank you for stepping in, Poppy." Laura pulled a face. "Fitting in the extra commitment of the PPG was getting difficult now that my mum isn't well and can't manage the kids like she used to. Richard, my hubby sometimes has to work evenings, the odd Saturday, too – like this one. It's a relief not to have to worry about finding childcare. Enjoy your freedom while you can, Poppy, before marriage and kids claim you!"

Poppy swallowed hard, her good humour evaporating like mist in the morning.

Laura's innocent remark was a stark reminder that Poppy was twenty-eight and still single. Had life gone in a different way, she would have had a partner and children herself by now. Unintentionally, her colleague had hit a raw nerve. While she claimed to be a career girl now, what would it be like when she was older? Lonely, said little whisper.

"No problem." Poppy threw Laura what she hoped was a cheerful grin, trying to ignore the sting of tears. "One of the bonuses of being on my own, no one else's needs to cater for. Lucky me, and I plan to keep it that way!"

Determinedly, she focussed her mind on Saturday morning's PPG event, mentally running through her wardrobe as she strolled home. She would need to look presentable, which meant wearing something other than shorts or jeans, her usual off duty attire. The weekend weather forecast was warm and sunny. She had a couple of nearly new cotton frocks that were ripe for an airing. It would be an opportunity to wear something pretty. A soft yellow one with a tight bodice and flared skirt was her favourite.

Teamed with a gold locket and her soft-knit, white cardigan it should do nicely.

Poppy suppressed a grin. After the PPG event she planned to drop by the estate agent's office again. It would be interesting to gauge Mr Kerslake's reaction when she looked all glam and feminine. Would he take more notice of her? She suspected the answer would be yes. Men – even old ones - were all the same really, easily swayed by appearance. Poppy giggled. Maybe she would add a slash of red lipstick, too, like a femme fatale.

"All ready for tomorrow?" Sam's deep voice made her jump.

She hadn't been aware of anyone behind her, least of all Sam. Poppy guessed he'd come out of the local grocery store, judging by the bulging carrier bag he held.

"Yes, I ... " but her words were cut off by the ring tone of Sam's phone.

Poppy hesitated as he glanced at the screen for caller ID, then scowled.

"Sorry, I'd better take this." He stepped aside, and indicated that she should go on ahead. "Listen, Michelle, I know. She's with you? Good, she's safe then. I said I'd ring her later, and I will. But I can really do without all the drama. If it's over, it's over."

Embarrassed, Poppy couldn't help but overhear. She walked swiftly on. Some telephone conversations were best kept private. But who was he talking to, and what about? It sounded like an ex-lover might be the subject. An ex who didn't want to be an ex. Perhaps Sam was a free-spirited kind of guy who distanced himself the minute a relationship showed signs of becoming serious. Unsurprised, she wrinkled her nose. She knew the type; this served as a timely lesson why it was wise to limit contact with Dr Sam Brocklehurst.

⌐∾

Saturday dawned clear and bright. Poppy treated herself to a lie in before eating a leisurely breakfast of poached eggs on toast, washed down with a large mug of tea. She showered, then slipped on the yellow frock and studied herself critically in the narrow, full length mirror that a previous tenant had left propped up in the corner. Nice! Except that the image staring back at her was, she had to admit, better suited to a girl poised to go out on a date. A work-related event called for a longer hem and something a little less frivolous.

Reluctantly, Poppy swopped the flouncy, yellow creation for a smart, navy polka dot dress with pearl buttons down the front. Its skirt swished gently as she walked. A smudge of lipstick, pillar box red sandals and a matching, short, red jacket lifted the outfit. With a nod of approval at her reflection, she coiled her hair into a neat French plait. Nearly ready!

To complete the outfit, she fastened a pair of pearl stud earrings. Yes, still trendy but far more suitable for a work event. A spritz of perfume and she was done. Poppy dug out the smarter of her two handbags, and thrust in tissues, purse, and keys before leaving the flat. The morning had a mellow warmth, heralding the start of a period of fine weather. She set off for Bramblewood, revelling in the fresh air and azure blue sky. Perched on a chimney pot, a rook cawed, eying her inquisitively with its beady, black eyes.

She arrived at the venue to find it full to capacity. Hailed by Julia, keen to introduce her to the other PPG members, Poppy smiled in response.

"This is Kate, our wonderful community dietician who is the key speaker today." Julia beamed as the figure behind her stepped forward. "Kate has very kindly given us talks before. I say kindly because as a PPG we have no designated budget for speakers, apart from travel costs, although we hope this will change in the future. So, we're asking our presenters to give up a chunk of their free time. A big ask, as I'm sure you'll agree."

"Hi Poppy." Kate smiled ruefully. "Afraid I'm the bearer of bad news. My expert patient slot at the end will need rejigging. Glenda, my expert patient lined up for today, has had to renege. A domestic problem of some sort."

"Oh dear, that is unfortunate." Julia's brow furrowed.

"Hmm, indeed." Kate continued. "A water leak, apparently. She has to wait in for an emergency plumber. So, unless you two can think of anyone available to step in at short notice, the expert patient talk is off" Kate eyed them hopefully. "Any ideas, either of you? They'd have to be able to get here pronto, of course. It's a very eleventh-hour request."

There was a silence. Julia, brow furrowed, remained quiet.

"Glenda has a dairy allergy." Kate added, looking more hopeful. "Not uncommon. I bet someone in the room here right now has it. I begin my session with an overview of the foods we all need for a balanced diet, then focus on allergies and special diets, busting a few myths along the way. The expert patient slot is at the end, so ... "

"Will you be touching on Coeliac disease and gluten free diets?" Poppy nibbled her lip. An idea took hold if only she was brave enough to put it into action.

"Briefly." Kate nodded. "Why, do you know someone with a Coeliac diagnosis who'd be prepared to talk about it? That would work."

"Yes, me." Poppy pulled a wry face. "I'll be your expert patient. Although I warn you, Kate, I haven't stood in front of a room full of people and talked about myself before."

"Marvellous!" Kate clapped her hands. "OK, I'll rejig my spiel, putting the emphasis on Coeliac disease rather than dairy intolerance, and pave the way for you to take over as I conclude. Don't worry, you'll be fine. Just speak from the heart, Poppy and tell everyone what life is like for you on a daily basis. The words will come, they always do."

Poppy declined a coffee and fetched a glass of cold water instead. Already her mouth felt dry and her knees wobbly. She hated being the centre of attention. What on earth had made her volunteer like that? Yet deep down she knew why she had put herself forward. Myths were rife about Coeliac disease. It was important to raise awareness when you had the opportunity – because, if you hoped for change, someone had to be brave enough to speak out. Today she was that someone. There was so much misunderstanding about Coeliac disease and what it meant for sufferers. Everyone needed to play their part in educating the public. Now it was her turn.

She'd been given an opportunity to highlight the condition, even if she'd have preferred more warning. Heavens, she had no notes to refer to, no preparation time, either. Zilch! What if she opened her mouth and her mind went blank? A not unlikely scenario. Poppy's breath came a little faster and her skin began to feel clammy. Hopefully, it wasn't too late to renege. Then she sat up a little straighter and gave herself a pep talk. She'd got this, she really had. What did a few nerves matter? Besides, what was the worst that could happen if she messed up. Her new found confidence held for all of five minutes.

Poppy listened, trying to ignore the butterflies in her stomach, as Julia opened the event and introduced Kate. The talk was underway to a full house. There was no sign of Sam. Poppy glanced round the room, relieved not to see him. As anticipated, he must have been held up by the boat purchase. She relaxed a little. If she did make a fool of herself, at least she'd know that Dr Sam Brocklehurst hadn't been in the audience to witness it. She nibbled her lip. Hadn't Sam asked her to do something for him - what was it? Ah yes, pass on his apologies to Julia. No time to catch her for a quick word now, though, Poppy realised. Clipboard underarm, the practice manager was firmly in organisational mode, bustling about chatting to folk. Hopefully, there would be a chance to see her at the end.

Kate's session was underway now. The dietician spoke with ease and assurance, regularly referring to the slides she had brought with her, preloaded into an overhead projector. Poppy was impressed by her professionalism. Kate must have given similar presentations many times before yet she managed to keep the freshness. Everything went without a hitch. A barely perceptible nod from Julia told Poppy that her turn was near, and she felt sweat snake down her spine. Why, oh why, had she opted to do this? She had never enjoyed public speaking.

The room felt uncomfortably hot. Poppy's pulse began to race as she rose to stand close to the front, ready to be introduced. Even the change of position made her feel exposed. She hardly dared to glance around the room now. There were so many people here, so many expectant faces that all too soon would be focussed on her! Was it too late to decline, admit she'd made a mistake, and she'd really rather not do this? No, she refused to let Kate and Julia down. She had volunteered and she would see it through.

Desperately, Poppy sought a distraction from her racing thoughts. Had Sam bought that boat? Maybe the Sea Nymph was his already. What sort of boat was she? She didn't recall him telling her. In fact, no, she was sure he hadn't. An image flashed through her mind: Sam at the helm of a sleek, ocean-going vessel, a schooner of some sort. He wore a navy, cable knit fisherman's sweater, his curling, dark hair windswept as he masterfully navigated the ship's course through rough seas. A picture to behold indeed!

Poppy suppressed a giggle as her heart give a little skitter. In reality, the Sea Nymph might be no more than a rowing boat, or a sturdy, little tug, not a sleek, ocean-going schooner at all ... although she suspected Sam would look the part, regardless. Like Jane Austen's Darcy, Sam was the archetypal romantic hero. The type of guy that girls would have swooned over in times past. And, if truth be told, most girls in times present, too. Heavens, where was she going with this fantasy? Poppy swallowed, mindful that she was treading on dangerous ground. Images she'd conjured up for the sole purpose of distraction were swiftly banished. Hastily, she turned her attention back to Kate as the dietician expounded on the benefits of eating healthily. This was a much safer topic to focus on.

"Next, our expert patient slot." Kate smiled. "May I introduce Poppy Lambert, one of our practice nurses. Poppy will tell us how she copes with a diagnosis of Coeliac disease."

CHAPTER FIVE

Sam jogged towards Bramblewood Dental Practice, giving a wry grin as he pictured Julia's face on seeing him pitch up in running gear. Not the attire she would expect to see him in, he'd lay a bet on it – but he rather liked giving management a jolt every so often. Anyway, it was a Saturday; he wasn't officially on duty yet. Sam suspected this might be his last free weekend for a while. At least he'd kept his promise to put his nose round the door for the last part of this PPG event. If they wanted him suited and booted, they'd have to whistle. Besides, this gig was targeted at health, so what better garb to arrive in. It didn't do any harm for the patients to see that he was a doctor who practised what he preached.

How to gain access to the building? Julia hadn't mentioned that. Sam found the main entrance locked and a 'closed' sign displayed in the window. He stepped back from the red brick, ivy clad front and sought another entry. A side door had been left ajar. Sam followed his instinct and slipped inside; hearing sounds above, he mounted a wide staircase. It didn't take a genius to work out where he should go next. The spacious lecture room upstairs, the one Julia had told him the PPG used for meetings, looked full to capacity. There was standing room only. Dutifully, Sam joined the line and stood at the back with the rest. A white board and projector slides afforded him an overview of the subject matter.

Sam frowned. The current topic was Coeliac disease. Had Julia said this would be under discussion? He didn't think so. However, he didn't anticipate being called on to add anything to the presentation. According to the practice manager, this morning he was merely there to say hi. Then Sam did a double take. This was an expert patient slot, and the speaker was Poppy! She held the floor with aplomb, looking ravishing in a navy, polka dot dress. If she felt nervous it sure as hell didn't show.

Sam was impressed. Her hair was in a neat French plait today, he noted. With small pearl earrings and that stunning dress, she looked poised and elegant. Yet why was she giving the talk? Then the penny dropped. Of course, Poppy had Coeliac disease. Sam listened intently, his gaze trained on her.

"To recap." Poppy smiled at the audience. "Coeliac disease isn't an allergy. It's an autoimmune disease which affects the whole body. Right now, research is ongoing, but following a strict gluten free diet is the only treatment option. A nuisance, yes, but I remind myself there are worse things. Any questions before I continue?"

A hand shot up from the audience. "Kate said that not everyone experiences the same degree of symptoms, or even any symptoms at all in some cases. How has being a Coeliac affected you, Poppy? When did you first notice something was wrong?"

Did he imagine it, or did Poppy hesitate before answering? Sam studied her intently.

"I was diagnosed over a year ago," Poppy's smile wavered, "and I'll let you into a secret. This is the first time I've talked about it in such a personal way. OK, here goes, the clues that something was wrong. Vague symptoms to begin with; I felt constantly tired – TATT, tired all the time in medical terminology. A debilitating fatigue that sleep doesn't improve. Blood tests showed anaemia, and I was prescribed iron without any further investigations – repeated courses of iron as my Hb kept dropping. I picked up infections easily, not great if you're working and keep needing to take time off. Back then, I was a young staff nurse in a busy hospital, and I worried about repeated absences affecting my job. I expect everyone knows that nagging sense of something being wrong, yet you've no idea what. It's like trying to find the missing piece of a jigsaw puzzle. When you find it suddenly everything slots into place."

She paused to take a sip of water and there was a hush in the room.

"Despite being a nurse, it never occurred to me that I might have Coeliac disease." Poppy gave a deprecating shrug. "And oddly, no one suggested testing me for it. Then, when I began feeling sick on occasion and experiencing a few digestive issues, it was easy to put it down to a stint of night duty upsetting my body clock. Even anxiety, or whatever." Poppy shrugged again. "My ex-partner used to say that my breath smelt bad when we kissed, not great for a girl's self-confidence. Despite the dentist insisting that my teeth were fine, I remember the feeling of embarrassment and spending a fortune on mouth washes."

Poppy had dropped her guard. The professional mask was off, and she was speaking from the heart. She'd been in professional mode at first, Sam realised, shielding herself with medical speak. Now her words had a rawness that held the room. This was the benefit of educational events having an 'expert patient' slot. Folk heard the lived experience. It grabbed the audience every time. Textbook signs and symptoms couldn't compete. However, it took a brave person to lay themselves bare to a group of strangers.

"I've mentioned fatigue." Poppy continued. "What I didn't mention is the impact that has on those closest to you, when you're always too tired to do anything. You stop being a fun person, or a fun partner. It seems like you're constantly making excuses not to go out when, in truth, it takes every ounce of energy to hold down your job." She paused to take another sip of water.

"Kate touched on fertility issues. My own diagnosis came after a second miscarriage. I had an emergency hospital admission and struck lucky getting a consultant who was keen to explore the underlying issues. He started the ball rolling by ordering a specific blood test – the IgA – an inflammatory marker for Coeliac disease. The result was positive."

Sam felt the collective holding of breath in the room as Poppy took a moment to compose herself before concluding.

"That led to referral for an endoscopy, which revealed inflammation and villous atrophy of the upper end of my small intestine. A biopsy, the gold standard test together with a positive IgA, confirmed Coeliac disease." She gave a small shrug. "And, hey, that's my story."

"So, how were things after diagnosis, Poppy?" Kate gently prompted her. "On a day-to-day basis."

"I wish I'd known what was wrong earlier, but at least I know now." Poppy said. "If I stick to a gluten free diet, I'm symptom free. Oh, and for those of you who might be wondering," she grimaced theatrically, "gastric inflammation was responsible for my bad breath. All sorted, so there's no need to worry about me getting close to you if you have a practice nurse appointment at the surgery and I roll up."

A ripple of laughter greeted her last comment, followed by another question from the audience. "A gluten free diet seems quite restricting. Can't you cheat every so often?"

"The first six weeks of going on the diet were the toughest." Poppy pulled a wry face. "That's when you experience the worst food cravings. I could have killed for a real Cornish pasty, still could sometimes if I'm honest. I am adjusting, though. And there is support out there, including referral to a dietician like Kate for advice after diagnosis. The reward for sticking to a gluten free diet is a much better quality of life. It's great to feel more energised; that's the pay off. I don't have odd skin rashes or migraine headaches anymore, either. So, no, if I want to stay healthy, cheating is out. Even a small amount of gluten will trigger a reaction and cause damage. It's not worth playing around, the price is too high."

"Thank you to our Practice Nurse, Poppy Lambert for stepping in at the last minute and being our expert patient today." Julia stood. "Before she concludes and I take over, does anyone have any final questions?"

"I have one." A hand shot up. "How else has being a Coeliac affected you, Poppy? You said it's an autoimmune disease and involves the whole body."

"That's right, and Coeliacs are predisposed to other autoimmune conditions." Poppy nodded. "So, yes, I'm mindful of that, too."

She smiled at the questioner. "My best defence is trying to stay as healthy as possible. Research into the condition has shown that about 30% of those with a Coeliac diagnosis are hyposplenic – that is, their spleen under functions. This contributes to reduced immunity to infection. Therefore, I need to be up to date with my vaccinations. On diagnosis, it's common practice now for Coeliac patients to be re-vaccinated against meningitis C, HIB, 'flu and pneumonia. Also, it's important for bone health to be assessed. Like most Coeliacs, I've had a DEXA scan to check bone density. Calcium absorption is often affected pre-diagnosis, leading to the risk of osteoporosis and fractures in future years. In fact, many Coeliacs experience vague aches and pains in the long bones."

The audience was rapt. Sam had to hand it to her. She was a natural.

"I'll finish where we started: diet." Poppy took a breath. "Gluten is in loads of foods that you wouldn't even suspect. For example, it's used as a thickener in gravies and sauces. And wheat flour is even sprinkled in packets of grated cheese sometimes to keep the pieces separate. Wheat, barley and rye are the key things to avoid, and I read the labels on everything now - checking each ingredient is a pain, but slip ups have consequences."

"How about eating out?" Someone queried. "Isn't that tricky?"

"True and accepting an invite to eat out still makes me anxious," Poppy agreed. "But I've stopped worrying about being a nuisance, or offending folk. I'll happily quiz anyone about what's on the menu. If they don't get why I need to be careful, that's their problem. Obviously, there are family implications, too. These days I live alone, which is far easier than being with a partner who doesn't understand the ramifications."

Sam marvelled at Poppy's composure, delivering what he guessed was an understatement. His gut instinct had been spot-on. Poppy had been hurt by someone in the past. His mouth twisted as a spark of anger flared. Unconsciously, Sam balled his hand into a fist, wishing he could take a well-aimed swing at whoever it was. OK, he didn't know the guy, but how hard was it to be supportive to a partner whose welfare you were supposed to care about. Especially a partner who had conceived your child and was coping with the fall out of a miscarriage as well as a life changing diagnosis. One thing was for certain; she was better off without the oaf.

"We conclude, but before everyone goes home may I introduce Bramblewood's new GP, Dr Sam Brocklehurst. Hopefully, he is here. He did say he'd try to drop in today." Julia cast around the room, her eyes alighting on Sam. "Ah yes, step forward, please, Sam."

Sam edged past the others, with a wave to Julia as he grinned at the assembled group. They regarded him with interest as he came to the front. He noticed Poppy's shocked expression and half wished he hadn't hung around. Quite obviously, his presence had thrown her. If he'd slipped out as her talk concluded she would have been none the wiser. Hell, he'd only dropped in to say hi. Now she looked decidedly flushed and embarrassed. Suddenly it was important that Poppy thought he had only just arrived.

"Hi, I'm Sam Brocklehurst." He stood beside Julia. "Slipped in at the eleventh hour. I'm afraid I only just made it today, but I promise a timelier arrival for future PPG events. For those of you who haven't heard, I'm your doctor representative now that Andy Doyle is stepping down. I don't think It's necessary to delay you folks further by saying more. Hats off to Andrew and Julia for putting on such an informative event. And, of course, to Kate for her part in the organisation – and to all of you for attending. You're what makes it worthwhile. Right, the sun is shining, off you go and enjoy the rest of your weekend. I intend to do likewise."

Sam nodded to Julia and spun on heel. He had an idea. His gaze sought out Poppy. What were the odds on her agreeing to have lunch with him? If she was free, of course, and there was no guarantee that she would be available. It was a Saturday, after all, and she was looking particularly gorgeous today. It would be no surprise if she already had plans, or a date lined up. Hell, she was a beautiful young lady, she was bound to have plans. Ridiculous to think otherwise. But it didn't hurt to put the question, Sam decided. He'd better get a move on, though, or the lovely young practice nurse would have disappeared. Dammit, she was halfway through the door already.

"Lunch?" The look on Poppy's face would be comical if Sam had been in the mood for laughing. She looked like he'd asked if she fancied a spot of firewalking.

"Yes, lunch." Sam raised an eyebrow. "You know, that meal people have in the middle of the day. There's a nice little bistro not far from here. I thought we might grab a bite to eat while I show you a pic of the Sea Nymph, my new acquisition."

"Wow, you bought her," Poppy clapped a hand to her mouth, her colour rising, "how exciting!"

"Yep." Sam grinned. "You're looking at the proud owner of a 19.5-foot cabin cruiser. She's a beauty. Play your cards right, Nurse Lambert and I'll take you aboard one day."

"Sounds like you can't wait to show her off." Poppy laughed. "OK, the bistro it is. I'm going into town anyway. I need to pop into my Letting Agent's Office and make an enquiry this afternoon, but I can do that afterwards. I'd love to see your new acquisition." She bit her lip, a shadow crossing her delicate features. "Maybe only a drink for me, though, depending on what this bistro has in the way of a gluten free menu. I don't know at what point you came in, Sam, but I have Coeliac disease. That's why I stepped into the expert patient slot when Kate's original speaker couldn't make it."

She made a face.

"Only a drink is fine," Sam shrugged, not wanting her to feel it was a big deal. "Entirely up to you. We can see what else is on offer once we get there."

In truth, he knew the bistro he had in mind did have gluten free options. By chance he'd noticed the menu board earlier. However, he wouldn't pressurise her. If Poppy chose to stay with a drink because that's what she felt safest with, that was her prerogative. Sam didn't give a direct answer as to when he'd arrived, not wanting her to feel embarrassed. If she thought he'd missed the bulk of her talk, then so much the better.

"You're looking very nice today," He nearly said sexy, but caught himself in time. Sexy implied that he was coming on to her. Yet nice was such an ordinary word, and Poppy

Lambert was far from ordinary. "Summery." He added for want of a better description.

"Thank you." Her cheeks reddened at the compliment. "Well, I decided to make an effort. It's the weekend, the sun's shining, and all that."

"The effort has paid off." Sam winked. Then he threw caution aside, deciding it was ridiculous not to say what he thought. "Hell, what I meant to say is you're looking drop dead gorgeous, Poppy Lambert. I can only apologise for my own lack of sartorial elegance."

Her blush deepened. Sam watched her, thinking this really was a girl unused to praise. A cardinal sin, in his book, for a guy not to compliment his lady. Damn it, if she went out with him, he'd soon change that! Hell, where had that thought sprung from! Sam steered her in the direction of The Marmalade Cat. Poppy was a lady with complications. Sweet she may be, but the girl had baggage. Not that that bothered him, but she'd had trauma in the past. She needed space to heal, it didn't take a psychologist to work out that one. Friendship was fine, but he'd be wise to proceed with caution when it came to anything else. Against his better judgement he admitted he was tempted, though.

Sam wondered whether Poppy had had any form of grief counselling after the miscarriages. Hopefully, someone would have suggested it. How far along had the pregnancies been? Early, he guessed, by the sound of things – but a loss even so. Sam reminded himself he was only trying to get to know her better to enhance their working relationship. They were both newbies to the area. It was mutually beneficial to spend a bit of time together. Wasn't it? Anyway, that was the spiel he'd give her – and himself, for now. Then he grimaced, because who was he trying to kid! Wise or not, he desired her.

The Marmalade Cat lived up to expectations, and then some. They grabbed a secluded table on the terrace, Poppy oblivious to the male heads that turned in her direction. Unlike most females, she seemed unaware of how attractive she was, Sam noted. Either that, or she deliberately ignored the attention she drew. He ordered a latte for her and a mocha for himself, then waited for her to reach a decision about food.

Surrounded by appetising aromas, it didn't take much persuasion by the waiter to tempt Poppy with something from the specials' menu board. They were both drawn to the sea bass, cited as catch of the day.

"I see you've broken your tea only rule." Sam indicated her frothy cup pf coffee as they waited for their meals to be brought.

"It's only a latte," Poppy smiled, "which I do drink on special occasions. And today does feel a bit out of the ordinary." Her expression clouded. "I hope my talk was all right, Sam? I mean, I didn't expect to speak at all. Obviously, I had no preparation time, and ... "

"Your talk was brilliant," Sam placed a reassuring hand over hers, "and being unrehearsed only added to the authenticity. The part that I heard, at least. Congratulations, Poppy, you highlighted the complexities of Coeliac disease very well."

"Thanks." Poppy shifted awkwardly in her seat. "I'd have done better with time to prepare. I'm sure there were things I missed. I hope I got the key points across, anyway."

Their food arrived and they tucked in with relish. Sam was pleased to see her look more relaxed. The next hour sped by as they lingered over a delicious meal of fresh caught, pan-fried sea bass with roasted vegetables. Poppy proved to be the most delightful company. Unable to resist, Sam drank in the peachy softness of her skin, drawn to her full, red lips just ripe for kissing. He wondered how she'd react if he leant over and did exactly that; not good, probably. He reminded himself that she was probably a whole lot of trouble – but it didn't seem to matter. She had applied the merest hint of eye shadow, making her grey eyes appear seductively smoky. Down boy, Sam told himself, hailing the waiter to request a jug of iced water. One false move and the delectable Poppy Lambert would bolt.

"Fancy a pudding?" Sam queried. "Don't know about you, but I always think homemade ice cream rounds off a meal nicely."

"Agreed." Poppy smiled back, then pulled a wry face. "I must check if it's gluten free, though."

It was, so they both ordered two scoops of vanilla flavoured ice cream to complete the delicious lunch. Eager to see the photos he'd taken of the Sea Nymph, Sam grinned as Poppy leant forward. He held out his mobile to show her another pic and found himself enjoying her company more and more. She wasn't his type, she really wasn't – yet there was something about Poppy Lambert that he didn't seem able to resist.

"You really must come out in her," Sam held her gaze, "when the conditions are right. Soon, if you fancy it. The weather looks set fair at the moment. And I do have a skipper's licence in case you're worried." He chuckled. "You'll be in safe hands. Ever done any sailing before?"

The invitation was a tad premature, Sam realised after he'd issued it. Hopefully, Poppy wouldn't be scared off by such a direct approach. He couldn't withdraw the invite now, though. Besides, he wasn't used to reigning in his attraction to a female. He'd never had any reason to tread carefully with a woman before. However, if he read her right, her expression was purely one of excitement.

"That would be great!" She exclaimed, her grey eyes sparkling. "Thanks, Sam. But I warn you, I've no idea what sort of a sailor I am. I've never been out in a boat before, apart from a little dingy when I was about ten. Heavens, I might get sea-sick while the Sea Nymph is still moored."

"You won't." Sam chuckled. "We'll choose a calm day and hug the shore in case a squall does blow up. And that dingy experience you mention will come in handy. We have to take a dingy out to the Sea Nymph's mooring."

He ignored the voice in his head that said, hang on, you were only meant to take her to lunch, colleagues getting to know each other. Be careful; you're angling for a date now.

"Really?" Poppy's face was a picture. "You mean she's not tied up at the end of a pier somewhere nearby?"

"Afraid not." Sam chuckled again. "She's a drive away, moored near Instow on the estuary of the Taw and Torridge."

"Gracious, that is a drive!" She seemed to reconsider. "How do we get there?"

"I drive is how we get there," he said, "and pick you up en route. By the way, I'm told that area is referred to as 'heaven in Devon.' The converging rivers flow out into the Bristol Channel and the winds and tides can really be something."

"Wow, I bet." Poppy gave a reluctant glance at her thin, gold wrist watch. "Lunch was lovely, Sam, but I'd best make tracks. I'm not sure of the letting agent's opening times at the weekend, and I do want to catch him. Shall we call for the bill? And, before you say anything, it's only fair to split it."

She reached for her bag and Sam put out a hand to stop her.

"No, you're here at my invite, Poppy." He held her gaze. "My invite, my shout. I get the bill. Call me an old-fashioned kind of guy, but that's the way it is. No argument, I'm afraid." He winked to soften his words.

Sam saw that she was flustered. For a moment he thought she was going to spin him some yarn about always paying her way – which would have served as another black mark against her ex. A chap Sam was fast beginning to loathe. Then something in his expression must have made her capitulate. Poppy shrugged and closed her bag.

"OK then, thanks, Sam." Her soft mouth curved into a smile as she said, "I'll return the favour next time. In fact, I'll show you the Tarka Trail one day in return, if you like."

"You're on, lady!" Sam gave a silent whoop, keeping his tone deliberately light.

"That's a deal, then." Poppy stood, wrinkling her brow. "Mr Kerslake may close the office early on a Saturday, I'd better get a wiggle on. 'Bye, Sam, enjoy the rest of the weekend. See you at the surgery on Monday."

"Cheers." Sam rose, too, out of courtesy. He indicated to a passing waiter that he was ready for the bill. "See you, Poppy. Enjoy your afternoon."

His gaze tracked her to the exit, noting the sassy sway of her hips. She moved like a dancer, poised and elegant. The navy polka dot dress clung in all the right places, flaring gently at the waist, and swirling at her knees. Sam suppressed a grin, thinking lucky letting agent! He wondered what she needed to enquire about so urgently. Something to do with her flat, no doubt. As he recalled, the man in question, Mr Kerslake, was on the elderly side and rather curmudgeonly. Well, the sight of Poppy Lambert ought to put a smile on the old boy's face. That's if he was there on a Saturday, of course. Sam wouldn't be surprised if Poppy did find the office closed.

The important thing was that she had agreed to come out on the Sea Nymph – not only agreed but offered to show him the Tarka Trail in return. Sam gave a silent cheer.

True, it was a loose arrangement and they hadn't exchanged mobile numbers. However, that was a small detail. He slipped his credit card into the machine proffered by the waiter, nodded his thanks and added a hefty tip. The food had been excellent, but the tip was warranted for the company alone.

Poppy left the bistro and headed towards the town centre. Her heart beat a little faster. Lunch with Sam had been unexpectedly good. She sensed that working with him was going to add a certain frisson to her role at Bramblewood Surgery. All she had to do was remember to keep firm boundaries. At least she'd made the effort to dress up today.

Not that she'd done it for that reason, Poppy reminded herself hastily. It was just nice to spend time with a guy without having him try to jump her bones within the first ten minutes.

She caught her breath, hardly able to believe she'd offered to show Sam the Tarka Trail. The words had slipped out before she had considered the implications. She hadn't visited the Tarka Trail for years, but the experience would be magical, she was sure of it. All she had to do was ensure their relationship remained platonic. How hard could it be.

She reflected on their lunch together. At least, Sam hadn't made an obvious pass at her. Poppy couldn't kid herself she hadn't noticed the way his molten brown eyes raked her when he thought her attention was elsewhere. But attraction was fine so long as neither of them acted on it – wasn't it? Even a bit of mild flirtation. Maybe, just maybe, Sam was being honest when he'd shrugged and said that, like her, he sought only friendship. They were both newbies and it would be pleasant to spend time together with no strings attached. And company would be welcome as they both found their feet in the area. Ha, you're a sucker if you believe that, Poppy Lambert, said a little whisper!

Poppy sighed. She must learn to trust folk more, believe what they said – something she'd never been able to do with Mark, her ex. Despite giving him chance after chance.

She walked briskly, thinking of the chores she needed to tackle over the weekend. Household tasks had mounted up, although with such a small flat Poppy usually breezed through them swiftly. Yet there was something more important to be done first. She entered the letting agent's office. A girl at the desk informed her that Mr Kerslake himself rarely came in on a Saturday. Poppy's heart sank; a wasted journey. Still, she was there now. She may as well make enquiries with the young receptionist. She swallowed her disappointment and queried the situation concerning Rowan Cottage. Did the girl have any update with regards the property going on the market?

Poppy fully expected the young receptionist to look blank and claim ignorance, so was startled by her reply. Yes, the owner was planning to sell the cottage, most definitely, and soon. It was likely to come on the market any day now, certainly within the next couple of weeks. Did Poppy have a mortgage agreement in place? No? Then the girl strongly advised her to seek an appointment with a bank or a building society and sort that out, pronto. Although she felt duty bound to inform Poppy that Rowan Cottage may not come on the open market at all. Tapping her pen, the girl leaned forward conspiratorially. Nothing was settled yet, but it could end up being a private sale, she said.

Poppy gasped. The receptionist explained there was another interested party keen to purchase both Rowan Cottage and the cottage adjacent. She'd heard that planning permission would be sought to knock the two properties together. Permission was likely to be granted without a problem, as further down Lantern Lane a similar project had been done which set a precedent. Indeed, the council were known to be in favour.

Poppy blinked, feeling suddenly light-headed. Then it was true, the mystery buyer existed! If such a transaction went ahead, financially Rowan Cottage would be out of her reach.

It might not happen; buyers had been known to change their minds, pull out of a deal. Poppy took a steadying breath, holding onto the words 'nothing settled yet.' Tentatively, she queried what the asking price might be and tried not to balk at the answer. Who would have guessed a lowly fisherman's cottage would command such a price!

"It's the proximity to the sea," the young receptionist explained, "that's always a strong selling point. In fact, the market is so hot at the moment, I wouldn't be surprised if it ends up going for over the asking price. We do have cheaper cottages on our books, if you'd care to take a look at those and don't mind an inland location."

The girl swivelled to the shelves behind and reached deftly for a file. She proceeded to lay it open on the desk between them.

"Hmm, no thanks." Poppy forced a smile. "I'm only interested in Rowan Cottage. The place holds memories. It once belonged to my gran, you see. And I've always dreamt of owning it myself one day."

"Oh dear, that's tough." There was sympathy in the girl's eyes as she put away the property portfolio she had been poised to flick through. "Yes, I understand. Listen, situations do change, including what you may feel about the purchase of a different property. Why not apply for a mortgage anyway, then at least you'll be prepared. And keep in touch with us regarding how things develop with Rowan Cottage. You can check on-line, too."

Poppy doubted very much if the young receptionist did understand. No one did. It was like a yearning deep down in her soul. However, the girl's advice was good.

With a hasty goodbye, Poppy beat a retreat before she blubbed. Once out in the High St., she scanned the area for the nearest building society. Did it matter which one? She realised she didn't have much of a clue about financial affairs, so resolved to try them all. She could approach her bank, too. Poppy took care to live within her means, so her track record was sound – even if her savings weren't very healthy. She grimaced; she had Mark to thank for that. He'd borrowed money from her too often, money that had never been paid back. How could she have been such a fool!

She walked on, rehearsing what she'd say when she applied for a mortgage. After all, confidence counted. She'd enquire about monthly repayments in a tone that indicated she didn't anticipate a refusal. Today was about information gathering. Vaguely, Poppy recalled her father telling her the importance of obtaining quotes before she committed to anything. Wise advice, she realised now.

It was good she'd had the foresight to pop a couple of relevant documents into her bag before setting off that morning. Everything else could wait. The hunt for the best mortgage deal took priority. Fingers firmly crossed, Poppy took a deep breath, and pushed on the swing door of the first building society she came to.

"I'd like to talk to someone about a mortgage application, please." She addressed the young man who sat behind the reception desk.

She took a seat, as requested, and waited while he disappeared to find the appropriate member of staff. Hopefully, this was her lucky day. She had fingers and toes firmly crossed. But it was only the start. Poppy determined to plead her case and try every avenue possible.

She wasn't ready to give up her quest for Rowan Cottage without a fight.

CHAPTER SIX

"I'd like to run some blood tests, Tania." Sam studied the wan, young lady in front of him. "Initially, I want an FBC – a full blood count. That's a pretty standard test and will give us a clearer picture of what could be the problem. You'll need to see one of our practice nurses, Laura, or Poppy, for the blood test. Wait a day or two for the results to be in, then book to see me again. How does that sound? In the meantime, do you feel well enough to return to work, or do you need a certificate? I'm happy to sign you off while we explore what's going on."

"A certificate, please, Doctor." Tania twisted her fingers nervously.

Observing her, Sam had the impression a strong breeze might blow her away.

"No problem." He printed out the certificate and handed it to her. "Here you go. OK, book in those appointments at reception. If there's a problem with availability of dates, tell them that I'd like you to be fitted in without undue delay. Ditto, an appointment to come back to see me. In the meantime, treat this as your 'r & r' time – rest and relaxation. Get plenty of walks in the fresh air, too."

"Thank you, Dr Brocklehurst." Tania returned his smile, her own distinctly tremulous as she prepared to leave. "I can't understand it. I haven't felt well since I picked up a gastric bug from one of the pupils. I'm normally so full of bounce. I need to be in my job as a classroom assistant with lively eight-year-olds."

"Gastric bug?" Sam pricked up his ears at this information. "How long ago was that? I don't see anything on your notes."

Could this be coincidental or was it a missing piece of the puzzle?

"Ah, a month ago, maybe nearer two." Tania shrugged dismissively. "It was vicious while it lasted, but the symptoms were over quite quickly. I didn't see a GP at the time, that's why there's nothing on record. But I haven't felt properly well since."

"Hmm, in that case we'd better send off a stool specimen, too." Sam leant down to fish out a specimen pot from the drawer of the clinical cabinet. He attached a label. "Best to check there's no lingering infection. Leave it with the nurse when you come for your blood test. In fact, while you're at it, bring along a urine sample, too. Ask the nurse to do a routine dipstick test while you're with her." He turned to retrieve a different specimen pot. "Let's cover all the bases. We'll talk further at your next appointment, Tania, but don't hesitate to ring if you're worried and need advice before that."

There was something about this patient that made Sam take notice. He scanned his computer screen after she left, reviewing Tania's medical history to ensure there was nothing he had missed. Tania Croft had been squeezed in at short notice. Of necessity, the consultation had had to be brief. Basic observations had been fine, albeit her pulse rate was slightly raised. However, her pallor was marked. Ditto, her lethargy. When the blood test results were available would be the moment to probe further. Hopefully, Tania's diagnosis would turn out to be straightforward. Various possibilities sprang to mind, but Sam always heeded his gut instinct – and with this patient it was putting him on amber alert.

Sam leant back in his chair, stretched and rolled his shoulders. His first ever session at Bramblewood was proving busy but enjoyable. A typical Monday morning when folk pitched up with an array of symptoms they'd been sitting on over the weekend. Busy was fine; he had no complaints. In fact, it was his preferred way of starting a new post, straight in at the deep end, no time to faff. A fast pace suited him, made the adrenaline flow.

He checked the computer screen for details of his next patient and gave a wry grin. He liked being left to get on with the job. Not that he was above seeking advice if it was warranted, but he didn't need to be mollycoddled. Sam glanced up as a sharp rap on his consulting room door heralded Bramblewood's senior partner, Andrew Doyle.

"Hi Sam, how's it going?" Andrew's bespectacled face peered round the door. "Any problems? Just poking my head in while you're between patients."

"Hi, Andy." Sam gave him the thumbs up. "No, I'm OK, thanks. Working my way through the patient list nicely. Another couple to see and I'm done."

"Fine, fine." Andrew beamed. "Then I'll leave you to it. Remember I'm only down the corridor if you do need anything. David and Liz are around somewhere, too."

Giving a cheery wave, Andrew disappeared. Relieved there were no issues to sort, Sam guessed with another wry grin. No matter how tolerant other members of staff were, the reality was that everyone preferred a new medic who was able to slot in and crack on with a session without too much fuss. Beyond the obvious need to know queries, a barrage of questions when surgery was in full swing could be tedious for everyone. That was the benefit of moving posts frequently to gain experience. It had left him adaptable, able to grasp the salient points quickly. Less important details could be gleaned later.

Sam strode to the waiting room to summon his next patient, and spied Poppy, albeit the back view of her. Today she was the consummate professional, looking neat and efficient in her navy uniform of tunic and trousers. Unexpectedly, she glanced round, perhaps feeling herself watched. Their gaze met and a smile lit her face. She gave him a quick thumbs up before vanishing into one of the treatment rooms.

Sam experienced a warm glow of pleasure. Gone was the timid fawn look with which he was familiar. Nurse Lambert was chilled in his presence – result!

"Mr Gerald Robertson, please." Sam glanced at the assembled group as he called for his next patient.

An old-fashioned approach, perhaps, but he preferred to call his patients in person, rather than rely on a buzzer. Apart from anything else, Sam liked the exercise. Otherwise, doctors risked sitting behind their desk for overly long periods.

⌒

"Oh Poppy, your next appointment has cancelled." Flo, one of Bramblewood's three receptionists, frowned. "Can you see a Miss Tania Croft instead, please? Dr Brocklehurst wants her bloods done a.s.a.p. and there isn't much availability the rest of this week. She's over there. I've asked her to wait while I sort out something."

"Happy to oblige, Flo." Poppy nodded, and invited the patient to follow her.

It made sense to see her, particularly if Sam was concerned enough not to want a delay.

She invited Tania to sit and roll up her sleeve, chatting as she prepared to take the blood sample. Poppy checked the computer screen to see exactly what bloods Sam had requested, then fished out the required bottles and a syringe. As often happened with patients, Tania was more relaxed in the presence of a nurse. Poppy listened to Tania describe how she'd been feeling, and alarm bells rung. Why, oh why did some patients fail to give their doctor the whole story. It would make diagnosis so much easier if they did! Also, more importantly, it could affect what blood tests were ordered.

"And you didn't mention the nausea to S – to Dr Brocklehurst?"

"N - no, it's only occasional. I forgot." Tania nibbled her lip. "I fancy it's getting worse, though. But this wretched tiredness is the main thing I'm worried about. I've started to get indigestion, too ... that's a new thing. Only mild, but I suppose I should mention it to Dr Brocklehurst when I see him again."

What best to do? Poppy was undecided. Surgery was in full swing. Unless there was an emergency, grabbing a GP wasn't likely to be easy. At best, it would mean Tania waiting again, and she might not wish to be delayed. Poppy made a swift decision.

"If it's OK, I'd like to add in another blood test while you're here, Tania. It has a long name; the IgA anti-tissue glutaminase antibodies test. Quite a mouthful, eh!" She winked to reassure her patient. "Just to screen you for one more thing while I'm taking blood anyway."

"Fine, whatever." Tania shrugged as Poppy deftly found a vein and slid in the needle.

"Done." Poppy lay down the syringe, and placed a small swab over the penetration site. "Press down firmly on this, please, Tania – no, don't bend your arm, keep it straight. Most of the results should be back by Wednesday. The IgA test will take a longer."

"Thanks, Poppy, expertly done. I'm not keen on needles, but I hardly felt a thing." Tania looked relieved. "Oops, I was supposed to leave you a couple of specimens if my bloods were done tomorrow. What shall I do about those?"

Poppy smiled. "Pop out to the toilet and spend a penny, I can test your urine now. The stool sample you can drop off at the surgery to be sent to the Lab tomorrow morning."

Poppy waited for her patient to return, unsure if Sam would object to her adding in the IgA test. She hoped not but there hadn't been an opportunity to check with him first. Yet she experienced a niggle of worry.

Tania's urine specimen was clear. Poppy pulled off her gloves, threw them in the clinical waste bin and gave her patient a reassuring smile.

"All fine. You're free to go now, Tania."

She placed the blood samples in the out tray ready for collection to go off to the Lab. Would Tania's IgA test come back positive? A long shot, but it would be interesting to see.

The result took a little longer than most routine blood tests, and went to a different Lab to be tested. The more immediate question was how would Sam feel about the test being added in without specific instruction? As a practice nurse her remit was to follow the GP's directive, competently carry out procedures but not diagnose. If she was worried about a patient or felt something had been overlooked, then she was expected to refer back to the patient's GP. This was the standard protocol, although she'd had flexibility in her last post.

Should she send Sam an explanatory email? No, better to catch him and explain in person. However, the pace remained relentless. When Poppy was free to look for Sam, she discovered he'd left, called out on an urgent visit to one of the local nursing homes. Due off duty shortly, she decided to seek him out in the morning. She still felt vaguely uneasy. It would be OK, wouldn't it? Some doctors did get a bit precious about not being consulted first, but surely Sam wasn't the type to bite her head off. At least, not if she explained her rationale to him. She said cheerio to Laura and stepped out into the sunshine.

If Poppy thought Monday had been hectic, Tuesday topped it – by miles. She arrived at Bramblewood only to discover that Laura had been poorly overnight and rung in sick. The practice nurse appointments had to be rejigged to allow patients to be seen according to priority. Faye, as senior nurse specialist, took charge of triage. Poppy did what she always did when the workload was heavy: put her head down and got on with it.

She barely glimpsed Sam and, once more, he'd disappeared again by the time her session finished.

Almost before Poppy could breathe it was Wednesday. With Laura absent until Thursday, the pressure intensified. Faye shared the load when able but had her own patient list to manage. Julia regularly made murmurings about them needing a bank practice nurse to call on, Faye said darkly, but to date that's all they were – murmurings. Poppy consoled herself with the thought it was the PPG meeting that evening. She could ask Sam for a quick word then. Not ideal, she thought ruefully, as Tania's blood results may have been viewed already – and he'd have seen the added in test, if not the result. She groaned in frustration.

"I'll take your next couple of appointments." Faye appeared as Poppy was about to call in her next patient. "You've been flat out all morning. Take a lunch break, Poppy."

"Thanks, Faye." Poppy smiled. "I promise to be quick. It won't take me long to wolf down a couple of sandwiches."

For the sake of convenience, Poppy remained in the practice nurses' treatment room. She fetched a fresh drink from the water cooler and took a sip. She had only just sat down again and taken a bite of her sandwich when there was a peremptory rap on the door.

"Come in." Poppy glanced up, half expecting Faye to enter with a reprimand for not having gone to the staff room, or out for some fresh air.

There really wasn't time, though. They were all going to be late off duty as it was. Besides, she could snatch a break before the PPG meeting. She opened her mouth to say this, but the words died as Sam strode in. He shut the door behind him, looking displeased. Poppy saw his expression and felt her heart sink. It wasn't hard to guess his agenda.

"Sorry to interrupt your break, Poppy, but I need to speak to you about Tania Croft." His tone had an edge, and there was no twinkle in Sam's deep brown eyes now.

"If you mean, why did I add in the blood test for coeliac disease," Poppy decided attack was the best form of defence, "Tania shared a bit more with me, and I thought she was displaying some of the symptoms. As I was taking blood anyway, and she hates needles, it seemed sensible to check for that at the same time. Rule it in or out. There wasn't time to run it past you first, Sam, but it's not an expensive test. I'm sorry, I did try to find you afterwards and explain, but if you remember Monday was hectic and ... "

Her voice trailed off. Poppy swallowed, aware that Sam was looking increasingly irritated.

"It's not about the cost of a blood test, Poppy." He stood with folded arms, regarding her sternly. "If I deem it necessary, I will order whatever blood test I think is warranted. What I don't do is order a blood test without first talking to the patient and explaining the reason for it. I don't slip in the unexpected on a whim. Does Tania know that she's being checked out for coeliac disease? Did you discuss it with her?"

"N - no. I only mentioned doing one more test while she was with me." Poppy cleared her throat, wilting under his steely gaze. "I asked if she was OK with that, and she said fine, do whatever needs doing. Then she told me she didn't like needles and I felt I'd made the right decision ... I mean, save her from coming back again for something I could do there and then."

"Not quite the question I asked, Poppy." Sam scowled.

"I didn't think it necessary until the result came back." Poppy hesitated.

"So, you didn't enlarge on the reason you added in another blood test." Sam paused to study her. "Which, again, isn't the key point here. As doctors, when we investigate a patient's symptoms it's common practice to start with the simpler things first – because, where general practice is concerned, in most cases the cause does turn out to be simple. We don't immediately jump to the rare and obscure. We explore more complex conditions after we've eliminated the obvious. Coeliac disease is not the most obvious diagnosis to jump to."

Heavens, he was giving her a proper dressing down. Poppy felt her face heat. She realised she was seeing another side of Sam. A side she didn't much like. Suddenly she had had enough of his lecturing. She was a professional in her own right, for goodness' sake.

"With respect, Sam, coeliac disease is missed repeatedly by GPs." No longer nervous, she determined to defend her corner. "I know from personal experience that's a fact, yet it's such an easy test to add in. I apologise if you think I've overstepped the mark, but I wish someone had had the foresight to test me earlier on! The docs at my last Practice didn't mind me adding in something extra if I thought it might be helpful."

As soon as her words were out, Poppy knew they were ill advised. Sam's expression changed from stern to forbidding, and a chill ran down her spine. She had dug a hole for herself by inferring he'd missed something. Heck, why couldn't she have apologised, ask demurely how he'd prefer her to act in future and left it at that. Then they both could have saved face. She replaced her unfinished sandwich in its container and discarded it, her appetite gone.

"In my experience, doctors who are happy to let their practice nurses have that level of responsibility are medics who need to sharpen up their assessment skills." There was no mistaking the steely glint in Sam's eyes now.

"Or, to put it bluntly, they're lazy and knowing their requests will be scrutinised is a useful backup. By all means, shout out if you feel something has been missed – no one is infallible – but otherwise please stick to the bloods that have been ordered, Poppy. Trust me, in the long run it will make everyone's life run smoother."

"And the patient?" Poppy couldn't stop herself. "How will it make Tania's life run more smoothly, for example? Surely it doesn't matter who first thought of doing a test that reveals something. What counts is that someone was proactive, whether that be the doctor or the nurse. You might think otherwise, Sam, but I really don't view every patient who comes my way as an undiagnosed coeliac, just because I have the condition."

Inwardly, Poppy seethed. She was a good nurse, a professional in her own right. A fact that Sam had chosen to ignore. And she refused to be spoken to like that.

"I've no more to say on the matter." His body language indicated the subject was closed. "See you at the PPG meeting this evening. Although, if it drags on, I won't be able to stay to the end. There is a proposal I want to put forward with regards Bramblewood's walled garden at the rear. No doubt you've seen it, a wilderness at the moment. With a team of volunteers that space could be transformed and put to very good use. Research shows the benefit of community gardening ventures. Fresh air and companionship can be a better mood enhancer than any medication. Anyway, we'll discuss that further tonight."

With a cursory nod, he was gone. Poppy blinked, wondering if she'd imagined the scenario that had taken place. As for the swift change of tack, she felt furious. How dare Sam think he could shut her down so easily. For her part, the subject was definitely not closed. She resolved to tackle him at a later date when she felt better prepared. Poppy suspected it was going to be a long day.

As for the PPG meeting, if Sam thought she was going to pick up the baton for a community gardening venture in his absence, he could whistle! This was his pet project, and he could spearhead it. How could she have ever thought him charismatic! Poppy discarded her sandwiches and went in search of Faye. She chose to ignore her colleague's look of surprise on announcing that she was ready to start the afternoon session. Anger proved a good fuel for flagging energy.

It was another late finish. At the end of her session, Poppy changed back into jeans and a neat, pastel coloured top. There was just enough time to relax with a mug of tea and finish her sandwiches before going across to Bramblewood Dental Surgery for the PPG Meeting. Hopefully, the hot drink would give her a needed lift. She had taken a sip when a cheery hello indicated the arrival of Julia, with an offer to accompany her.

"Excellent idea, a snack before we convene." Julia beamed. "Wish I'd had the foresight to bring sustenance. Right, if you're ready, off we go. The format for these things is quite straightforward. We follow an agenda which Allan Harcombe will chair. Alan is our current PPG leader, if you recall. Tonight, we'll be reviewing last Saturday's event, and exploring ideas for the next one. My role is to bring the PPG up to date on any surgery news. Then there's space at the end for A.O.B. Apparently, Sam is keen to put forward his thoughts on our rather neglected Victorian walled garden."

Nothing unexpected here. Poppy nodded, increasing her pace to keep up with the Practice Manager's brisk step. Catching Julia's expression, she felt a response was in order.

"How many PPG members does our Practice have?" Poppy searched for something pertinent to ask. "Did they all attend on Saturday? I think I met about seven."

"No, we have ten if everyone turns up." Julia laughed gaily. "We'd like more but drumming up interest is an on-going challenge. Any ideas on how to do that welcome, by the way. Sam's suggestion, a poster in the waiting room to ask for specific gardening volunteers might be worth a try. Folk who will be attached to the PPG, but not committed to attend every meeting ... but I'll let him talk about that later. I won't steal his thunder."

"Hmm." Even to her own ears Poppy's reply sounded less than enthusiastic.

Ah, so he'd already collared Julia, had he! Well, the two of them could organise whatever they wanted as long as it didn't involve her, Poppy thought waspishly. Perhaps it wasn't too late to withdraw from her involvement with the PPG, admit to Julia that she found the extra hours too much after a long working day. What, after attending one meeting, an inner voice countered. No, she would have to give it more of a go than that, or think up a different excuse. Like be honest and say that she'd rather not be in proximity with Sam. Poppy sighed, aware that excuse wouldn't do, either. In any case, who else was there to replace Laura. Poppy trailed after Julia, feeling disgruntled.

A small group, Sam among them, had gathered in the upstairs galley kitchen where refreshments were being organised. Immediately, Poppy's heart sank.

"Excellent, someone's on tea making duty." Ever jolly, Julia ushered in Poppy. "This is the hub of the place when we have a PPG meeting, Poppy. And I've brought along chocolate hobnobs; pass me a plate, please, whoever's closest to the cupboard. I'm sure we can all do with a bit of light refreshment."

No good for her, though, Poppy thought with gritted teeth. Julia's bland expression said everything. Already she'd forgotten about the talk Poppy had given.

Tired of always telling folk not to worry, it didn't matter, Poppy felt her smile freeze as the biscuits were offered around. She waved them away. The truth was it did matter, and she was fed up with folk not understanding dietary restrictions. Had Julia paid no attention to her expert patient spiel? Obviously not.

"Ah, chocolate biccies, a welcome addition to my flapjacks." Smoothly, Sam produced a box and opened the lid. "Here you are, folks, courtesy of a wonderful bakery I've discovered just round the corner. Gluten free, too, by the way. Do we have another plate in that cupboard? I'll put them out separately."

Poppy remained silent. If this was meant to be a peace offering, she wasn't in the mood to accept it. Not for the first time Sam's actions put her in a quandary. A second plate was thrust into her hands and she allowed herself the merest glance at the flapjacks.

"Great." Her tone was flat. "You needn't have bothered on my account, though, Sam. I've just finished eating the packed lunch I didn't have time for earlier."

There, that would show him! She moved away, attempting an air of nonchalance. However, her departure wasn't fast enough to avoid Sam's gaze. Their eyes met and she saw an unmistakable twinkle. Why, he was laughing at her, the beast! Heat scorched her cheeks. She turned and stalked into the main room, almost flinging the plate of flapjacks down onto a low coffee table. Where guys were concerned, she should trust her instincts. The charmers were always rats!

Other members of the PPG had wandered in now. Poppy found herself a chair, and sat and watched as folk milled around, chatting. She sighed. It felt like this was going to be a very long evening.

"OK everyone." Julia clapped her hands for attention. "It looks like we're all here, so let's start." She indicated Poppy. "For those of you who haven't met her, this is Poppy Lambert, our new practice nurse. Poppy has taken over from Laura."

In the pause that ensued Poppy realised belatedly that Julia expected her to say a few words. Quickly, she pasted on what she hoped was a cheerful smile and not a grimace.

"Hi, yes, I'm Poppy." She cleared her throat. "Pleased to meet you all. I'm interested to see what goes on at PPGs." A white lie tonight but what else could she say. "This is my first experience of anything like this. My last GP practice didn't have one, you see."

The room quietened amid nods and smiles. Poppy found a sheet with the minutes printed out and studied it dutifully, trying to ignore the rumble of her stomach. She had fibbed about finishing her packed lunch, she hadn't done any such thing. There had barely been time for a nibble before Julia breezed in to collect her. Moreover, Poppy felt sure that Sam knew this. Perhaps pride should be ignored, and she could take a flapjack. Just one, when he looked the other way. It would be so easy to reach out and lift it off the plate. They did look delicious, and heaven alone knew what time she would be home tonight. Too late to want to cook anything, that was certain.

Poppy almost stretched out her hand. Almost! However, she didn't intend to capitulate now, even if that meant she had to stay hungry.

"Shall we start with feedback from our recent event," Julia continued. "Excellent reviews from those who attended. I will, of course, pass comments on to Kate. And the Expert Patient slot was very well received, for which we have Poppy to thank for stepping in at the last minute."

CHAPTER SEVEN

Sam suppressed a chuckle. He hadn't intended to laugh, he honestly hadn't, but Poppy trying to pull off aloof really didn't work. She was angry with him, that much was obvious. Regretful though he was about that, because he much preferred her shy smile, Sam was clear on one thing. They were a team at Bramblewood, and efficient teams had robust boundaries. Where patients were concerned, his staff needed to trust him to order the appropriate investigations and make a diagnosis. Not jump to their own conclusions and add in something extra without referring to him first. He didn't doubt Poppy had tried to find him for a word afterwards, but that was hardly the point. Especially as she'd failed, and Tania had rung in to query an extra blood test he'd had no recollection of ordering.

With hindsight, though, Sam admitted his reaction hadn't been entirely fair. He wished he'd told Poppy about the ensuing telephone consult with regards to Tania. It was this urgent request for a call back that had been the trigger for him to seek out Poppy. However, he could have handled things better. Poppy hadn't been aware Tania had had a sudden worsening of her – previously unreported - indigestion, vomited, and noticed frank blood. Scared, she had rung the surgery and he'd arranged an urgent endoscopy.

Further delving had resulted in Tania sharing symptoms she'd hitherto not mentioned – to him, anyway. Namely, a history of stress related cluster headaches that she managed by self-medication. Warning bells had rung on that one.

Tania's drug of choice, an anti-inflammatory, had resulted in over-use of NSAIDs – a habit that Sam was pretty sure had damaged her stomach lining and was responsible for a bleeding gastric ulcer. The anaemia, too, in all likelihood. Her iron levels were low, and the results of her stool specimen indicated the presence of occult blood.

Even a trickle of blood over a lengthy time could lead to anaemia, which in turn would lead to the chronic fatigue that had brought Tania to the surgery. In Sam's opinion, adding in the test for coeliac disease only served to muddy the waters. Yet Poppy's stony expression made him regret the way he had approached her. Tonight, he had to leave early. So, there was no chance of catching her for an explanatory word afterwards.

The PPG meeting underway, Sam focussed on the reason he was there. He listened courteously while someone read through the minutes, and Julia gave feedback on the recent PPG educational event. Popular, judging by the comments. Poppy's talk had received particular praise which he was glad about.

"Now I'll hand you over to Sam," Julia nodded at him, "who has a wonderful suggestion to make with regards Bramblewood's neglected Victorian walled garden. I expect you've all seen it, tucked away behind the parking area. He votes that we, the PPG, take over the upkeep and put the space to good use."

"Practical and therapeutic use with the aid of extra volunteers, obviously." Smoothly, Sam picked up Julia's cue. "We can advertise specifically for gardening vols. Folk who don't need to be involved with the PPG in any other way. In fact, some of you may already know people keen to be involved in such a project." Briefly, he outlined his ideas for use of the garden space once it was tidied up. Concluding,

"With regards loneliness and depression, evidence-based research shows the benefit of community and folk getting out in the open air. I see our gardening vols as having a mix of ability, ranging from skilled right down to never done it before, but keen to try. I hope the venture will attract those who enjoyed gardening previously, and no longer have their own plot, plus folk who are looking for a small patch of earth to grow veg., for example."

"I like the idea of the surgery using the outside space for mums and toddlers, too." Marie, one of the younger PPG members spoke up. "From experience, I know what a nightmare it is trying to placate a fractious toddler when the wait is prolonged. There'd have to be some health and safety stuff, too, like checking for obvious trip hazards."

"Indeed," another voice interjected, "and ensuring no one grew anything toxic, you know what kids are like for putting stuff in their mouths."

"Hmm, and there is a small pond at the top, if my memory is correct." Julia pursed her lips. "That may need covering over. Right, how about we look at wording and design for a poster to go on display in the surgery waiting room, with a date – say three weeks hence – for another PPG meeting specifically to address the garden project? Before we proceed any further, let's see how much interest this plan generates."

"We'll need to crack on." Alan frowned. "Summer is the optimum time for gardening and there's plenty of work to be done before it's anything like a usable space. We'll need two teams of vols., those able to help with the heavier physical work and those happy to weed and potter, as well as grow stuff."

"Why not involve Liz, our patient co-ordinator?" Poppy spoke up. "After all, she's the one who signposts folk to beneficial groups and activities. She could add 'gardening group' to her list of strategies to help with anxiety and low mood."

Sam felt pleased to see Poppy join in, her expression more animated. As enthusiasm for the project grew, the suggestions put forward became more ambitious. They wouldn't be able to accomplish everything this year, of course - and, if wise, they would start small. That didn't matter, though. Big ideas captured interest and fired enthusiasm.

The ideas kept on coming, and Sam grinned. As long as folk were aware those plans would need reshaping as the project evolved, it was fine to think big and bold. For the moment, they were exploring options, testing what was feasible. No one had tackled the thorny issue of finance yet. Even small projects cost money. Sam glanced at the wall clock and frowned. Unfortunately, he needed to leave.

"Apologies," he pulled a face, "I'm afraid I must go, but please carry on with the discussion in my absence. This project has legs. Julia, if you would kindly pass on my email contact, Alan can forward me the minutes of this evening's meeting and I'll see you all when we next convene. Thanks for your input tonight, everyone. Cheers."

With that he stood. Out in the warm evening air, Sam half regretted his decision to leave early. It meant an opportunity missed to invite Poppy to the pub afterwards and, hopefully, walk her home. A friendly overture to prove there was no ill feeling regarding their earlier altercation, on his side, anyway. But the anguished call he'd taken from his little sister played on his mind. With limited time to talk, he'd promised her a call back and something in her tone had made him feel he didn't want to leave that call overly long. From past experience there was bound to be a bloke involved. Sam's lip curled. What was it with sparky females who repeatedly picked the wrong guys? He really thought his little sis had wised up in recent months, but obviously not.

Poppy's face flashed into his mind. She'd been paler than usual and tired tonight, he could tell. A fact not helped by a missed lunch. Sam felt a pang of guilt. He wondered exactly how poorly she had been pre-diagnosis. Yet, from what he'd heard her say at the PPG Event, she was healthy now. Yet full recovery was an individual thing. It took some folk longer than others.

Sam scowled as he strode across to his car, parked in a patch of mellow evening sun. Someone needed to tell Poppy to rest more. Not him, obviously, but someone. Then he had an idea. The Sea Nymph was ready, and the weather forecast looked set fair for the weekend. Ideal conditions for messing about on the water, something he'd been itching to do for ages. Sam grinned. Why not invite Poppy to come out in the boat with him on Saturday. After all, she had shown a keen interest.

The more he considered it, the more the idea appealed, if only to get their relationship back on an even keel. He'd cobble together a snack of some sort to tide them over, then drop anchor close to a riverside pub for a proper meal. The place Bill had shown him on the Sunday, when they took the boat out together, would be perfect. Sam decided to check the menu for gluten free options in advance to ensure Poppy had a stress free, relaxing day out – if she agreed to accompany him, of course. He guessed the odds were not in his favour.

Back at Rowan Cottage, Sam opened the 'fridge door and grabbed a lager. He carried the can through to the front room, flipped the lid, and took a gulp. The cool, amber liquid felt like nectar as it ran down his throat. He waited a moment, relishing the sensation, then reached in his pocket for his mobile. Better prepare for the long haul! What was happening with his little sis now? He stretched out on the comfortable but rather worn sofa. His call answered on the second ring, Sam tensed. All was about to be revealed.

As anticipated, the phone call proved lengthy. Even after it was over, Sam wasn't entirely sure he had grasped the salient points. Uncharacteristically, his sister had been weepy, her sobs making it difficult to hear everything she said. This alone had been enough to worry him. Continually, he'd had to ask her to slow down, take a deep breath and repeat herself. Sam still felt like he needed more clarity.

The only girl amongst four rowdy brothers, he'd never quite understood why it was him that his little sis turned to when things went awry. Thankfully, she had sounded calmer when they'd said their goodbyes. One thing was for sure, though; things were not resolved, and he couldn't leave the situation unsorted. Not after the news his sibling had just imparted. Aware that dusk had fallen, Sam stood and stretched; emotional baggage was certainly draining! So far, he'd been fortunate to escape without too much of his own.

It might be wise to rethink issuing an invitation to Poppy, though.

He walked to the uncurtained window, and stared out a moment before turning to switch on a table lamp. Immediately the pale cottage walls took on a welcoming, rosy glow. Yes, he could picture himself making a home here, Sam thought, particularly if he was able to purchase the property next door. In that respect all the omens were good, as his little sis would say. However, he'd made his offer, and it was a fair one. Sam wasn't one to hang around. If the owner shilly-shallied too long then he may just find the offer withdrawn.

Sam folded an old throw he'd found for the sofa, trying to imagine Poppy as a child, coming to stay here at Rowan Cottage with her gran. Did she find the place much changed, he wondered. Maybe, when they were on friendlier terms again, he'd ask her. Not ready for sleep, he decided to sift through another couple of packing boxes. It was gone midnight, with a silver moon sailing across a starlit sky, when eventually Sam's head hit the pillows. He slept soundly, undisturbed by nocturnal shadows and the odd creaks of an old house.

The next day the pace at Bramblewood Surgery was as fast and furious as the one before. Indeed, Sam was beginning to suspect this was the norm. Not that he objected, he liked being kept on his toes. He kept an eye out for Poppy but, annoyingly, she proved to be elusive.

After futile attempts to catch the young practice nurse, Sam gave up, resigned to glimpses of her as she disappeared with yet another patient. He frowned. Friday was only a day away, and the weekend almost on them. He kept his head down and concentrated on his own patient list, deciding it prudent to wait until later to issue his invite. His list held nothing too challenging, mostly run of the mill cases for a GP – although a lot of diagnoses to make in the allotted ten-minute consultation slots. Much as he might wish to spend more time with folk, things were as they were. Yet Sam was never complacent, ever alert for the more serious presentations hidden amongst the mundane.

The morning wore on. A call came in from one of the district nurses; a request for a repeat prescription for an end-of-life patient's syringe driver. Fine, except that he'd never set eyes on the patient in question. Sam took a moment to scan the woman's notes. Once a syringe driver had been set up troublesome symptoms tended to be much better controlled – which was, of course, the aim. Indeed, this seemed to be the case for Mrs Cartwright. The district nurse reported that, bar one tweak to the medication advised by the last specialist hospice nurse to visit, things remained stable.

It seemed no one from Bramblewood Surgery had reviewed the patient for a while. A further scroll through the notes indicated that a GP home visit wouldn't go amiss. Happy to issue the repeat 'script, Sam asked the nurse to inform Mrs Cartwright's family of his intension pop in after lunch. The situation sounded well managed and the district nurse hadn't requested a doctor review, but he wanted to eyeball things for himself.

Equally important, Sam wished to see the patient's partner and assess how the man was coping. The needs of the carer often became eclipsed by the needs of the patient – and they could be silently drowning in a relentless sea of physical demand overlaid by emotion.

No one noticed the carer's quiet struggle until things fell apart. Plus, there was a thirteen-year-old in the family, Sam noted. Harry, a young lad poised to lose his mum at a critical time. Teenage was said to be the worst age to lose a parent, although how data like this was assessed Sam didn't know. Surely any age was bad if you were a kid! Whilst nothing could be done to reverse the situation for Harry's mum, in the coming weeks what the boy needed most was a functioning father. Sam determined to access every support available for this little family.

Towards the end of his morning session, Sam took a call from the Matron of one of the local nursing homes, a request for the assessment of an elderly resident after a fall. It sounded urgent although precise details were scant. He shrugged philosophically and grabbed his medical bag. It wasn't the first-time lunch had had to be put on a back burner.

On arrival at The Gables Nursing Home, Sam immediately saw the odd angle of the elderly man's leg. A fractured femur, common in the elderly after a fall. The man had not been moved, but kept warm and made as comfortable as possible where he lay in the corridor. Sam administered a pain killing injection and organised ambulance transfer to hospital. An Xray would be needed to confirm diagnosis, followed by admission for surgery. In fact, he was mildly surprised the Home hadn't gone ahead and summonsed an ambulance in the first instance. Had someone in authority ever said not to in times past? Sam made a mental note to enquire with the matron about in-house staff training. An update was due!

Whilst still at The Gables, he was asked to see another resident attached to Bramblewood: increased dementia, query infection related. On examination, the elderly lady did indeed have a chest infection. Sam's mobile rang again with another urgent call even before he'd written out a 'script for antibiotics.

He noted the address as he left the building and the afternoon wore on. Frustratingly, Poppy had left by the time Sam returned to the surgery. He'd have to nab her on arrival at Bramblewood first thing tomorrow morning, his last chance as it was Friday. Like him, Poppy tended to arrive early. He would suggest they grabbed a coffee together in the staff room, under the pretence of two colleagues having a catch up. With luck he would find her in a more receptive mood.

Sam's focus switched to his sister. The telephone conversation had been a revelation. Although, if he'd understood Tizzy correctly, it seemed that for once her relationship was going well. To date there had been no great dramas. Strangely, this was what had upset her, because it was so out of the norm that she couldn't trust it was real. For the life of him, Sam hadn't been able to fathom out why. Or what there was to discuss so urgently about a relationship that was coasting along smoothly ... but guessed that he, a mere male, must have missed something.

Then his little sis had dropped her bombshell, and left Sam feeling like he'd been side-swiped by a steamroller! He wasn't even sure if Michelle knew yet, though he supposed she must. Hell, he needed to talk to Tizzy face to face. Therefore, he'd asked her to stay at the cottage. He grimaced on recalling his phrasing; insisted might be a more accurate term. After a lengthy debate of dates, she had agreed and he had to be content with that.

Sam shouted good night to his colleagues as he left Bramblewood and strode out into the sultry evening. He wasn't on call. The lure of a beach run was strong, and he'd always had a penchant for translating mental energy into physical. A blustery coastal wind picked up, making the treetops sway. The pull of the elements won. In no time he'd reached Rowan Cottage, and parked neatly in the layby opposite. The beach called like long-lost friend.

Sam donned his running gear and set off again at a jog, reaching the sands in record time. He quickly found his stride, increasing his pace as he pushed forward against the stiff, offshore breeze. He dragged in lungfuls of fresh, salty air, feeling the day's tension dissipate. Out at sea, foamy white seahorses topped the waves against a noisy backdrop of circling gulls. The one thing missing tonight was Poppy. Sam wondered if she might be down on the beach, too, and found himself looking for her. There were other runners but Poppy's leggy, gazelle-like form wasn't among them. A pity.

With no distractions, Sam focussed purely on the run. A fine sheen of sweat on his brow, he felt his muscles burn as he pushed himself to the limit. Eventually, when the first stars populated the evening sky, it was time to head back to Rowan Cottage.

Sam unlocked the oak front door, the original, he suspected, peeled off his running gear and headed for the shower. He stood a moment under the cool needles of water, then adjusted the temperature control and began to wash. A bar of slippery soap necessitated all manner of contortions to retrieve it, and he had a sharp reminder of the size of his washing space. Was it his imagination, or had the shower cubicle shrunk? It certainly felt that way.

Hopefully, a remedy was on the horizon. Sam tipped back his head, rinsed his hair, and remembered a voicemail from the letting agent inviting further dialogue. Mr Kerslake's tone had been positive. Sam's bid to buy both cottages had piqued the owner's interest. So, if he would care to call back for a proper discussion, they'd be only too willing, et., etc. Tomorrow was Friday, always busy, but he determined to find a moment to return the call.

Sam frowned as he towelled himself dry. Unless or until Rowan Cottage went on the open market, his was the only offer on the table. If sensible, Kr Kerslake would advise the owner to accept and save himself marketing fees.

There was the price to consider, Sam mused. The owner was bound to try it on, of course, starting off ridiculously high. Sam wasn't bothered. He'd make a sensible bid after an independent valuation. Courtesy of his wealthy uncle's inheritance, he was able to enter the fray as a cash buyer. Despite the supposedly 'hot market,' any serious vendor would be daft not to see the benefit of that. Hell, he expected the owner to bite off his hand!

Sam grabbed the bathrobe hanging on a hook at the back of the bathroom door. No point in getting dressed again only to whip up a cheese omelette. Tired now, he planned to wolf it down with a hunk of bread, leave the plates and pans to soak in the sink, and crash. Then, as he knotted the belt, he stopped short, remembering who had last worn this towelling robe: Poppy. She'd looked a good deal sexier in it than he did! He fancied the scent of her still lingered. Sam pictured her standing in his kitchen, skin aglow and damp tendrils of hair framing her delicate boned face, remembering how she'd stared at him with her luminous grey eyes. Hell, the lady had started to haunt him! Sam pulled a wry face as he went in search of supper. He needed to get a grip, and fast.

Friday dawned clear and bright. Overnight the wind had died down and the weekend weather forecast sounded ideal for taking out the Sea Nymph. However, his plans thwarted, Sam was disappointed to find Poppy not at work. On enquiry, Julia wouldn't be drawn, saying only that Poppy had put in a late request for an annual leave day. Nor did Laura give away anything, merely commenting that she thought Poppy had to attend to something urgent. It was protocol, of course. Staff matters needed to be kept confidential. Sam felt a flash of irritation despite being aware that personal information was sacrosanct. It was too late now to wish he'd had the foresight to take her mobile number. Now there was no opportunity to issue an invite to go sailing this weekend.

It wasn't meant to be. Fate had stepped in to keep them apart. At least, this was the conclusion anyone sensible would reach. Sam scowled; he didn't feel very sensible where Poppy Lambert was concerned. Mid-way through his morning patient list, a solution presented itself. It was a long shot, but why not drop by Poppy's flat on his way home from the surgery. If she was there, fine, if not, so be it. Forget about the Sea Nymph. He'd offer an apology for the way he had spoken to her on Wednesday. Then, hopefully, they could both move on. A decision made, he scanned the computer and rose to call in his next patient.

Mary Wilson, a lady in her mid- fifties, needed a review of her blood pressure medication.

"How long have you been experiencing ankle swelling like this, Mrs Wilson?" Sam bent to take a closer look. "Hmm, that looks uncomfortable."

Not only were both feet and ankles visibly oedematous, but the skin was stretched tight and shiny, too. Obviously, it had been a struggle for Mary to prise on her shoes. Sam winced at the discomfort his patient must be in.

"About eight weeks." She shifted nervously. "I know I should have come in before. Things were OK until my blood pressure started to creep up again and the dose of my pills was increased. Dr Doyle keeps on at me to exercise more. I do try, Doctor, but this swelling is getting worse and my legs always ache – quite apart from the struggle to get my shoes on. Oh, and do call me Mary, please Doctor. Mrs Wilson makes me feel ancient."

"Well, Mary," Sam smiled encouragingly, "first we need to play around with your medication and see if we can find a drug combination that suits you better."

He consulted the computer screen to confirm his treatment rationale.

"You've been taking amlodipine," Sam named her prescribed drug, "without side effects until this last increase in dose, is that correct?" At her nod of agreement, he continued. "So, what I propose to do is to lower the dosage again and bring in another drug alongside. Lisinopril. But we'll need to monitor your renal function more closely with this one. Let's see when you last had bloods done."

A glance at the screen confirmed the date. Sam noted it wasn't long ago. Happily, Mary's renal function had been within the normal range at that point. This gave him no undue concern about prescribing Lisinopril. He explained to his patient that although Lisinopril was considered a renal guard it could also, on occasion, adversely affect the kidneys. Hence the need to proceed cautiously and monitor her via regular blood tests to keep an eye on things, especially at the start of treatment. A new 'script printed off, Sam handed it to Mary with instructions on how to take the medication and when to book in for a repeat blood test.

"Talk with the practice nurses, too." He paused, fishing for Bramblewood's new leaflet on hypertension. "Here you go, not the most riveting bedtime reading, I grant you, but you should find some useful tips. Book in for another blood test in two months' time. Ask the nurse you see to help you explore a few lifestyle changes. But hold fire on more exercise until that swelling has reduced. Another tip: make sure you keep your skin moisturised to minimise the risk of damage and infection. If you have a more suitable pair of shoes, wider ones, I'd advise you to wear them – forget about fashion for now." He winked to soften his words, having noted that Mary was a lady who liked to dress smartly. "See me again a few days after you've had your next blood test."

He smiled to indicate the consultation was over.

"Thank you, Dr Brocklehurst." Mary gave a watery smile. "My blood pressure, though ... I know the other doctor said it's up more than he was happy with, but wasn't that only the lower reading? What I mean is, why not see how I go on the original tablets and dosage?" She twisted her fingers. "I wasn't even symptomatic before. And this new drug does sound rather involved, especially with the need to monitor my kidneys."

Sam leant back, not wanting to give Mary the impression of being rushed. An extra five minutes' informative chat now could pay dividends in the future.

"That's right, it's the diastolic reading, the lower figure, that is raised. But we take as much notice of that as we do the systolic, which is the higher one. Your systolic reading is only marginally outside of normal range." He paused. "That's good, but your diastolic reading has been consistently high for a while. We do need to address that. High blood pressure if left untreated will cause significant damage over time, whether or not you're symptomatic. In fact, many people are unaware anything is amiss until something like a heart attack or 'stroke' happens."

Sam proceeded to outline the cardiovascular risks. Despite the leaflet he'd given her doing exactly the same, he knew from experience that once home leaflets were often pushed to the back of a drawer. He guessed Mary had had these risk factors explained to her before, but it wasn't unusual for people to need things repeated before they fully grasped the implications of their condition. The holy grail was that, once they understood the rationale, patients were more likely to be compliant with treatment.

"With regards renal function." Sam held her gaze. "Yes, we need to monitor your body's response to Lisinopril. This is an effective medication that goes well with Amlopidine to lower blood pressure when increased doses of that drug alone isn't well tolerated."

He let her digest this, then continued.

"If it suits you, hence the need to monitor its action. But it's important to remember that high blood pressure itself, if left untreated, will also damage your kidneys."

"I see." Mary's expression was suitably chastened as she clutched her handbag. "It's quite involved, isn't it. Thank you for taking the time to explain, Dr Brocklehurst. To be fair, Dr Doyle tried, but then his list got busier, or whatever, and he suggested I book an appointment with you. He talked about lifestyle changes, too, but then ... "

"Then you weren't ready to hear it." Sam grinned as her voice tailed off. "You'd be surprised how often that happens before the penny drops and folk realise effective care is a two-way process. Doctor and patient must work together. Nice to meet you, Mary, and let's see how things are at your next appointment."

Ah, so Andrew Doyle had slipped Mary his way for a new approach, had he, the wily old fox! Sam suppressed a grin. Was that meant to be an accolade, or a learning curve? The old dog teaching the young pup that, despite entering general practice with the best of intentions, some patients had a fixed mindset. And you were never going to get them on board as partners in their medical care. As if he didn't know that already, Sam thought with a flash of irritation. Surely it didn't mean that a doctor should ever stop trying. You may not win over everybody, that was impossible, but by the law of averages you'd win some. With a wry twist of his mouth, Sam updated Mary's notes.

At last surgery was over for the day. Sam strode out into balmy fresh air that was heavy with the scent of blossom. He loved evenings like this. The sun was low in the sky, throwing a soft, rose-gold mantle over the rooftops as he made a detour to Poppy's flat.

It wouldn't be long before the sun disappeared, slipping below the horizon and leaving what was left of the day bathed in purple shadow. Was Poppy at home? He was about to find out! Sam frowned, stopping by the entrance of the tall building she had vanished into the other night. Faced by a panel on the wall, he debated which bell to press. There were six options, and it was pure guesswork which flat was Poppy's. Hold on, hadn't she mentioned a view? Decisively, Sam pressed the bell to the top flat. He could imagine her living there, but if wrong he'd try again. Hell, he'd press every damn bell until he found her!

It seemed an age before the intercom crackled into life with a voice he didn't recognise. Ah, wrong flat! About to apologise and try again, Sam heard whoever it was ordering him to stay exactly where he was, she was on her way down. Excellent result, especially if this person knew Poppy. However, he was unprepared for the door to be flung open and a distraught young woman demand to know if he was free to stay, then grab his arm to haul him inside.

Apparently, this was Poppy's cousin, Maisie - and she'd received news that her mother had fallen, fractured a wrist, and sustained concussion. Maisie urgently needed to go home, which meant that someone else needed to stay overnight with Poppy. Sam felt his eyebrows shoot up. What on earth was going on!

"Stay - with Poppy? Why?" Sam stared at the white- faced woman, wondering if he had heard her correctly.

"Yes, obviously with Poppy." Maisie looked at Sam as if he was a halfwit. "She's had her procedure under sedation and mustn't be left on her own tonight." The young woman acted as if he knew all about it which he most certainly did not. "Look, just come up. Please."

Sam's frown deepened. Much as he was in the dark, one fact stood out. Poppy had been on the receiving end of a medical procedure and needed someone with her until fully recovered from the after effects of sedation. That much he grasped. This was not quite the visit he'd anticipated but he was free, and he'd stay. There would be time enough to glean the finer details later. There was a split second while the frazzled woman in front of him stood waiting for his answer. It was obvious that she itched to leave.

"Lead the way, then, Maisie." Sam's tone was curt. Hell, this woman didn't know him from Adam. He could be an axe murderer! "Wait, though. How do you know who I am?"

"I'm sorry to pounce on you with barely an intro." Maisie motioned for him to follow her up the wide staircase. "You're Sam Brocklehurst, the new doc at Bramblewood Surgery, right? Poppy described you. She had her repeat endoscopy today and she's sleeping again, still a bit away with the fairies. They were supposed to take her down at midday, but the timing had to be rejigged 'cos of an emergency, or something. So, it was quite late when they took her down and we haven't been back long. I can't just abandon her, but Mum's on her own and the hospital wants to discharge her. They need the bed." She spread her hands in a helpless gesture. "It's all a bit of a mess."

"Hmm, sounds it. Listen, I'm here now, just go." Sam's response was short. "Luckily, I'm not on-call."

He could tell by Maisie's expression that that possibility hadn't occurred to her.

"Phew!" Her relief was palpable as she bade him continue on upstairs. "Sorry, hope you're fit. Afraid Poppy's flat is up in the eaves. Look, I know if I woke her, she'd say don't worry, go home." Maisie sighed.

"And maybe I wouldn't feel so bad about doing that if she'd had her procedure this morning. But she is quite woozy. Anyway, here we are."

Maisie nudged open the door, listening before she beckoned him in. She put a warning finger to her lips. Apparently, Poppy was fast asleep. As if to verify this information, Sam heard a gentle snore coming from what he guessed must be the bedroom. Maisie pointed to the tiny kitchenette, snatching her jacket and bag as she told Sam to make himself at home.

"Plenty of milk for cups of tea, or whatever, so do help yourself. By the look of things, she won't wake for ages. OK, I'm off. My car is parked round the corner. Please tell Poppy I'll ring and update her on mum."

The whirlwind that was Maisie disappeared without waiting for his reply. Sam heard the sound of her heeled sandals clattering on the stairs as he stood in the middle of Poppy's small lounge. He grimaced; he must have been in medical mode when he agreed to Maisie's plea so promptly. Better make himself a coffee and wait, he supposed. That's if

Poppy had any coffee, of course. He strolled into the kitchenette to explore the contents of her neatly stacked cupboard. A jar of a passable brand sat on the shelf. Sam filled the kettle and flicked the switch, drumming his fingers on the work surface as it boiled. An unopened packet of digestive biscuits sat on the side, obviously bought for Maisie who wasn't here to eat them. Easy enough to replace, Sam thought as he ripped open the cellophane. At least they would stave off a few hunger pangs.

Gingerly, he sat down on Poppy's small sofa, and stretched out his long legs. If this was where he'd be spending the night he'd better try and make himself comfortable. A folded blanket and pillow lay on the sofa's armrest. Useful, although he didn't anticipate a need for the blanket. The evening was too warm for covers.

Silence enveloped him and he realised Poppy had stopped snoring. She still appeared to be asleep, and according to the oracle that was Maisie, she'd sleep through to the small hours. The next question: whether to turn on the television and risk disturbing her, or flip through a discarded newspaper lying on the floor instead? With a shrug Sam reached for the newspaper, trying not to rustle the pages. Not much of interest, so he gave up and scrolled through his 'phone instead.

It was dark outside now, a soft indigo summer dark. Sam rose to switch on a table lamp. It wouldn't do for Poppy to wake and feel disorientated, wander out and trip. From what her cousin had said, there'd been enough accidents in the family already. He wondered what Poppy's reaction would be when she discovered his presence. Not best pleased, he suspected, but that was tough. Hell, what had he got himself into?

Sam debated whether to fetch a tumbler of water and leave it by her bedside, then decided against it. She might have one already. Besides, it was best to let her sleep. His attention was caught by a corner bookshelf. He wandered over to inspect the contents. It had been a while since he'd had an opportunity to read for pleasure. One hardback looked particularly interesting. He reached it down and began leafing through the pages. The title, West Country Legends, had several chapters devoted to the folklore of Dartmoor and Exmoor, plus a short section on Bodmin Moor, too. The book was illustrated by stunning photographs – rugged landscapes dotted with sheep and ponies, and vast sweeps of yellow gorse and purple heather. All interspersed with granite rocks and tawny streams. Details on the dust jacket claimed that the author was local. Sam was impressed.

He began to read, still stood by the bookcase where the light was best. Then a noise made him spin round and almost drop the book. Poppy!

Bathed in a rosy glow of lamplight, she hovered in the bedroom doorway, staring at him. For a moment Sam could only gape, too. Hair all mussed, her luminous, grey eyes looked huge in her pale face. Barefoot, she wore the skimpiest of pink, cotton nightshirts. A frown creased her brow as if she was trying to work out what he was doing there.

"S -Sam?"

"You're awake, then." Sam heard the gravelly tone in his voice.

"Yes, but what – what are you doing here?" Poppy sounded like she was struggling with a particularly difficult clue in a crossword.

A good question, Sam thought. What was he doing here? Even with mussy, just woken hair, Poppy Lambert was one delectable lady. She swayed slightly and held onto the doorframe for support. Sam dragged in a breath as he moved to steady her, his gaze drawn to a pair of coltish legs that seemingly went on forever. Lord, she was beautiful !

"D – did something go wrong and someone have to call you?" She looked anxious. "B – but you're not my doctor! Why did ... "

"Hey, relax, Poppy." Sam growled. "Nothing's wrong. I'm not here in a medical capacity."

The room was too dim, adding to her disorientation, Sam guessed. Once sure she wasn't about to fall over, he switched on the overhead light. But the sudden glare only served to make her gasp and screw up her eyes.

"Oops, a bit too bright." Sam tried to inject a note of humour. "OK, I'll switch it off again." Doctor or not, momentarily he was at a loss to know what to do next.

CHAPTER EIGHT

Her tired mind must be playing tricks. Poppy rubbed her eyes; dream seemed to be merging with reality. The man in front of her had to have been conjured up by some weird side-effect of the sedation she'd had – midazolam could do that – because Sam couldn't really be here in her flat. Could he? She had been given a higher dose of sedation this time, she recalled the anaesthetist saying so. After the procedure she'd come home and fallen asleep again. There had been only her cousin with her, she would swear to it. Now there was no sign of Maisie, and Sam stood facing her, so close it felt dangerous.

Her mouth felt dry. A sip of cold water, that's what she needed. Her head still felt muzzy, but she could wrestle with the strangeness of it all afterwards. That's if Sam hadn't morphed back into Maisie by then. A pity her legs felt wobbly. She attempted to sidle past him into the kitchenette, but he moved to block her way with panther like speed.

"Sit." Guided by strong hands, Poppy found herself steered towards the sofa and pushed down. "You want a drink? Fine, wait there. I'll get it."

Poppy obeyed, taking a steadying breath as she pulled ineffectually at the hem of her nightshirt. Sam's touch had felt real enough. Yet why was he here and where on earth was Maisie? Had something out of the ordinary occurred and she'd needed medical assistance? That had to be it. Even so, it didn't explain everything. True, Sam was a doctor, but he wasn't her doctor! No one would have summoned Sam to attend her. Her head began to ache as she struggled to solve the puzzle.

Maisie must have the answers but where was she? She'd give her cousin the worst earbashing of her life. Heavens, Maisie had given her solemn promise to stay!

The sound of a tap running was followed by footsteps. A cool glass was pushed into her hands. Poppy clutched it. Water, that's what she needed. When had she last had something to drink? Ages ago! Obviously, dehydration had messed with her brain.

"Th- thank you." Thirstily, she took a swallow, and checked again. It most definitely was Sam, and his nearness unnerved her. "B – but I really don't understand what ... " Her voice trailed away.

"What I am doing here?" Sam raised a dark eyebrow, expression sardonic. "Good question, Poppy. If I give you the bare bones, perhaps you can fill me in on that one."

Poppy listened with a growing sense of shock. She felt sorry for her Aunty Bea, but whatever had Maisie been thinking of to drag Sam in off the street like that! Heavens, he'd only dropped by to exchange a few words with her. In fact, it was a miracle that Maisie had guessed who he was. She had only described him in general terms during idle chit chat while they both waited at the hospital.

"Maisie shouldn't have asked you to stay." Poppy cleared her throat. "She should have woken me and explained the situation. I'd have been OK on my own. I mean, what's going to happen? Nothing! I'll just have a drink and go back to sleep. I do apologise, Sam. My cousin was out of order. You must have felt put on the spot. Honestly, you're free to go now."

The sooty eyebrows rose higher, causing her to shrink back.

"You've had a procedure under sedation, Poppy. I'm staying." Sam's expression brooked no argument. "You know the rules: someone with you overnight. Let's not waste energy arguing about it." His voice was testy.

"Anyway, why the repeat endoscopy? Is it linked with your coeliac diagnosis? Are you symptomatic again?"

The questions were gun fire rapid. Poppy opened her mouth to declare it was none of Sam's business, then felt herself flush, aware that wasn't quite true. He'd volunteered to stay with her, hadn't he. Therefore, the quizzing was justified.

She took another swallow of the deliciously cool water, and gave him the backstory.

"My consultant has a particular interest in research, and he's keen to explore any genetic links. I don't have a living relative with a Coeliac diagnosis, but my mother fitted the profile – regular bouts of anaemia, fatigue, thyroid problems, food intolerances, you name it, she had it. Fertility issues, too, which was why my parents only had me, I suppose." Poppy experienced a wash of emotion as she recalled her own miscarriages. "Mum died of a rare cancer, a T-cell Lymphoma, which has been found to have a link with Coeliac disease. This leaves me at a higher risk for complications. The repeat endoscopy was to confirm that any gastric inflammation has resolved."

"And has it?" Sam's expression was unreadable.

She sensed him still as the weight of her words hit home.

"Yep, all OK. These days they report on findings before you leave the department; no being kept in suspense for results to be sent on later. I shouldn't need another endoscopy, only the routine annual IgA blood test in future, like every diagnosed coeliac, to check I'm being compliant with diet." Poppy felt tears threaten. "If only a GP had thought of testing Mum for coeliac disease. I'm convinced she must have had it, too."

"How old were you when she died?" Sam's voice was gentle as he sat beside her.

"Five months off my twenty-first." Poppy sniffed and dashed away a tear. "About to take my nursing finals. Mum never saw me graduate. Dad was in bits. Once he decided I was settled enough to leave, he sold the family home – too many memories, he said – took early retirement and moved to Spain. He helps run a little bistro out there. There's a lady friend on the scene, Jill. She's nice, I've met her several times, but Dad always says he won't remarry. For him, Mum was the only one. I never stop thinking of her, either."

"If her daughter is anything to go by, she must have been a remarkable lady." Sam gave Poppy a swift hug.

The touch was her undoing. Suddenly she was crying, unable to stem the flow of tears. A dam had burst, and she was grieving all over again, or that's what it felt like. Sobs wracked her body as Poppy wept anew for everything she'd lost – including her unborn babies. Vaguely, she wondered if it was a delayed effect of the sedation, or maybe the time of year. Both her miscarriages had occurred in the summer. Grief was a strange thing.

"Hell," Sam swore gently and pulled her roughly into his arms, "everything's going to be OK, sweetheart. Don't talk anymore if it makes you sad."

He was wrong, though. Things hadn't been OK for ages. Sometimes Poppy felt as if life would never be OK again. There were days when the pain of loss threatened to tear her apart. She ached for her mum as she burrowed her face in Sam's shoulder and howled. Only her mum would know what to do as she mourned her lost babies, and her mum wasn't here. Sam rocked her until the sobs abated. His firm body felt reassuringly solid, all hard muscle and very male. Safe. She, on the other hand, was a snivelling wreck, and had soaked his T-shirt with her tears. Embarrassed, she stared at the damp patch.

"Oh, s ... sorry." Poppy tried to wriggle away. "I really didn't mean to cry."

"Shh." Sam's grip on her tightened. "Cry on my shoulder if you want, Poppy Lambert. Like I said, I'm not going anywhere."

The minutes ticked by as they sat wrapped in each other's arms. Poppy sniffed, inhaling Sam's very male scent. It was a long time since she'd been this close to a guy. Tentatively, her arms slid round his neck as he dropped a kiss on her head. The feel of Sam's rock-stolid body triggered all sorts of emotions. Suddenly she needed more. Poppy nestled closer, aware of a sense of coming home, of belonging. It was too complicated to analyse, so she didn't bother to try.

She exulted in Sam's low growl of response as she began to run her fingers tentatively through his dark, newly cropped hair. Aware of feeling drowsy again, she closed her eyes. Then a memory stirred. He'd called her sweetheart, the word murmured like a caress. With her head resting on Sam's chest, she could hear the steady beat of his heart. Tentatively, she opened her eyes and met his smouldering gaze. And knew in that moment that he wanted her as much as she wanted him.

"Take me to bed." It was a bold move. She'd never asked a man to bed her before, didn't know how it was supposed to be done. "Please, Sam," she whispered.

Initially he didn't respond. Her pulse rate quickened as she watched a myriad emotions flash across his rugged features. Then, with infinite care, he lowered his dark head to kiss her again. But the kiss was chaste, a mere touch of his lips with hers. Sam cupped her face as his thumb brushed a lone tear sliding down her cheek. Poppy blinked, not understanding. Then he stood, pulling her up with him, his look regretful as he took a step back.

"Don't think I don't want to, Poppy." Sam's voice was gruff. "Dammit, I'd sleep with you in a nanosecond but not now, not like this."

"Why not?" Poppy felt her face flame. How could she have got things so wrong, misread all the signs? "Tell me why not, Sam? Is there someone else?"

"There's no one else." Sam pulled a face. "Dammit, Poppy Lambert, you've been on my mind since the moment we met. But you've had a procedure today. I'm only here to keep an eye on you. Hell, I'm not about to jump your bones when you're recovering from sedation."

"I -I'm OK now." She stared at his set face. "Honestly."

Sam took her gently but firmly by the shoulders. "Good. But you're going back to bed, strictly solo and I'm kipping on the sofa. If you need anything, shout. Tomorrow, if you feel like it, we'll take out the Sea Nymph. After that let's just wait and see what happens."

He steered her towards the bedroom, placed a fresh glass of water on her bedside cabinet and left. About to plead with him that she was fine and completely lucid, Poppy bit back words that would sound too much like begging. And she wasn't going to beg for any man. Miserably, she slid under the duvet, shivering despite the warmth of the evening. Enough pretence, her immunity to guys – sexy guys like Dr Sam Brocklehurst - had worn thin and she'd left it too late for a booster injection. She was at risk and exposed.

Poppy swallowed. Tonight, Sam had shown her that he was the real deal, but she'd offered herself to him on a plate and he'd refused. He didn't want her. Mortifying! How would she ever be able to face him at work now. She listened to Sam move about in the lounge. His phone rang, but he cut the call. She heard him tersely tell the caller he couldn't talk now. Odd, why not? Her last waking thought was that sleep was going to be elusive.

When Poppy woke next her flat was quiet apart from birdsong. As she listened to the dawn chorus, early morning light streamed through her bedroom window, and she could almost believe she'd imagined the events of last night. At least, she fervently hoped so! Her throat felt dry. Poppy gulped the last of her water and grabbed a towel, eager to brush her teeth and wash.

"Morning, Poppy. Tea and toast?" A yell from the kitchenette brought her up short. "It'll be on the table when you're ready."

Poppy froze as she emerged fresh from taking a shower. Sam really was here, she hadn't dreamt him – and he hadn't gone home yet! Hadn't the deal been that he would stay overnight and leave in the early hours? By rights, he should have let himself stealthily out of her flat when the first pearly wash of dawn lit the sky. The toast smelt good, though. Poppy dragged a brush through her hair, dressed hastily, and tried to compose herself before she entered the lounge.

"Thanks, Sam." Demurely, she avoided his eyes and took a bite. "Hmm, this tastes nice. It's barely six o'clock, though. Listen, I'm fine now, honestly. Please go home. I – I'm sure you must have better things to do than babysit me. After you've finished your own toast, I mean. Sorry I only have gluten free bread."

She tried to hide what she knew must be a fiery blush.

"And sorry about last night, me behaving like a ... a ... well, anyway, sorry." She attempted a shrug. "Blame it on the midazolam. I don't normally throw myself at men."

"I'm glad to hear it." Sam chuckled, holding her gaze.

She saw that his warm brown eyes twinkled.

"And stop with the apologising, Poppy. There's no need. If you must know, I was flattered."

Unable to think of a suitable reply, Poppy remained silent and drank her tea. Sam drained his own mug and stood to rinse it in the sink. Cautiously, she watched him pull on his trainers and stretch. She guessed he felt stiff after a night on her worn sofa.

"Can you be ready in, say, an hour?" He shot her a grin. "I need to go back to Rowan Cottage to shower and get changed. Then, if you fancy a sail today, I can drive back and collect you. We'll head over to Instow where the Sea Nymph is moored and pick up some grub on the way. Trust me, you'll love it. The weather's perfect. Just relax on deck and enjoy being out on the water while I navigate."

"Wow!" Poppy gasped. Sam's invite hadn't been an empty gesture when they'd lunched together at the Marmalade Cat. The words had been meant. "That sounds wonderful, Sam. Yes, I'll be ready." She experienced a rush of pleasure.

"Great! See you in a while." He threw her a wink and disappeared.

On her own again, Poppy was left in a frenzy of indecision. What was de rigueur for a day on the water? Swiftly, she rifled through her limited wardrobe.

The morning was set fair, Sam had been right. Maybe they would drop anchor and swim off the boat somewhere. It didn't hurt to be prepared. She opened a drawer and pulled out her favourite hot pink bikini, planning to wear it under a pair of cut off denim jeans and a cerise, cotton top. Rain wasn't forecast; however, the weather could be changeable along the coast. Also, it might become chilly as the day wore on. Poppy frowned, selecting a navy, fleece lined jacket and folding it to go into an olive-green holdall.

For good measure, she added a rolled up stripey beach towel. Then paused, debating the issue of underwear. Which set to bring, old or new? No contest, it had to be the new – not that Sam was likely to see it, of course, she told herself hurriedly. Before Poppy could rethink the matter, she pulled open another drawer and grabbed a pair of wispy, white cotton panties and matching, lacy bra. A bottle of sun screen was pushed into the bag, too.

Next to go in were tissues and lip balm. Poppy hesitated, wondering if she had forgotten anything. Ah yes, sunglasses! Sunlight reflected off water could be dazzling. Then, after fastening a thin, gold chain around her neck, she twisted her hair up into a neat coil and donned a jaunty little sunhat left behind by Maisie. Her cousin wouldn't mind. Thinking of Maisie, Poppy found her mobile and sent a quick text to enquire after her Aunty Bea. 'Ring later,' she remembered to add. However, within minutes she heard the ring tone of her own 'phone.

"Poppy, you're up! I didn't dare call before in case I disturbed you." Maisie's voice sounded breathy and excited. "How are you? Apologies for dashing off yesterday. Is that dishy doc still there? I must say he's a ... "

"I'm fine, Maisie. But listen, how is Aunty Bea?" Poppy stopped her cousin in mid-flow, determined not to enter into a discussion about Sam. "Tell me what happened."

"Mum slipped on a wet pavement." Maisie sighed. "Sprained ankle, bruises, and a Colles fracture of her wrist, not to mention a touch of concussion. Did a proper job, poor thing! I'll be staying here a while, I'd imagine. Wait, let me put her on. You can talk to her yourself."

The line crackled, there was a pause and then her aunt's voice took over.

By the time Poppy had finished chatting to her aunt and had a final exchange with Maisie - not forgetting to chide her for collaring Sam the night before - another twenty minutes had gone by. She slid her mobile into her bag just as the toot of a horn sounded outside. Poppy hurried to the window and spotted his car parked by the kerb. Quickly, she pushed her feet into trainers, let herself out of the flat and ran down the three flights of stairs.

"Hallo there, sailor girl." Sam grinned, looking relaxed and confident behind the wheel. "I like the hat, very apt."

"It's Maisie's. She left it behind." Poppy smiled back as she slid into the passenger seat. Her holdall tucked down by her feet, she clipped on her seatbelt. "It does have a nautical touch, doesn't it. I only hope the thing stays on my head if it gets breezy."

"Though you aren't going to object too much if it gets blown into the river." Sam threw back his head and let out a roar of laughter. "Payback time for your cousin leaving me with you yesterday. How is your aunt, by the way? She had a fall, didn't she."

He released the brake, indicating as he eased out of the narrow alleyway into the steadily increasing flow of traffic. His eyes on the road, he listened as Poppy updated him.

"Aunty Bea's going to need Maisie around for a while. It's lucky she was able to drop everything and go, otherwise I'm not sure how she'd have coped, bless her."

"No other family members to step in?" Sam raised a questioning eyebrow.

"Only my dad over in Spain." Poppy chewed her lip. It was at times like this that having a small family could be tricky. "I know he'd have dropped everything and flown back, if necessary, though."

Sam nodded.

"He and Aunty Bea are siblings." Poppy continued. "They've always been close. In fact, Maisie and I are more like sisters than cousins. Growing up that was nice 'cos we're both only kids. How about you, Sam? Do you come from a big family?"

"Awash with siblings, I'm afraid." Sam chuckled. "We do our own thing, give each other space, but if ever anyone's in trouble we're there for them. That's the deal, the positive side of family. And cross one of us, beware. The Brocklehurst clan can be a formidable bunch when we gang up together. Looking back, we certainly gave our teachers some hassle. I have three brothers, two older, one younger, plus a little sister. The baby of the family."

"One for all and all for one, like the Three Musketeers?" Poppy heard the wistful note in her voice.

"Something like that." He grinned. "Only we'd be the five musketeers. Or maybe that should that be four. I'm not sure if a mere girl can be a musketeer. I'm sure Tizzy would contradict me, though."

"Tizzy?" Poppy glanced at him.

"A pet name we still use for her sometimes." Sam said. "She hates it now that she's all grown up, of course. But it suits her. Right from a baby, she was always getting in a tizz over something."

The day was young, with a shimmer of sea mist that would burn off as the sun broke through. Already the heat was building; Poppy followed Sam's lead and lowered her window, revelling in the wind in her hair as the car ate up the miles. Sam commented on the route as he drove and she was surprised by how quickly the time passed.

The picturesque drive to Instow had Poppy enthralled. They stopped once en route for Sam to dash into a village grocery store to purchase fruit and soft drinks. Poppy was impressed to discover he had a cool box in the boot to ensure everything remained fresh.

"My original plan was a proper picnic to take on board." He checked the dingy on the roof rack was secure and grinned at her. "Afraid that'll have to be for next time."

Ah, Poppy thought, today's invite wasn't a one-off; he'd mentioned a next time! All right, so she didn't want another relationship. But that didn't mean she couldn't enjoy the company of a sexy guy like Sam. The sun shone on a day filled with promise and a delicious tingle ran down her spine.

"Hey, what's that?" Sam pointed. "Look, a bird of some sort. A curlew, maybe. See over there, Poppy."

"Hmm, I'm not sure from this distance." Poppy shaded her eyes.

Carried on the wind came the lone call of a sandpiper. Or was it a dunlin? She knew the two species were often mixed up with each other. Both were stocky waders, to be found along the rocky North Devon coastline. Although, being only June, it was rather early in the year for the purple sandpipers which bred elsewhere but liked to winter along the North Devon coast. For a moment Poppy felt sad.

"Penny for them." Sam caught her expression.

"Oh, nothing." Poppy shrugged as the bird flew off, still unidentified. "It looked like a sandpiper and reminded me of being here with my gran during the winter months. We often spotted them on walks. Did you know the collective noun for them is a bind? A bind of sandpipers. Whenever I hear one, it's like a call back home."

"And do you feel you've answered it?" Sam stilled. "The call back home, I mean."

"Yes, partly, by relocating to Woolacombe." Poppy faltered. "But home was always Rowan Cottage and I ... I'm not there. I'm staying in a rented flat that's practical but not very homey."

"I get it," Sam nodded. "Renting is all very well but, at some point, you need your own place. I feel the same."

He paused as if to say more, then glanced at his watch; state-of-the-art diver's watch, Poppy noted. "Anyway, not far to go now. Let's drive on."

Soon they reached their destination. Sam parked and prepared to row them across the river to the Sea Nymph's mooring. Under his instruction, Poppy clambered into the sturdy little dingy. She felt the teeniest twinge of trepidation. Yet was an ideal day; weather and water were both calm.

It didn't take long to reach the larger vessel. Poppy took Sam's hand, grateful for his help to climb aboard the Sea Nymph. He secured the dingy and weighed anchor. She felt the lift of the ketch as he steered her out into deeper channels. Poppy's offer of help dismissed, there was nothing for her to do except relax on deck and enjoy being out on the river. She let her mind drift with the tide, relishing the warm sunshine and balmy breeze. Things augured well.

Sam proved to be an excellent sailor, just as she'd imagined. She felt utterly confident in his hands and experienced no fear when he suggested taking the Sea Nymph further. The estuary lay ahead. Out in the open sea there was more tidal movement, yet nothing that caused her to feel nervous on a calm day like today.

After sailing round the headland, Sam steered the cabin cruiser back into the estuary and upriver a way before dropping anchor in a tranquil inlet. By tacit agreement, they both stripped down to their swimwear and stretched out on the warm deck to soak up the rays. The boat rocked gently as they dozed.

Caressed by the warmth of the sun, Poppy had fallen asleep quickly. Just as well, Sam thought ruefully. Her hot pink bikini left little to the imagination. It showed off her slim, lightly tanned legs to perfection, not to mention the display of toned midriff and tantalising curve of her breasts. He'd had to try hard not to ogle her, though she seemed oblivious of the effect she had on him. Somehow, he hadn't expected her to own a bikini quite so ... quite so what? He frowned, struggling to find the right word; revealing was all that came to mind. No objection on his part, though.

"Enjoying yourself?" At length, Sam opened an eye to glance at her.

"Hmm, this is heaven." He saw her roll over and sit up. She treated him to a wide smile. "It's hot, though, isn't it. I'm ready for a dip, if you are."

"Let's do it." He stood to offer her a hand up. "Best keep close to the boat, but it's pretty safe around here. Are you OK jumping off the side? Or there's the ... "

His answer was a splash as, running past him, she climbed on the side and leapt overboard. Belatedly, Sam realised he hadn't asked how well Poppy could swim. Although not far from the sandy river edge, she'd be out of her depth. He'd chosen a spot shallow enough to drop anchor, yet deep enough for the Sea Nymph not to run aground. He heard her squeal as she hit the water, throwing up a shower of silvery droplets.

"Ooh, it's cold … lovely, though!" Poppy trod water as she laughed up at him. "Come on, Sam, get in. It's really refreshing."

He gave a pretend yelp as she cupped water in her hand to throw at him, then dived below the surface. Sam tensed as she disappeared, poised to leap in after her. Then she emerged several yards away. He chuckled as she gave him a cheeky wave and dipped below the surface again. He realised he had no need to worry about Poppy Lambert's swimming ability! She darted and dived like a silvery fish.

"Hey, Captain, why are you still onboard?" Poppy circled and trod water again.

"OK, OK." He grinned, stepped up on the side and executed a neat dive, surfacing close beside her. "Right, Miss Lambert, think you can swim, do you. See that buoy over there? Race you!"

"You're on." There was mischief in her eyes as she struck out, doing a surprisingly fast front crawl.

Sam liked the way Poppy was up for a challenge. They reached the marker within seconds of each other and each grabbed a handhold, panting. They exchanged smiles.

"A tie." Sam recovered first. Holding her gaze, he grinned. "How's about that, Poppy Lambert? Seems we're in perfect sync."

"It does indeed, Dr Brocklehurst." She shook back her hair, dislodging more silvery droplets of water while sunlight played on the river.

Her wonderful grey eyes changed shade like the sky, Sam noticed. Right now, they were luminous and sparkling. He enjoyed seeing this different side of Poppy, totally given up to having fun. He sensed there hadn't been too much fun in Poppy's life of late.

For a second, Sam was tempted to lean across and kiss her but that risked breaking the spell. No doubt, she would retreat. Restraint was the name of the game even if his desire for her was off the Richter scale. The rest of the day lay ahead, and he was going to make damn sure nothing happened to mar it. He kicked away from the buoy, then did a leisurely breast stroke. Poppy was right about one thing; being in this crystal-clear river felt sensational.

"We'll swim for a bit, then dry out on deck before going further upriver." He yelled across to her. "There's a great waterside pub I heard about where we can moor the boat and have lunch. Serves food all day, apparently. How does that grab you?"

"Sounds wonderful." Her voice was carried on the coastal breeze as she pushed off and swam in the opposite direction. "And don't worry, I expect there'll be a jacket potato, or something that I can eat. Most places offer a jacket spud. Sorry, I know this gluten free thing is a bit of a pain."

Ah, so she thought he'd forgotten to check out the menu. Well, she was wrong there! Sam suppressed a grin. With a non-committal grunt, he flipped over on his back and floated, listening to the gentle river sounds. This was one of the best days he'd had in a while.

At length, aware time was going on, he yelled to Poppy and pointed to the Sea Nymph. Sam reached the boat first and hauled himself over the side. He began to towel himself dry as he watched her follow in his wake. As she reached the boat, he leant down, ready to catch her hand as she scrambled up. There was a moment when she nearly slipped, and he tightened his grip to steady her. Sam chuckled; jumping overboard was the easy part, the climb back on board always proved trickier. Her luminous grey eyes focussed on him trustingly but the touch of her smooth skin triggered a jolt of awareness. In that moment, Sam felt as though the earth gave a seismic tremor.

He tried not to notice how Poppy's wet bikini clung to her svelte body as they stood only inches apart. Immediately she regained her balance, he dropped her hand and turned away. The sexual chemistry was strong; ignoring it wasn't going to be easy.

Weighing anchor, Sam fired the motor and took the helm. He steered the Sea Nymph out into deeper water and navigated upstream, with his gaze steadfastly fixed ahead. Behind him, Sam was aware of Poppy having a rub down with her own towel. Once finished, she donned her hat and stretched out on deck. He glanced at her soaking up the rays, and noticed that she looked drowsy again.

"Sunscreen?" Sam lifted an eyebrow. "You have fair skin, Poppy, you need to be careful, especially if you fall asleep. I know you applied some earlier, but ... "

"But the water will have washed it off and I don't want to burn." Poppy sat up and delved in her bag. "Quite right, Dr Brocklehurst. Thanks for the reminder."

Hastily, Sam looked away as she slathered lotion over every inch of her delectable body. He realised belatedly that she was asking him to do something, and spun round.

"What? Yes, of course." He slowed the boat before gingerly taking the bottle she was proffering. He tipped it, and rubbed the cool suncream onto her back.

Her skin was satin smooth under his tentative hands. Sam groaned inwardly, feeling like he was being put through some kind of exquisite torture.

"All done." His voice was gruff. "Right, if we want lunch, I'd better concentrate on navigating this vessel. Don't know about you, but I'm famished after that swim."

Sam pulled a wry face as he took the helm again. What he hadn't said was that he was hungry for more than food. Poppy stared at him in consternation.

"Oh Sam, why didn't you say! I'm sure we have some fruit left in the cool box. Lemonade, too. I'll fetch it."

She went in search of the hamper. Soon they were both sucking on juicy, ripe nectarines. Sam pointed to her chin, laughing as she blushed. Quickly, Poppy fumbled for a tissue and dabbed at the offending trail of juice. The innocent gesture was unexpectedly sensual, causing him to look away swiftly. As the Sea Nymph gathered speed, he stared fixedly at the horizon. Surely the little jetty they were heading for ought to be in sight now. He damned well hoped so, otherwise there was a strong chance that, wise or not, he might jump Poppy Lambert's delectable bones – and that would never do!

Resolutely, he switched focus. Hopefully, she'd be happy with his choice of venue, 'The Mud Lark.' An upmarket pub, the weathered old building stood in solitary splendour on the banks of the river Taw.

Access was via boat or a stony track that became so muddy it was virtually impassable in mid-winter, when the venue shut down, and did no favours to a car's suspension whatever the season. At least, that's the information Bill, the former owner of Sea Nymph had given Sam when the boat transaction had been completed early on that first Saturday morning. Generously, Bill had given up his Sunday to take Sam out on her, happy to show him something of the area.

Sam shaded his eyes, spotting the wooden landing strip at last. Poppy wriggled into her clothes while he guided the Sea Nymph safely in. He threw the heavy rope and coiled it securely around a nearby mooring buoy to hold the ketch steady before they clambered out. Then he caught Poppy's hand as they walked down the jetty, eager to nab one of the rustic tables set up in the shady riverside pub garden.

The menus were on display, including alternative allergen free options, but customers needed to go inside to place their orders. Poppy made her choice swiftly: a gluten free version of the roasted veggie lasagne with a mixed leaf side salad to accompany it.

"Sure?" Sam stood, ready to order. "Think I'll go for the steak. Fancy a drink? I'm told they do great juice cocktails here if you'd prefer something non-alcoholic."

"No, thanks." She smiled hesitantly. "A jug of iced water for the table will be fine. But you go ahead and have a drink if you want, Sam."

"Apparently, their apple and elderflower mix is popular." He scanned the drinks list. "Natural ingredients, nothing added that would pose a problem for a Coeliac." A sixth sense told him that she was anxious about saying yes to something new and didn't like to trouble him to check out the ingredients. "Ditto, most of the other juices, but it's your call, of course. I'll order a jug of iced water anyway."

In the silence that ensued Sam added for good measure, "If you're wondering how I know about the juice cocktails, I rang ahead and checked the menu in advance when I thought of bringing you here."

He winked.

"Oh, I see." A pleased expression crossed Poppy's face. "OK, then. Apple and elderflower juice does sound tempting on a hot day, doesn't it."

She wriggled in her seat, reminding Sam of an excited child on a day out.

"Although," Poppy nibbled her lip, studying the drinks list, "there's this, too. Lychee and mango juice cocktail with a sprig of mint may just top it. May I change my mind and have that instead, please?"

"A lady's prerogative." Sam chuckled as he strode away, leaving her to sit on the wooden bench and gaze out over the tranquil river Taw. He flung over his shoulder, "Back in a jiffy."

Their table, under the shade of a large beech tree, was exactly where he'd have chosen if he had booked ahead. The queue at the bar moved steadily. Soon it was Sam's turn. He returned with their drinks and placed them on the table. Then sat opposite her and raised his glass of lager.

"Cheers. Here's to a delicious lunch and thanks for being my shipmate today."

"Cheers." She clinked glasses with him. "Thanks for the invite, Sam. I'm having the most fantastic time."

"Glad to hear it." Sam cleared his throat. "My plan all along."

'The Mud Lark' was crowded. He suspected this was par for the course during the summer months. Yet suddenly it was as if no one else existed but the two of them. He held Poppy's gaze. Was it only him, or did she feel it, too - the atmosphere heady with anticipation like the inexorable pull of an unstoppable tide? Her grey eyes darkened to smoke, and Sam knew that she did.

Their food arrived and the spell was broken. His steak was medium-rare, cooked to perfection. However, as they dug in, he found he hardly tasted it. He was aware of Poppy's every nuance. When had been the exact moment things changed? She was an enchantress who had woven a spell. There was no other explanation. The cynical side of Sam said nonsense. It was the age-old attraction of male to female, nothing more than biology. A strong sexual chemistry.

He'd been without a woman for too long, that was the problem. The purpose of today's trip was to put their relationship back on track - as colleagues, Sam reminded himself hastily.

"How did you find this place?" He realised she was staring at him. "I mean, you're new here, Sam, whereas I'm coming home." She shrugged. "At least, that's what my heart says."

So, he told Poppy about Bill, the sprightly chap who had sold him the Sea Nymph, and how the two of them had taken her out on the river to let him get the hang of her. And he'd pointed out the Mud Lark. Bill had proved an excellent tutor, teaching Sam how to navigate the local waterways. In turn, Sam had promised the older man trips out in the future, including loan of the Sea Nymph on occasion, should Bill wish it.

"That was kind, Sam."

"Not so." Sam pushed away his empty plate. "It's reciprocal. Bill's a great bloke, a good friend to have made. Right, I'll settle the tab. When you've finished, Poppy, we need to make a move to catch the tide." He grinned. "Remember that old adage about time and tide waiting for no man. I'm afraid it's true out here on the water."

Sitting contentedly under the spreading branches of the beech tree, it was easy to forget that nature had her own constraints. And it didn't do to ignore them.

"Sounds like trying to catch the traffic right." Poppy laughed. "OK, I'm nearly done."

Once aboard again, resisting her proved impossible. Like a rip tide, the pull was too strong. They entered a quieter stretch of water and Sam slowed the boat. He held her gaze.

"Let's drop anchor here for a last bit of sunbathing, or ... maybe go below deck and get to know each other better instead." He grimaced. "Hell, that didn't come out well. Poppy, what I'm saying is this. I want you. Dammit, you're gorgeous! Will you sleep with me?" He watched a slow smile spread across her sun kissed face.

"Dammit, Sam, I thought you'd never ask. The answer is yes. Drop anchor, Captain."

CHAPTER NINE

Determined not to rush things, Sam led Poppy below deck, his fingers linked with hers. The cabin, complete with makeshift bunk, afforded a welcome privacy. He felt the wild beat of her heart as he pulled her close. Or perhaps it was the thud of his own, he couldn't be sure. They both breathed faster as the heat ramped up a notch. Gently, he removed her top, helping her shimmy out of her jeans. He reached for the ties of her bikini. It was in the way, superfluous, stopping him from seeing all of her. Soon, the offending article lay crumpled at her feet, a froth of pink, and Poppy stood naked before him.

"You're beautiful, sweetheart. Do you know that?" Sam gave a low whistle of appreciation as he slid his hands along her satin smooth back. He kept the pace slow, burying his face in her hair as he murmured, "I've wanted to do this since the first moment I saw you, Poppy Lambert. I just wasn't sure if you felt the same."

His answer was the flare of desire he saw as she slipped her arms round his neck, stood on tiptoe and commenced her own slow kissing. Her lips tasted faintly salty. She began to tease him with her tongue. Aware that her fingers were fumbling with his belt now, Sam gave a guttural growl. At this rate, he wasn't going to last long.

"I need to see you, too." Her shy whisper was his undoing. "Undress for me, please, Sam."

He scooped her up in one easy movement, and deposited her on the bunk. It took only seconds to strip off his own clothes. Soon he was lying naked beside her. Poppy's slim body seemed to mould perfectly with his. He kissed her deeply, exulting in her breathy gasps as, pressed against him, he felt the hard nub of her nipples.

They began a tantalising exploration of each other's body. Vaguely, Sam was aware there must be more comfortable berths. However, right now that didn't matter. The bunk on this 19.5-foot cabin cruiser did just fine. Then it hit him like a wash of cold water.

"Poppy?" Sam raised himself on one elbow and gazed down at her. In the throes of passion there was one important question neither of them had addressed. "Are you protected? I mean, contraception. Do you need me to use a condom?"

"Oh!" He watched her amazing grey eyes fly open and widen with understanding, a blush staining her cheeks. "It should be OK. I had a coil fitted after – you know. Though I've no idea why. Mark and I were well and truly finished. B – but ..."

"But use one anyway." He threw her a grin. "OK, just give me a moment."

Sam was back within seconds, picking up seamlessly from where they'd left off. Her ready response to his touch delighted him. Cave men of old must have felt this way after they claimed their women, he guessed. Triumphant! Like they'd searched the whole land through until they found exactly the mate for them.

Sam had slept with other women. Hell, he enjoyed sex as much as the next bloke. Yet sex with Poppy felt different, it took the act to a whole new level. There was no hurry, none at all. He wanted to know every inch of her. As their union reached its climax, a ray of sun slanted through the oval cabin window. It touched her hair and made the light brown strands glint like spun gold.

Sated, Poppy nestled half asleep in his arms, it dawned on Sam what had just happened. With Poppy it was more than just sex. They had made love together. Dammit, he was close to falling in love. The knowledge felt like a punch to the solar plexus.

Sam tensed, unsure how to handle this revelation. It was women, not blokes, who were supposed to feel the earth move. Hell, what had he got himself into? Careful not to disturb her, Sam removed his arm, and eased himself away. He'd said 'no strings,' yet even so ...

"Rest, sweetheart." He dropped a feather light kiss on Poppy's brow. "I'm going up on deck for a quick dip."

"Aye, aye, Captain."

Her voice was so quiet that Sam could barely hear her. Lulled by the boat's gentle sway, she drifted off to sleep again. Sam tugged on his discarded swimming trunks and chuckled. He stood a moment, his eyes drawn to the light dusting of freckles on her nose that had hitherto gone unnoticed. The sun must have brought them out as it did for some folk. Poppy had a birthmark, too, at the top of her thigh, although you had to look hard to see it. Her skin had a healthy glow now, with no trace of pallor, Sam was pleased to note.

He watched her long lashes flutter. He'd leave her to snooze undisturbed while he took a last swim. Hell, he needed to do something to cool off, otherwise he'd be tempted to ravish her all over again. Already Sam could feel the tell-tale stir of desire.

The initial shock of his cold plunge had the desired effect. Sam had intended only to jump in, cool off and climb out again, but he struck out in a lazy front crawl. His arms sliced effortlessly through the sparkling water. At length, libido under control, he flipped over on his back and floated. A sense of peace washed over him as he stared up at the azure blue sky. What did they say about North Devon? Today, it truly was a little bit of heaven.

The sound of a splash made him glance towards the boat. Back in her bikini, Poppy had entered the water, too. Within seconds she was level with him.

He grinned, returning her breathy "Hi."

"Hi yourself. I thought you were asleep."

"Nope, only resting." She giggled, a happy, joyous sound. "Don't want to miss out on a last swim."

"Any plans for tomorrow, Poppy?" An impulse made him put the question before he considered the ramifications. "We won't be back until late. Want to stay over at the cottage tonight and do something on Sunday? Make a weekend of it." He added quickly, "no strings attached." If he said that last phrase often enough, it might sound convincing.

"Hmm, let me see. What exactly had you in mind Dr Brocklehurst?" Poppy pretended uncertainty, her grey eyes sparkling with mischief. "I'll have to consult my diary."

"Oh, late breakfast, a stroll on the beach, maybe a drive somewhere for lunch." Sam shrugged. "See what we feel like when we wake up, I guess. How does that grab you for a nice, lazy Sunday?"

The truth was he hadn't formulated a plan. The invite was merely a ruse to avoid saying goodbye to her. Delaying tactics. Well, they could see how the day rolled, and go with the flow. Spontaneity was good sometimes. Off duty, Sam preferred not to be too organised.

"It grabs me, Dr Brocklehurst." Poppy's slow smile widened. "Right, I'm going to swim now."

She kicked out, totally at home in the deeper water.

"All you need is a tail." Sam chuckled as he drew abreast of her. "And gills, perhaps. You're a fish in disguise. Where did you learn to swim like that, Poppy?"

"I've swum since I was little." She switched to a leisurely backstroke. "I did have lessons later, and did some competitive swimming in my teens, but my dad taught me to begin with. He's the same, loves the water. Another benefit of living in Spain, I suppose, a better climate and the sea on his doorstep."

"You don't miss him too much?" Sam swum alongside her. "Or he, you? Though I guess having a parent in Spain makes for great holidays. Where is he based, the Costa del Sol, by any chance? I've heard that's an area ex-pats like to settle."

"Yes, a sleepy little fishing village near San Pedro." Poppy wrinkled her nose. "It is lovely over there. We keep in touch, and I go over when possible."

"But not this year," Sam probed, "or maybe you've been already?"

"Actually, Dad plans to return to the UK for several weeks in October, one of the reasons I decided not to visit this summer." Poppy splashed lazily. "That and starting a new job, of course."

"Hmm, a busy time." Sam flipped onto his back and floated beside her.

Inevitably, their quick dip turned into a proper swim, racing each other for the sheer thrill of it. At length, treading water, Sam noted the subtle light change. The sun, a golden orb, had dipped low on the horizon. He was aware of a current, too, as the drag of the tide became stronger. Nothing to worry about yet but they needed to stop swimming now. He yelled to Poppy and pointed to the boat. It was time to climb aboard, and head back to the Sea Nymph's mooring at Instow.

"Unless you're planning on staying here until midnight." Sam grinned in answer to her plea to stay longer. "It's later than it seems."

"Hmm, imagine that, lying on deck under a canopy of stars." Poppy sighed wistfully. "Glorious. Let's do it one day, Sam."

"We'd need better provisions than a mere half bottle of lemonade." Sam laughed as he struck out for the boat, Poppy in his wake. "OK, let's get out of the water and on with those life jackets. The tide is definitely turning, I can feel it, and the current will be much stronger soon. The winds and tides have to be respected out here on the open water."

On board again, Sam retrieved his clothes and left Poppy to change in the shelter of the cabin. Up on deck, he towelled himself dry and stripped off his wet trunks, unconcerned with the lack of privacy. After all, who was there to see him out here. Soon, he was back in denim shorts and T-shirt, ready to weigh anchor. He checked Poppy was prepared for the increase in speed, fired the outboard motor and steered a course for Instow. They were travelling faster now. At speed, the return journey wouldn't take long.

Poppy joined him on deck and leant over the prow, watching the scenery flash past as the cabin cruiser ate up the knots. Sam caught the rapt expression on her face.

"Enjoy the trip, sweetheart?"

"It's been amazing." Poppy turned towards him and gave a wide smile. "I've loved every minute! Thank you, Sam."

Her meaning was clear. Sam held her gaze. "My pleasure."

They were fast approaching the mooring. He cut the engine and made the Sea Nymph secure, then helped Poppy into the waiting dinghy. Seeing her relax and trail her fingers in the water, he determined to eke out every precious moment for her. He chose to ignore the dinghy's own outboard motor, grabbed the oars and rowed them to the landing slip.

The distance wasn't far. Sam had inherited one of the closer moorings and, all too soon, they'd reached the jetty, and were homeward bound. Poppy helped him remove both the outboard motor and oars, to stow them inside his waiting vehicle. She watched as he secured the dinghy to the roof rack.

"You don't leave the dinghy at Instow, then?" Sam grimaced, as her gaze alighted on several other dinghies moored nearby. "I intended to, but Bill warned me off. This little outboard motor is fairly new, bought after he had the last one pinched. Anyway, no problem with storage. I'm renting one of those garages behind Rowan Cottage."

He saw her frown, then her face clear as she pictured where he was talking about.

"Ah, I know where you mean. They stand in a row, don't they, all the doors painted different colours. Handy."

"Yes, indeed." Sam nodded. "I've stored some packing boxes in there, too."

He bit back the comment the lease would do until the purchase of the two cottages went ahead and both properties could be joined together. Then, after some clever architectural reconfiguring, he'd end up with his own garage – plus, a small parking space. Already he'd had a voicemail, requesting him to contact Mr Kerslake's office at his earliest convenience. Apparently, there was news to impart; his bid to buy had been successful. This didn't feel like the right moment to tell Poppy, though. Also, it wasn't unheard of for a prospective sale to fall through. No, better to wait until exchange of contracts and surprise her with a done deal.

"Hungry?" Sam revved the engine, raising a questioning eyebrow as he glanced at Poppy. "Fancy grabbing a pizza en route - of the gluten free variety, of course."

At her nod, he grinned.

"Great, let's go. There's supposed to be a nice little Italian place tucked away that isn't too much of a detour. Eat in or take-away, whichever you prefer."

In about forty minutes they'd located the venue. Poppy decided on the take-away option. Soon, together with pizza boxes and a fresh bottle of mineral water, they were back on the open road. Sam kept a sharp look out until, spying a clifftop parking spot, he indicated and swung off the main highway. It was an ideal place for a picnic supper. Soon, they were sprawled out on a thick tartan rug on a wide, grassy verge overlooking the shimmering sea, enjoying the warm evening air.

"Wow, this is delish." Poppy licked her lips as she balanced the cardboard container on her knees. "I haven't had pizza for ages. Now here I am eating Pizza Fiorentina, my favourite."

They munched in companionable silence. Then Poppy paused mid-bite.

"Tell me, Sam – how did you know that little bistro would have a gluten free option? I mean, before we tried it. Not all places do, by any means." She eyed him curiously.

"Simple." Sam cleared his throat aware it was time to 'fess up. "I charted our route after I first suggested the trip, picked out a few likely looking eateries, and checked them out in advance. Didn't take very long but you're right, of course. A surprising number of places don't cater for Coeliac customers. I was shocked, to be honest."

"Welcome to my world." Poppy made a face. "Only I'm not shocked anymore, just resigned." She looked down. "Sorry. I'm afraid going out with me is rather complicated, isn't it, Sam?"

Something about her expression touched him, yet at the same time made him furious. Who the hell was responsible for making this gorgeous girl feel like that about herself?

"You listen to me, lady." Sam growled, pushing aside his own pizza box. "If you're apologising for having a Coeliac diagnosis, stop right now! There's no need. It's part and parcel of who you are and it's my privilege to spend time with you. Got it?"

"Got it." She gave him a tremulous smile. "Thank you, Sam. And put it down to the shrapnel, as I call it. The fallout from my previous relationship. Mark, my ex always liked to do things on the spur of the moment. Nursing, with shift work and unpredictable finishing times made that difficult enough. He'd never have coped with my Coeliac diagnosis, too. He'd have found it the biggest pain if I had to keep checking the list of ingredients and saying I couldn't go somewhere because the menu choice was too limited."

"Selfish bastard." The words were out before Sam could censor them. "Apologies, Poppy, I shouldn't have said that even if I do happen to think it."

"No, you're right. Mark was exactly what you said." Poppy sighed, picking up another slice of pizza. "Unfortunately, it took me a while to see it. Anyway, enough about my ex. He's history. How about you? No one special in your life before you came to Woolacombe?"

"Girlfriends, yes, but none serious enough to want to marry, if that's what you mean." Sam studied her. "Perhaps I've not stayed in the same place long enough for it to happen."

"Don't you want to settle down and have a family, Sam?" Poppy nibbled her lip. "You know, do the traditional thing."

"Yes, in the future, I guess." Sam shrugged, unsure where she was going with this line of questioning. "All my brothers have ... but, as I said, for me all that's in the future."

There was a split second where he thought she was going to say more. Then, a succinct change of subject instead.

"Wow, look at that glorious view, isn't it just magical!"

Sam glanced in the direction she pointed and, sure enough, the view was breathtaking. As the last vestiges of daylight disappeared, a pale moon rose, casting an ethereal glow over the darkening ribbon of sea. Magical, indeed. Yet, if truth be told, it was the view in front of him that really held him spellbound. Sam's gaze returned to Poppy.

"What?" He saw her blush as she turned and caught him staring at her. "What is it, Sam – have I got pizza on my chin, or something? Ooh, I bet I have! Where are the tissues? The topping tastes fantastic but this cheese is all melting and ... "

"Poppy, come here," Sam growled, "and please stop talking."

Deftly, he removed the last pizza slice from her fingers, pulling her to him as he crushed her lips with a kiss. She uttered a soft moan. Sam saw her pupils darken, the grey eyes becoming smoky before closing as she gave herself up to his kiss. The sounds she made, little whimpers of desire, almost undid him. With infinite care, he brushed back a stray lock of her silky brown hair, tucking the wayward tress gently behind her ear. In the fading evening light, dimpsy as Devonians called it, he could see the rosy flush of her skin. Dammit, she was beautiful! As Poppy twisted towards him, her top rode up. Sam slid a hand beneath the thin material and cupped her breast, feeling her nipple harden in response. Poppy nestled closer; her arms wound seductively round his neck. Oblivious to their surroundings, they both missed the sound of another vehicle pulling up until alerted by voices and the slamming of car doors.

"Oh no, people." Poppy murmured but remained in his arms.

"I want you, sweetheart," reluctantly, Sam set her aside, "best not here, though." He gave a crooked grin. "Not unless we want to get ourselves arrested. Ready to go, or do you fancy a stroll along the clifftop first?"

"I'm ready." Her voice was a whisper. "Let's go."

As Poppy scrambled to her feet, she caught his wrist. "Promise me something, Sam. This has been such a perfect day. Will you bring me here again sometime?"

"I promise, sweetheart." Sam bent to gently kiss her.

The drive home was achingly slow. Lantern Lane was in darkness when they arrived, Sam having managed to convince Poppy she had no need to stop at her flat first. There was a spare toothbrush she could use at Rowan Cottage, and her clothes could go straight in his washing machine. By morning, the garments should be clean and ready to wear again. If not, well, there were plenty of ways they could amuse themselves whilst they waited for the damp garments to dry. The scent of honeysuckle from the hedge hung heavy on the night air as they ran up the path. Poppy lingered a moment to inhale it as Sam slid the key in the lock.

The old front door creaked open and they were inside within seconds. Sam pointed upstairs, offering her the first shower.

"Hang on a sec while I find you a clean towel."

He took the stars two at a time, aware of Poppy close behind as he went to the airing cupboard. He grabbed a fresh towel and threw it to her.

"I think we've played out this scene before." Her soft mouth curved in a smile. "It feels familiar."

"Believe me, if only that damn shower cubicle was larger, I'd vary it and suggest we got in together." Sam threw back his head and laughed. "Right, I know my lines. Leave out your clothes, sweetheart, and I'll shove them in the washing machine. There will be hot coffee waiting downstairs when you're done."

"Lovely." Her smile widened. "Herb tea might be better, though. Mint, if you have any. No worries, if not. See you shortly. I won't be long."

She disappeared into the small bathroom, holding the proffered towel. Soon there was the sound of water running as she turned on the shower.

Sam frowned; herb tea wasn't something he usually bought. Hang on, though! Hadn't he noticed mint growing at the end of the cottage garden? He was right. Sam grabbed a handful. Poppy could have her fresh mint tea, after all. Quickly, he scooped up the pile of clothes she'd left at the top of the stairs, and bundled everything into the washing machine. Everything apart from her bikini. A memory stirred of his sister only ever rinsing her swimming togs in the sink, before hanging them up to dry in the open air.

Several minutes later, with Poppy's bikini pegged out on the clothesline, Sam flicked the switch on the kettle. He placed the mint leaves in a mug and waited for the water to boil, debating whether or not to add a slice of lemon. Did folk add lemon to their mint tea? He had no idea. The noise of running water had stopped now. Sam chuckled; the lady had promised to be quick. A creak of the floorboards caused him to glance up. Poppy stood in front of him clad in nothing but the wispiest of underwear.

He felt his jaw drop. The lacey, white cotton bra and panties gave a 'barely there' impression. Not that Sam had any complaints, but he'd expected her to be wrapped in his towelling bath robe when he saw her next. Perhaps she hadn't seen it, though he was sure he'd left the robe hanging on the hook behind the bathroom door. Whatever – he guessed she must have missed it.

"Wow." Sam blinked. "Look at you, Miss Poppy Lambert. That's what I call an entrance."

"It's so hot tonight that I thought ... " A blush stained her cheeks. "Anyway, we'll be in bed in a minute." The blush deepened. "What I mean is ... "

"No explanation necessary." Sam's voice was gruff as he placed the mugs on the table. The drinks could wait. "I agree, clothes would be an utter waste of time."

The temperature had certainly ramped up a notch or two, that was for sure. And it was nothing to do with the sultry evening.

"Come here, sweetheart." He caught her wrist. "With your permission, I'd like to jump your beautiful bones."

He saw her eyes widen. Part of Poppy's allure was her oblivion to how drop dead gorgeous she was, Sam thought. Any other woman appearing semi naked like this would have had at least an inkling of the response they'd elicit. However, he could see realisation dawn as she stepped away. Perhaps she wasn't totally naïve, after all.

"Ooh, is that fresh mint tea?" Her eyes alighted on the steaming mug. "Hmm, it is, I can smell it! Sorry, Sam, but I'm going to have a sip of that before indulging in any hanky-panky. In fact, I insist on savouring it."

She threw him a teasing look as she took the slowest of sips

He saw the tantalising flick of her little pink tongue as she tasted the drink. Accidental, or on purpose, he wasn't sure.

"You certainly know how to torture a bloke." Sam gave a theatrical groan. "Right, shower time. A cold one, me thinks. Wait there, temptress. I'll be with you in five."

Sam left her in the kitchen and took the stairs two at a time. He stepped in the shower, and stood under a cascade of icy needles. It took mere seconds to soap himself vigorously, rinse and dry off again. A large navy towel wrapped round his waist, he headed down to the kitchen, half expecting to find Poppy gone. Something about her was ethereal like a will - o' the wisp. Yet no, there she was exactly where he'd left her.

Words were superfluous. Sam wasn't sure who moved first. It didn't matter. Suddenly she was wrapped in his arms, her luminous grey eyes darkening to smoke.

By tacit agreement they didn't ask any questions, just revelled in being together - loving each other in the hot June night. Nothing else seemed to matter. All that existed was the present moment, and the silvery moon as it trailed across a velvet sky, weaving its way between a blanket of stars. Sam didn't bother with pulling the blinds. There was no one to overlook Rowan Cottage. At least, not unless they were intent enough to climb a ladder and gawp through the bedroom window. And he didn't foresee that event happening.

Slumber didn't claim them both until the early hours. Sam stirred first. He turned to look at Poppy, check she hadn't fled in the night. She lay peacefully beside him, the dawn rays dancing over her face as she slept, her light brown hair spread over the white pillow. Long lashes fanned her cheeks, her breathing slow and even, giving him no hint of her dreams. Sam relaxed, waiting patiently for the day to unfold.

There were morning sounds outside now. It must be getting later. Gently, Sam eased himself away so as not to disturb her, wrapped a towel round his waist and padded downstairs to make a tray of tea. A nose in the kitchen cupboard unearthed a packet of plain rice cakes to go with it.

First, he made himself a coffee, hot and strong exactly as he liked it, and stood by the open window while he drank it. The scent of lavender drifted in on the morning air. Apart from birdsong, the cottage was silent. Or was it? He thought he detected a muted laugh, followed by a soft footfall and a creak of the floorboards. A shadow fell across the flagstone floor, lengthening before it disappeared into the cob wall. For a fleeting moment he sensed a presence – yet he was alone, Sam was certain of it.

Oddly, he didn't feel unnerved. The presence, whatever it was, felt benign. Someone from the past just dropping by to see who lived here now, perhaps. He wondered if he had passed muster.

Sam held no set views on the supernatural, though he was of the opinion the living were more likely to do folk harm than the dear departed. But it was interesting to ponder on. Carrying the tea tray, it occurred to him to wonder if Poppy or her grandmother had ever had any strange experiences at Rowan Cottage? He decided to ask her.

"Oh, you've met Sadie, then." Poppy sat up in bed, hugging her knees. "Rumour has it that she was a wise woman who once lived – and died – here." Her eyes sparkled with mischief. "Sometimes she makes herself known, but she won't cause you any bother. Did you know Rowan Cottage was built on a ley line? I've always felt the positive energy."

Sam felt his eyebrows shoot up. This was news indeed.

CHAPTER TEN

Poppy strolled hand in hand with Sam along Putsborough Beach, her heart full. Right now, she was living her best life. On waking that morning, she'd struggled to place where she was. The dim bedroom had been at once familiar, yet unfamiliar. Then came a joyous realisation as she rolled over and saw Sam lying beside her. He half stirred, edged closer, and slung his arm across her waist. The move had been possessive, proprietorial, the weight of it trapping her. Quietly, with no clear sense of what time it was, she'd watched the pearly grey, opalescent light playing over the strong contours of his sleeping face. And wanted to pinch herself because, surely, she must be dreaming.

Then Sam had woken, and lazily they'd made love again. Slowly, as if they had all the time in the world, they'd explored each other's bodies anew. Poppy drifted back to sleep; the next time she woke was to see Sam approach the bedside with a welcome tray of tea. His face had been a picture when she'd told him about Sadie, the wise woman said to haunt Rowan Cottage. Yet there was nothing bad here, she was sure of it. Her gran used to tell her the ley line that ran underneath the old cottage had a powerful female energy, making it a nurturing place for women who needed shelter. Maybe this was why she'd always felt protected under its roof.

Later, considerably later, they had showered and dressed and prepared a tasty brunch together before taking a stroll. At Poppy's suggestion, they'd opted for a leisurely beach walk, trainers off as they splashed in the shallows, laughing like children as they kicked up the spray. The breakers rolled in ever further up the sand, pressing forward on an incoming tide. Poppy watched the sun dance on the water and decided this North Devon beach, if not the best place on earth, was certainly her best place.

"You don't mind us staying close to home today?" She glanced at Sam. "I know you suggested a drive out on the moors and having a meal in an olde worlde pub and everything, which would have been great. We got up so late, though, and … ."

"And had other things to do." Sam shot her a teasing look. "Far better things, in my opinion." He chuckled. "Don't worry, Poppy, we'll do the moorland trip and lunch out another weekend. Start off early one Sunday and visit Witheridge. The Gateway to the Two Moors Way it's called, isn't it? Did you know Witheridge is said to be almost equidistant from Dartmoor and Exmoor. At least, that's what I read in my North Devon tourist guidebook."

Sam threw her a wink.

"Then that must be right, Dr Brocklehurst." Poppy giggled, reassured to hear Sam plan ahead. "Guide books don't lie. Anyway, I'm still full after that delicious brunch."

"Hmm, we've walked a fair distance. How about afternoon tea on the way back?" Sam laughed. "You'll have worked up an appetite by then, especially after we've had a swim. Remember that clifftop café we saw? We can try the menu there if you like."

They strolled a little further before sitting on the beach to chat a while. Then, when the sun began to make them feel uncomfortably hot, they ran into the sea to cool off. Sam wasted no time and dived cleanly beneath the rolling surf. Thigh deep, Poppy stood a moment watching him. She yelped as an extra big breaker hit, nearly knocked her off her feet. Despite the warmth of the day the water felt chilly.

"The secret is to get in quick, sweetheart." Sam laughed seeing her hesitation. "Just do it! It's fatal trying to inch in by degrees."

Poppy took the plunge, diving under the crest of the next big wave. She surfaced close to Sam. Although the sea was choppy, the tide was in their favour, each breaker pushing them shoreward. There was safety in that, she knew. However, by tacit agreement they didn't stay in long. The buffeting of the waves was fun, but became tiring after a while. Afterwards, they spread out towels to lie on further up the beach. The rays of the hot afternoon sun dried them as they dozed.

The word blissful sprang to Poppy's mind. She rolled over, boldly reaching out to run her fingers through the dark whorls of hair on Sam's chest. The feel of his toned, salt licked body triggered a frisson of excitement. His sharp intake of breath told her that he felt aroused, too.

"Little minx." He opened an eye and grinned.

"What would you have been doing this weekend, Sam?" Idly, her hand rested on his toned abdomen. "If you hadn't been with me, I mean."

"Pining for you, of course." Sam gave a throaty chuckle, catching her hand as it strayed downwards. "Best not go there, sweetheart, not on a public beach. Don't start something we can't finish without getting arrested."

Poppy pulled away, giggling, only to find herself swept up in Sam's arms and her mouth plundered with kisses. Eventually, he paused to answer her question.

"Hmm, I'd have tackled the garden, I suppose." He shrugged. "It's looking a bit unkempt. Part of the tenancy agreement states I must keep it tidy, so I need to up my game. I've spotted a few gardening implements in the shed, so I won't need to go out and buy any. But, to tell the truth, I don't think the last tenants did much, either."

"Maybe they were too short term." Poppy said. "It was a riot of colour in my gran's time. She was very green fingered; it was amazing the variety of plants she managed to grow. She had a veggie patch, too. And I remember the end garden wall was covered in wisteria. All gone now, of course. I'd love to see the garden prettied up again."

Sam thought a moment.

"Perhaps you'd like to help me with that." His dark eyes were soft as he cupped her face, running a thumb across her cheek. "It can be our project. If the memories won't make you sad, of course."

"Ooh, I'd love to!" Poppy beamed in delight. "But you're talking like you're planning a major overhaul, Sam. As a tenant, surely mowing the lawn and doing a spot of weeding is enough. Maybe plant a few flowers here and there if you want, nothing too expensive, just some colourful annuals to brighten things up. That shouldn't be too pricey. After all, you'll be leaving Rowan Cottage for a bigger place at some point, won't you?"

"Not anytime soon." Sam glanced away. "Rowan Cottage suits me fine for now. And you're right, I do relish a project.

Might as well be my own garden. Whatever ideas you have are welcome, Poppy."

Poppy detected a slight hesitation before Sam spoke. Strange, what reason could he have to be hesitant – unless he thought she'd be upset at the prospect of him making changes to her grandmother's old cottage garden. Nonsense, of course. There were changes aplenty already, especially outside. Although the bones of the place were the same, the cottage was different in so many ways. She could see that now, having spent more time there. Sam had put his stamp on the place and it felt a decidedly male domain.

Maybe the changes had invoked the spirit of the old wise woman, Sadie. Her spirit would settle again, Poppy felt sure if it. After all, Sam was a healer, too. Instinctively, Poppy knew his presence would be welcome. Sadly, by comparison, her gran's presence felt like a mere fading echo of times gone by. Rowan Cottage had entered a new incarnation.

"Let me know when you need help and I'll be along." She smiled. "If you're up for replanting the flower beds, or reconfiguring them, I can give you a few tips. We'll have a wander round a local garden centre. I promise to focus on low maintenance plants, nothing too expensive 'cos I know you will be leaving at some point." Sam made to speak and she put up her hand to silence him. "That's a fact. No need to deny it."

Again, Sam appeared to hesitate. Poppy wondered what was wrong. Had she sounded too enthusiastic over a garden space that wasn't her own? However, before she could delve further, Sam had jumped to his feet. He stretched out a hand to pull her up.

"Don't worry, the big make-over won't happen yet." He stooped to grab his towel. "And, speaking of gardens, don't forget we'll be expected to make a few token appearances on behalf of the PPG when this walled Victorian garden project at Bramblewood takes off."

"Any more developments on that front?" Poppy sensed he was trying to distract her but chose to go along with the ploy. "Too soon, I imagine, despite the nice weather."

"Exactly what I thought," Sam nodded, "but it turns out to be quite the opposite. Four patients have shown a keen interest already, I heard on Friday. And that was the first day our notice went up in the waiting room. I believe we've tapped into something."

"You're thinking along the lines of the gardening vols organising themselves, once this project is up and running properly?" Poppy queried tentatively.

Not keen on having too big a chunk of her own free time swallowed up, she felt a need to clarify that. "Loosely connected with the PPG but operating separately, like we discussed at the meeting?"

"Yep." Sam said. "I'm sure there'll be folk who are happy to join a venture like this, but don't want to be attached to something more formal like the PPG. Every so often they'll touch base with us, obviously, but otherwise – once things are up and running - the gardening vols can operate independently."

"What about the Health and Safety aspects?" Poppy chewed her lip aware this issue hadn't been broached. "Who will be in charge of that?"

"Hmm, good point." Sam grinned. "Julia would be proud of you, Nurse Lambert. I guess that's something we need to explore. As Practice Manager, it's her responsibility to check out the insurance aspect, public liability." He frowned. "We'll have to hope one of the gardening vols is up for the role of supervisor. All groups need a supervisor - to put together a rota, who's doing what in the garden, when. And who is paired with who, stuff like that."

"I can assemble a basic First Aid kit. It'll need to be accessible outside of surgery hours." Poppy added. "It wouldn't do for an accident to happen on surgery premises, even if out of hours, and find no one was able to locate a first aid box. Also, one of us needs to do a walk-through of the place, identify any trip hazards, etc. And won't the supervisor need to know if any of the vols have a physical disability, or any medical condition that may cause an issue?"

"You're more cut out for this than you realise, Poppy." Sam chuckled. "There was I, thinking you'd been railroaded into replacing Laura. Especially when you saw that Andy Doyle was stepping down, and you'd be left with me."

"Nonsense." She glanced away, feeling a fiery flush stain her cheeks, unwilling to admit he was spot on.

She was getting into the swing of it, Poppy acknowledged. Yet this was only because if she had to be involved with something she liked to know it was being done properly. As her old nursing tutor had once commented, thoroughness was in her nature. Besides, in Poppy's experience, there was likely to be far more angst when a project was undertaken without proper organisation beforehand.

"Just dotting the i's and crossing the t's, Dr Brocklehurst," she collected herself and gave him an answering grin, "but I'm glad you see my potential."

"Oh, I see your potential all right, Poppy Lambert." Sam stooped to brush her lips with a kiss. His dark eyes smouldered. "In fact, I'd say you have great potential."

The kiss became hungry and demanding. Poppy responded eagerly, her body yielding to his touch. She wrapped her arms round Sam's neck and began a gentle teasing with her tongue, exulting in his low growl of appreciation. His lips tasted faintly salty. This was one amazing man, Poppy thought. How lucky she was to have met him! She had no power to foretell the future – Sam had already indicated he wasn't ready to settle down - but, for today at least, he was hers. As for the rest, she could pretend. Her toes curled in the warm sand while he continued to kiss her. Sea and sky dipped amid the wild cry of gulls as she lost herself in the sensation.

At length they drew apart, breathing hard. Sam stood, offering her a hand up.

"Home time, sweetheart." He brushed back her wind-blown hair and grinned. "This next bit is best completed back at Rowan Cottage, me thinks."

Poppy felt a delicious shiver run down her spine.

Sam caught her hand as he broke into a jog across the golden sands, pulling her with him. His long, muscular legs set an exacting pace. She panted with the effort of trying to keep up. Poppy might be his match in the water, but on dry land Sam was definitely the one with more stamina.

"Sorry, sweetheart, too fast?" Sam slowed to keep pace with her.

"It's f – fine." Poppy puffed. "A g - good cardiovascular workout."

The sun's caress on her bikini clad body felt good; lifting her face to the offshore breeze, she felt like singing. If she had any air left! They ran along Putsborough Beach, soon drawing level with the rocks that separated Putsborough from Woolacombe Sands. After a debate, they agreed to forgo afternoon tea in favour of drinks in the garden of Rowan Cottage followed by an early fish and chip supper at Ben's Plaice. Careful now, they clambered over the sea sprayed rocks and continued on, skirting round family groups dotted about the sands. Reminded of Rupert, the small boy who had nearly drowned, Poppy asked Sam if he'd had any further update.

"Yep, and all good news." Sam nodded. "I'm told he responded well to treatment and has been discharged home. A close call, but the resilience of kids, eh!"

Poppy responded with a watery smile, feeling suddenly emotional. Sam squeezed her hand in understanding. Soon they were off the beach, headed for Lantern Lane. Rowan Cottage hove into sight, and Poppy experienced a twinge of guilt. She'd secured the offer of a small mortgage now. So, why not mention this to Sam. Nothing to be gained by keeping it a secret. She must be in with a chance, at least, despite the letting agent's initial rebuff.

This was Sam's home now. Any purchase would affect him, especially if what he claimed was true and he wasn't considering a move yet.

"Sam, I - I should have said something before." Poppy stopped and caught his arm. "A while ago I asked Mr Kerslake if Rowan Cottage might come on the market soon. Remember me saying I always dreamt of buying it one day? Well, he more or less told me, yes, but when it does come on the market the price will be out of my reach. He says there is another interested buyer, prepared to offer over the odds, and purchase the next-door property. If you can believe that! Anyway, I thought you should know."

Poppy wasn't sure what response she'd expected, but Sam throwing his head back and giving a loud guffaw wasn't it.

"Sam?" Puzzled, she stared at him, wondering if he'd understood what she said. "You did hear me say that Rowan Cottage could be sold soon?"

"If you're fretting about me being given notice to leave, relax sweetheart, no need." He grinned, pulling her to him. "My tenancy is secure. I can assure you I'm in no danger of being thrown out on the streets with my bags and baggage. Right, let's get inside and have a drink. Tea OK for you? If not, there's fresh juice in the 'fridge."

So, he'd remembered that tea was her preferred tipple. Poppy hid a smile. Oh, she enjoyed a latte on occasion, but tea was her go to drink. Even on hot days she found it refreshing. Heavens, she was fast turning into her Aunty Bea, Poppy realised with a jolt!

"Tea will be great, thanks, Sam. Shall I brew a pot? Why don't we take our drinks in the garden and have a chat about what you can do out there, if you still want to." She didn't know why he'd have the enthusiasm now.

"Great, the garden it is." Sam nodded, ushering Poppy through. He waved away her offer of tea making. "Find a shady spot and I'll grab us some seating."

He emerged from the shed with a couple of foldup, canvas chairs, instructed Poppy to make herself comfortable, then disappeared. The back door was ajar. Poppy heard the clink of cups and teaspoons as he rattled around in the kitchen. Without a task, she did as she was told and rested under the shade of a gnarled, old apple tree. The daisy strew lawn looked pretty in the late afternoon sunshine. A robin perched on the rockery only a few yards away, head on one side as it regarded her. There was certainly plenty to be done out here if Sam really was keen to do it.

Poppy listened to the low hum of bees in the mature lavender bushes that edged the winding garden path, and began to feel drowsy. She fancied she heard her grandmother's voice, carried on the balmy air. 'Those need cutting back, lass, grown a bit woody now.' Feeling nostalgic, Poppy pictured the elderly lady as she remembered her best - pottering in her beloved garden, taking cuttings of this and that, with a wicker basket on her arm, and her favourite pair of secateurs to hand. 'If you want things to grow well, my lovely, you mustn't be afraid to prune them.' How she missed her gran's soft, West Country burr – and the warm hugs that, whatever the problem, never failed to make things feel better.

What would her grandmother have made of Sam? A shrewd judge of character, Poppy very much hoped she'd have liked him.

"Here you go, sweetheart." Poppy's eyes flew open as Sam pushed a bowl of fresh fruit salad and cream into her hands.

He studied her a moment. "You looked miles away. Let me guess; you were thinking of being here with your gran. Happy thoughts, I hope?"

He was spot on, of course. How, she had no idea. It was a novelty, being with a man who was so tuned into her. In fact, being in sync with a guy was the biggest turn on, Poppy decided. There was no doubt about it, Dr Sam Brocklehurst was one sexy, Alpha male. And here she was spending her weekend with him. She wanted to pinch herself.

"Yes, definitely happy thoughts." Hastily, she cleared her throat and smiled, meeting Sam's molten, brown gaze. "This garden was gran's joy. She was in her element out here. I was wondering what her advice would be for you with regards prettying it up. I'm sure she'd have had some, starting with a good tidy up of that lavender." She glanced at the bowl resting in her lap. "Thanks, Sam, this looks tempting."

"To make up for the missed cream tea." He sat down opposite her and stretched out his long legs. "By the way, mind your feet. I put a mug of tea on the grass by your chair."

"Oops!" Poppy moved her feet swiftly out of harm's way.

"Admittedly not the safest place," he added with a chuckle, "but I haven't got round to buying a picnic table. In fact, I don't own any garden chairs, either. These must have been left behind by a previous tenant."

"Hmm, that was lucky." Poppy was rather taken with the bright orange, canvas fold-ups. "They're nice. You may as well use them."

The next few minutes passed in companionable silence while they both ate. At length, with a last lick of her spoon, Poppy was done. She glanced up to see Sam watching her.

The intensity in his gaze made her face heat. His dark eyes smouldered; there was no mistaking the drift of his thoughts. She felt her body tingle with anticipation.

"Finished?" His voice sounded gruff as he took her bowl.

Finished? Suddenly, Poppy knew that things had barely begun. Wordlessly, she stood, her heart skipping a beat as she followed Sam inside the cottage. She barely registered the sound of the dessert bowls being dropped in the sink. The next moment she was wrapped in his arms, returning kiss for passionate kiss. Sam's hand slid under her top, caressing and exploring, and she uttered a low moan of pleasure as he cupped her breasts. Poppy pressed closer, sighing. She wanted to feel him, skin to skin. Clothes felt in the way, superfluous; her fingers trembling, she fumbled with his belt.

"Hang on, sweetheart." Sam gave a wolfish grin as he captured her hands. "Best do this next bit upstairs."

He led her to the narrow wooden staircase. Wordlessly, Poppy followed him into the main bedroom, where the sheets were still rumpled from the night before. Rays of sunshine danced on the soft white walls.

Her last conscious action was to pull the blind, throwing the room into cool shadow before giving herself up to the blissful sensation of Sam loving her. Soon she was lost in ripple upon ripple of sensation, revelling in the feel of Sam's touch on her body. Without being told, he seemed to know exactly what to do to elicit her whimper of response. In fact, Poppy thought he was nothing short of a magician! She wished she was bold enough to ask Sam what he liked, check what felt good for him, too. Yet every time she opened her mouth to try, he silenced her with another kiss, each one longer and deeper than the last. Then she gave up trying, guided only by his low grunts of satisfaction.

Eventually, Poppy dozed, lying sated in Sam's strong arms. Earlier, he'd asked if she felt like she'd come home. Now she had the answer, and it was a yes. Poppy Lambert had very much come home.

⌣

She slept so peacefully that Sam was loath to rouse her. However, time was marching on. No doubt, Poppy would want to return to her flat tonight, and there was still supper to consider. Sam very much doubted either of them would feel like walking to Ben's Plaice for fish and chips now. No, it was wiser to order food in, although what type of food would she prefer? He frowned, debating the matter as he sat up and began scrolling through his 'phone to check out the take-away options. Poppy didn't stir, her breathing slow and rhythmic. He grinned, covering her with a sheet before he slipped out of bed and padded towards the shower. One of them needed to shift, and it might as well be him.

Hair all mused, Poppy's eyes were open on his return, with the dreamy look of the just woken. The weekend had given her peachy skin a sun kissed, golden glow. As she sat up, careful to wrap her delectable body in the sheet, Sam suppressed a chuckle. Why the embarrassment? It wasn't as if he hadn't seen all of her already. Remembering how she'd made him feel only a short while ago, he thought she really was the most delightful mix of bold and shy. He cleared his throat and suggested they order a take-away. The only problem was what to opt for. Neither of them felt in the mood for Indian cuisine. Chinese was out, Poppy said, because it was rare to find much on the menu that she could eat. Unfortunately, the local Italian didn't offer gluten free pizzas. However, there were several Thai dishes that she could safely eat, and there was a good Thai restaurant in town.

"Sorry, Sam." He saw her bite her lip regretfully. "It's a pain, I know. Please, have a Chinese if you'd prefer. Honestly, it's fine. We'll order from two different places. It's a shame 'cos I used to love it, but with most Chinese food there's usually very little on the menu that's gluten free."

"OK, Thai it is then," Sam lifted an eyebrow, "for both of us." She was apologising again, but he chose to ignore it. Hell, what was it with this woman; he was with her, wasn't he! In his book that meant he looked out for her, just as he'd expect her to do for him if the situation was reversed. "Tell me what you want, and I'll place the order while you shower."

"You're a great guy, Sam Brocklehurst." Her sweet mouth was curving into a smile. "Do you know that? Could you delay that order for a short while longer, though? And come here, please."

She lowered the sheet, exposing the swell of her breasts where the skin was paler. Her nipples peaked as the sheet dropped lower. Her beautiful grey eyes had darkened to the colour of a storm chased sky, her pupils wide in a clear message of arousal. All thoughts of the take-away supper fled as Sam gave a growl of approval. The next second, he had tumbled her on the bed, answering her invitation to make love again. This time he was determined to take it slow ... even if it ended with her begging him for release.

Dusk had fallen by the time they were ready to order their take-away. Sam suppressed a grin, thinking how lucky it was that Poppy wasn't here every night, or they would both be in danger of starving. He grabbed his mobile and rang the restaurant while she darted into the shower. When she emerged some ten minutes later swathed in one of his large, navy bath towels, he avoided his gaze. His turn to shower and no time for distractions.

The food delivery arrived without undue delay. They opted to eat outside and returned to their seats under the apple tree to enjoy the last of the summer evening. The fruit tree cast a long shadow on the lawn, toughing overgrown shrubs alongside the brick wall in soft indigo purple. The twitter of birdsong had ceased, most birds having returned to their nests for the night. A pale shape glided by, and they heard the hoot of an owl on the hunt.

Perched on one of the orange fold-ups, Sam was struck by how right Poppy looked sitting there in the garden of Rowan Cottage. There was no doubt about it, she had an affinity with the mellow stone cottage. Yet it had been quite a revelation to hear that she'd enquired about purchasing the place. How serious had she been, Sam wondered? That had been the moment when he should have said something, admitted he was the mystery buyer. Yet the property market was notoriously fickle. A lot could go wrong before completion of the sale. No, Sam thought, he would stick to his original plan and tell Poppy when there was something concrete to celebrate. After all, news of that magnitude was a special event. He pictured her raising a glass to him aboard the Sea Nymph.

Sam watched her lift the lid of each different container and sniff appreciatively at the exotic flavours. Suddenly he was hit by an instinctive knowing. Hell, this was the woman he wanted to settle down with. He'd dated many females, but Poppy Lambert was the only one who was a fit for him. The knowledge floored him like a punch to the solar plexus.

He shifted restlessly. The more pressing problem was what to do about it. He'd been in Woolacombe barely five minutes, dammit! Surely that was too soon to get serious about anyone. It crossed Sam's mind to wonder how she saw things, especially since they had slept together. Suddenly it was important that she didn't have too many expectations.

"Cards on the table, Poppy." His turn to have her under the microscope. "How do you see your life going in the next few years – settle down, children? What page are you on?"

He could tell the question had thrown her.

"Oh, er, I don't think too far ahead now." She glanced away. "After Mark, I ruled out relationships and decided to be a career girl. So, er, yes, I guess that's me. A career girl."

CHAPTER ELEVEN

"I couldn't eat another thing," Poppy sat back and licked her lips after she'd carefully stacked the empty containers, "that was delicious."

"No washing up, either." Sam chuckled. He pointed to the end of the garden, now shrouded in deep shadow. "Isn't that a rowan tree over there? Looks quite ancient, well over a hundred years, I'd imagine. Must be where the cottage gets its name from."

"Yes," Poppy nodded and followed his gaze. "Gran used to say that folk believed rowan trees had mystical properties. In olden days it was considered lucky to have one near your house, a protection against witchcraft and enchantment."

"Ah, that explains it, then." Sam raised an eyebrow. "The old tree must be working its magic. You've cast a spell on me, Poppy Lambert."

"I don't think it works like that." She smiled. "Careful, though – it's meant to be unlucky to chop down a rowan tree."

She stretched and stood, glancing up at the starlit sky. Sam read her tacit message and jumped up, too.

"Hey, leave everything, Poppy. It's late. I'll run you home and tidy up afterwards." He grimaced. "Otherwise, you'll be bushed tomorrow."

Aware that Sam was right, Poppy acquiesced. Her eyes felt heavy as she followed him out into the lane. Hopefully, she would sleep well after all the fresh sea air ... not to mention the other bonuses of the weekend. As she remembered what they'd got up to only a short while ago, Poppy felt her face heat. She stifled a yawn and laughed as she scrambled into Sam's car.

"Don't worry, I'll be asleep as soon as my head touches the pillow."

"Possibly before, by the look of you." He grinned, then fired the engine and engaged first gear. "Ready, seat belt on?" In answer to her murmured 'yes,' he checked the wing mirror and pulled out onto the clear road. "Right, let's go, sweetheart."

They moved smoothly away. Poppy reached her flat within minutes. Tempted though she was to invite Sam in, she didn't. Instead, she bid him a swift goodnight, mindful that he needed to be fresh for the start of a new working week, too. He'd been correct about one thing. She struggled to keep her eyes open and was asleep the moment she fell into bed.

Monday dawned bright and clear. Poppy thought Bramblewood Surgery seemed busier than ever. She scanned her computer screen for the day's booked appointments and suspected this was likely to be the pace for the whole week. As she ushered in her first patient, she caught a glimpse of Sam's dark head as he disappeared into his consulting room. Flashbacks of their weekend together made her heart do a little skitter.

"Please take a seat, Mrs McDowell." She smiled at the middle-aged lady. "I'm Poppy, one of the practice nurses. I see you're here to have bloods taken to check thyroid function. Is this what you're expecting?"

"Yes, that's right. I've been out of sorts recently. Quite achy and tired, vague things really. Dr Brocklehurst wants to review the dose of my thyroxine pills. I've had an underactive thyroid for a while now. Oh, and please call me Trisha. The other nurses usually do. Mrs McDowell sounds so formal."

"Trisha it is, then." Poppy said. She her invited Tricia to choose an arm and roll up her sleeve, and smiled. "Ah, good veins – this should only take a jiffy."

She placed a pillow under the patient's arm for support and slipped on a tourniquet, then deftly slid in the needle to take blood. Done! As anticipated, Trisha's veins were easily accessible. Task completed, Poppy placed the used syringe in the sharps box and labelled the specimen. The computer screen indicated that a routine urine sample had been requested, too.

"Oops, I nearly forgot." Trisha laughed as she fished in her handbag. "Here it is."

Poppy kept on her gloves and took the sample across to the basin. The urine was cloudy, with an offensive odour as well as traces of frank blood. It didn't need testing to tell her that Trisha had a rip-roaring bladder infection. However, she popped in a dip stick, unsurprised to find it registered positive to protein, blood, and leucocytes.

"I'll send this off to the Lab." After she explained her findings, Poppy invited Trisha to return to the waiting room while she tried to find a doctor for an opinion. "You'll need a course of antibiotics to combat this infection. No wonder you've been feeling rough. And I'll give you another specimen pot in case a repeat sample is needed."

"I hate taking antibiotics," Trisha pulled a face, "they always give me side effects. Really, I prefer not to take them.

Couldn't I just drink more, or something, and see if this infection clears up on its own?"

"Definitely drink more, that's wise." Poppy nodded. "But it's important to treat infections like this one with antibiotics, too. And finish the course, to ensure no bugs are left behind to develop resistance to the treatment prescribed or become a low-grade infection that rumbles on and flares again later. Left alone, UTIs – urinary tract infections – can cause kidney damage, Trisha. Even sepsis, in some instances."

"Gracious, I never realised a simple bladder infection could lead to that." Trisha looked suitable chastened. "OK then, I'll hang on while you find a doc."

Trisha rose to make her way back to the waiting room and Poppy followed, keen to nab the first medic she saw. As luck would have it, she caught Sam as he headed towards his consulting room. Great, as he was Trisha's own GP! Poppy increased her pace and called his name. Now she had no need to hover outside doors, waiting for a doc to emerge. Also, this was an opportunity to query Sam's thinking. Poppy was aware that some GPs preferred to wait on Lab results before they prescribed, whilst others may start a broad-spectrum antibiotic immediately.

"Hi Poppy, problems?" He swung round and raised an eyebrow.

She outlined the situation, trying not to blush as she held his familiar, twinkly gaze.

"You've sent the urine specimen off to the Lab?" Sam considered a moment. "OK, let's hold fire on prescribing until we know the exact antibiotic this bug is sensitive to. Tell

Mrs MacDowell to up her fluids and I'll ring her and prescribe once the result is back."

"Will do." Poppy hesitated.

"Anything else?" He threw her a sexy grin that made her cheeks burn.

"Um, no, that's all." She hesitated, feeling like a gauche teenager. "Thanks, Sam."

In truth, she'd been hoping he would grab the opportunity to suggest another date. Things had been left loose when he'd dropped her back at her flat the previous evening. Of course, Sam was in work today; being the type of doctor he was, he would be focussed firmly on medicine. Silly of her to think otherwise. In any case, Poppy berated herself, work wasn't the place to arrange dates. They had exchanged mobile numbers. He'd message her.

Also, hadn't Sam mentioned a busy week with a young GP trainee scheduled to join him? Plus, Poppy recalled, a couple of orientation sessions at the local hospital this coming weekend. He'd been serious about keeping up his A & E skills. No matter: he had her contact details now. She must wait for him to be ready. As Poppy stepped away, she almost missed Sam's quiet aside.

"Fancy a run this evening, Poppy?"

Poppy glanced up and nodded.

"Great." Sam flashed her a quick grin. "Meet you down on the beach. Not sure what time, I'll text you. Obviously, it will depend on when I finish up here."

"No problem." Poppy felt her face heat again. "I'm free all evening."

On return to Tricia, she explained Sam's decision and sent her home before calling through the next patient. Another blood sample required – unfortunately, the gentleman in question didn't have such good veins this time. However, she flashed him a smile and did her best to warm the chosen arm to encourage the veins to rise to the skin surface. Even so, the task proved tricky.

"Well done, Nurse." The elderly gentleman rolled down his sleeve. "Last time they couldn't manage it at all – and the docs were all busy, so they sent me to get my blood taken at the local hospital. But that's two bus rides away. Much better if I can have it done here. I'll ask for you next time, shall I?"

"If you like." Poppy laughed. "I'm happy to see you if I'm on duty. A tip, though: make sure you're really well hydrated when you know you're going to have blood taken. And try to keep your arm as warm as possible, too. I'm afraid the rest is all luck on the day."

Caught up in the momentum of work, the hours sped by. Lunch was a snatched piece of fruit and a bag of crisps. Later, between patients, Poppy glanced up as she was interrupted by a knock.

"Hey, someone's happy." Laura slipped into Poppy's consulting room to pinch a request form and gave her an old-fashioned look. "I do believe you've been smiling all day, Nurse Lambert. Every time I've seen you, anyway."

Had she? Startled, Poppy blinked.

"Can I help it if I'm blessed with a naturally sunny disposition?" She regarded her colleague innocently. "Anyway, I'm nearly done here. How about you, Laura?"

"Four more patients to see, not including the person this is for, who I'm with now." Laura grimaced as she waved the form. "I got behind when poor old Amy Beale had a wobble and needed a shoulder to cry on. Dear soul admitted she's been feeling low recently. And no wonder! Can't be much fun when you are eighty, you live on your own in a cramped flat, and have a pesky leg ulcer that refuses to heal. It would get me down, too. Happily, the ulcer looked better today, so that was better news."

"Hmm." Poppy chewed her lip. "I'm sure I did Amy's last dressing – you must have been off that day. She seemed rather low then, too."

An idea struck. "Do you think she'd be interested in the PPG Garden Project, Laura? Oh, nothing too strenuous, obviously, just a bit of light weeding after the vols have put in some raised flower beds. That should be happening in a couple of weeks' time. I bet she'd enjoy helping to tend those, not to mention the benefit of having a cuppa and chat with everyone. On Thursdays, I believe someone brings along cake to share."

"Excellent idea!" Laura beamed. "I'll give her a leaflet about it."

"Great," Poppy nodded, "and why not pass on her contact details to Suzy, our Care Navigator? There might be other activities she could suggest that would help lift Amy's mood. OK, let's share the remaining patients then we can both go home."

"Would you, Poppy? That would be marvellous." Laura blew Poppy a kiss. "You're a star."

Finished at last, Poppy waved cheerio to Laura and strolled out into the sun dappled grounds. Sam's car remained parked, an indication that he was still engrossed in medical matters. She scanned her mobile, hoping for a text - not that she expected one from him yet, not while he was still at the Practice. It didn't hurt to check, though.

En route home, Poppy bought a pint of fresh milk and some eggs for her evening meal. She had tomatoes and cheese in the 'fridge and planned to whip up an omelette. it occurred to her to wonder why Sam had told her to meet him on the beach. Why hadn't he asked her to come to Rowan Cottage instead, surely that would be simpler? After all, she'd have to go down Lantern Lane anyway. Swiftly, Poppy dismissed that thought as irrelevant. No doubt Sam had his reasons for suggesting the beach. Heavens, it didn't matter where they met.

The next hour was taken up with tidying her flat and doing a laundry catch up. Also, she made an overdue call to Maisie and her Aunty Bea to enquire how things were with them. As always, Poppy ended up chatting far longer than she'd intended. The one thing she missed in North Devon was the ease with which she used to be able to jump on a train to look in on them both. Her old flat had been a short walk from the train station, Bristol Temple Meads. She'd grown used to the noise of the big locomotives thundering by.

Her call ended with a promise to visit again soon. Time was going on and Poppy felt at a loose end. There was nothing for it but to change into suitable running gear and wait. Maybe Sam had been delayed by an urgent request to see a patient. Poppy wriggled into shorts and a vest top and tried not to count the minutes tick by. At last, she heard a ping indicating the arrival of a text message. Hopefully, it was from Sam. Eagerly, she snatched her mobile.

It was indeed Sam, his message almost curt in its brevity. 'Ready in 10. Meet you by the breakwater.' Poppy frowned. Which breakwater? There were several and she wasn't a mind reader. She supposed he must mean the one people reached when stepping onto the sand via the stony path direct from Lantern Lane. Or could it be the next groyne along where they had paused on the Sunday? Well, she'd take her mobile with her. If they missed each other, she could ring him – that's if Sam had his phone with him, too, of course.

Poppy hummed as she let herself out of the flat, and set off at a brisk jog. It had been another blisteringly hot day, but the heat was abating now. Down by the sea the early evening air felt refreshingly cool. An ideal running temperature, Poppy thought, revelling in the breeze tugging at her hair. The swoop of a gull drew her gaze skywards. The azure blue backdrop was fast fading into pale lilac and dusky mauve. It was a mackerel sky, heralding rain tomorrow if the cloud pattern was anything to go by.

The first breakwater in sight, her spirits lifted as she recognised Sam waiting for her. He responded to her wave and jogged across the sand to meet her. They exchanged tentative grins before Poppy found herself swept into his arms and thoroughly kissed. No words were spoken; no words were needed. Sky, sand, and sea disappeared as she closed her eyes and gave herself up to the moment.

Had she really told this gorgeous man she was a career girl now? She must have been mad! One word from him and she'd be happy to revise her plans. Sam Brocklehurst brought her weary spirits to life. It had only been a day but, oh, how she had missed him!

"Good to see you, sweetheart." Sam's voice was gruff.

"You, too." Poppy's eyelids fluttered open to meet his warm, brown gaze.

She sensed a restlessness about him tonight, a pent-up energy that needed release.

"Come on, let's run." He grabbed her hand and set off, setting an exacting pace as he pulled her along with him.

"Need to blow away a few cobwebs?" She glanced at his expression as she struggled to keep up.

"Something like that," Sam gave a rueful shrug, "and no better running mate than you, Poppy, so I hope that's OK? Apologies if I'm not very talkative tonight."

"No problem." She gasped. "We'll concentrate on running."

Sam drove them relentlessly on. They kept close to the shoreline, their trainers leaving footprints on the damp, hardpacked sand. She found it harder to keep pace with him now. Poppy detected a look of steely determination. Was he just 'in the zone,' wearing his serious runner's face, or was there something on his mind? She didn't know and didn't have enough breath left in her lungs to ask. However, there was definitely an edge of tension about Sam tonight. Hopefully, if something was worrying him, he'd share the problem in due course. Poppy hadn't known Dr Sam Brocklehurst for long, but he didn't strike her as the type of guy to be cajoled into baring his soul before he was ready.

For now, it appeared that Sam preferred to remain quiet. Taking her cue, Poppy did likewise until a sharp pain in her side forced her to stop.

"Ouch." She bent double and gasped. "Ooh, that hurts. Sorry, stitch, need a breather."

"Rest a moment, sweetheart." Sam placed a solicitous arm round her, waiting until she was recovered enough to be guided up the beach to where the sand was dry. As she flopped down and stretched out, he crouched beside her with a look of concern. "Feel better now?"

"Yep." Poppy inhaled cautiously and winced. "Only a stitch, almost gone now. Phew, I can breathe properly again."

"Let's hang on for a few minutes, anyway." Sam frowned. He turned from her and stooped to throw a pebble into the sea. "Listen, Poppy, this is as good a moment as any to tell you that my week's gone a bit pear shaped. Unexpectedly so, I'm afraid. I won't be free to see you for a few weeks."

"Oh?" Poppy blinked. "Well, you already said you have a couple of orientation sessions coming up at the hospital. I know about that. And I know Bramblewood is particularly busy at the moment, so ... "

"No." Sam ran a distracted hand through his hair. "It's nothing to do with work, Poppy. At least, yes, in part, I suppose, but there's more to it. Complications I hadn't bargained for." He was quiet for a moment, then grimaced. "You see, I took a call before coming out tonight and I have someone coming to stay. They're not in a very good place at the moment. To be honest, I'm concerned, and my time's going to be taken up with all the hoo-ha. Are you OK with putting our next date on hold until I'm free again?"

What was the real message here? Poppy felt a shiver of apprehension.

"Of course." She swallowed, wishing she could think of something more constructive to say. Difficult, as Sam didn't seem inclined to elaborate on the situation. "Anything I can help with? I have a good listening ear – if you need one."

"Poppy, that's very kind," He gave a terse laugh, "but from what I've gleaned you've had enough of your own relationship problems without being burdened further. Hell, I don't have a clue how this is going to pan out. Be patient with me, that's all I ask at the moment."

"It's a relationship issue, then?" She nibbled her lip, hesitant to dig deeper if Sam didn't want to break any confidences.

"Isn't it always?" He jumped up. "OK, if you're ready to move let's head back. I'd love to say come in, sweetheart, but there's stuff I need to sort tonight."

"It's fine, Sam, honestly." Poppy's voice came out stronger than she had expected. She scrambled to her feet. She could handle this, she really could. "Anyway, I have things to do back at the flat myself."

It was a lie, of course. There was nothing urgent awaiting her attention. If honest, she had been dreaming of another tumble in Sam's large double bed, revelling in the feel of his hands on every part of her. She grew hot at the direction her mind had taken. Better quash that image, fast! Poppy had the distinct impression that, although Sam had been keen to see her when he'd issued the invite, now he was distancing himself. Odd, but his attention was definitely elsewhere.

They broke into a jog, and she felt a wash of disappointment. But she mustn't become clingy, or – heaven forbid - paranoid and risk spoiling what they'd had together. Sam was being focussed, that's all, his concentration on the busy period that lay ahead.

It was nothing more than that. The friend he'd mentioned sounded like someone he'd known for a long time. It figured he would want to keep their confidence and hesitate to share the finer details.

"I can be patient." Poppy attempted nonchalance. "Actually, I was thinking about a visit to Aunty Bea this coming weekend. High time I see how she's doing after her fall and give Maisie a break."

"Great idea." Sam threw her a grin that Poppy thought was tinged with relief. "You'll travel by train, I suppose? Have a good weekend – well, I'm sure you will."

Did she imagine it, or was Sam's response a fraction too enthusiastic? All too soon, they were back in Lantern Lane. The ring tone of his mobile made him glance at the screen, stop dead and step aside. Poppy heard him tell the caller he couldn't speak now, he had someone with him. Then his voice took on a testy note as he repeated his promise to ring back later when he would have more privacy.

What was going on – and why couldn't Sam talk in her presence? Poppy hovered on the pavement, uncertain how to react. She had a distinct feeling that Sam wanted to be alone, and it was disquieting. He might have cut the call but his dark eyebrows were drawn and his mind elsewhere. As they walked on and drew level with Rowan Cottage Poppy determined not to pause. Instead, she increased her speed and broke into a jog, throwing him what she hoped was a cheery wave. There was no way she intended to hang around and see if he planned to kiss her ... because suppose he didn't.

"Bye Sam." She called over her shoulder. "Good luck with everything."

A banal thing to say but she didn't know what else.

Poppy frowned; there was no denying that their relationship had developed quickly. Had she allowed things to move too fast, too soon? She experienced a wash of embarrassment. Heavens, she'd practically slept with the guy on their second date – thrown herself at him like a hussy! What was it her best friend used to say? Slow burn was best. There had been nothing slow about her attraction to Dr Sam Brocklehurst, it had been red hot from the start. He'd lit a touch paper and ignited a fire!

Poppy stilled. A fire that threatened to burn her if she didn't take care. Yet it was too late to step away from the flames now. Too tired to think anymore, she ran faster, as if the very hounds of hell were at her feet, keen to put distance between herself and Sam.

Sam suppressed a groan as he watched her disappear, fleet of foot as a gazelle. If only he could have explained his sister's call, but he hadn't processed it fully himself. In fact, he was still reeling from the shock. What was it with women who were always attracted to the bad guys? True, he hadn't met this particular bad guy yet, didn't want to if honest – although Tizzy had hinted that she wanted them to meet. Normally a patient man, Sam balled his fist. Like his brothers, he had done a bit of boxing during his teens, and he had a good left hook. This new bloke of his sister's would be wise to steer clear of North Devon.

Yet it appeared to be more complicated than that now. Sam conceded he would have to meet the guy at some point. He only hoped he'd be able to rein in his temper when he did. In Sam's book, if you made a mistake, you stuck around. You didn't slope off and leave the fall out for others to sort. His lip curled as he entered the cottage. No, it was the right decision not to involve Poppy. She'd had enough relationship trauma of her own to deal with - he refused to land her with his own unexpected baggage!

Sam made a coffee, hot and strong, and paced the floor as he drank. He'd take a moment and then ring Tizzy. However, she beat him to it. His mobile pinged with the sound of an incoming message and he frowned as he read it. Another change of plan. He sighed. Now it seemed that Tizzy was debating a conciliatory chat with her ex and would ring later with an update on the situation. Strange, hadn't the bloke left her? Certainly, that was the impression Sam had been given. Well, he would know soon enough. Tizzy still planned to come down tonight, albeit later than first thought. Apparently, she needed space and time 'to get her head straight,' so would be on staying in Woolacombe with him for a couple of weeks.

Sam scowled, wishing he could get his own head straight about the situation. It didn't matter that he wouldn't be around much, Tizzy had said. She'd occupy herself with beach walks, painting and a browse in the local gift shops. Sam imagined how this lifestyle would appeal to his sister's artistic nature. She really should have taken up the place she'd been offered at Art College, and do something positive with her life. Instead, she seemed content to drift from job to lowly job.

He raised his eyes skyward. Now that Tizzy wouldn't turn up on his doorstep in the next few minutes, he had time to kill. Honestly, women! Hell, he could have invited Poppy in, after all. Poppy Lambert was the one female he knew who was uncomplicated and easy to be around – meeting her had been a gift. Yet tonight, he'd pushed her away. What sort of a fool was he! Suddenly Sam lost his taste for the coffee; draining his mug, he threw it in the sink. In the gathering dusk Rowan Cottage felt lonely.

An upstairs floorboard creaked. Sam laughed derisively into the echoing quiet. 'Don't worry, Sadie. If that's you, save your tricks; I know!'

More creaks followed, then a window banged and he felt a draught skitter across the floor. It lifted the edge of the mat and a spider scurried out. Briefly, the temperature dipped a degree or two. Sam was aware of the fine hairs at the back of his neck rising. There was no sense of malevolence, just a subtle shift in the atmosphere – so swift he could even believe he might have imagined it. 'Come on, Sadie,' he whispered, 'no more antics. I know you're there.' Then things reverted to normal and the place was silent again.

What had Poppy said about Rowan Cottage, he mused? Ah yes, it sat over a ley line that was supposed to transmit a powerful energy, of particular benefit to females. Its key properties were nurture and protection. Ancient wisdom, if you believed in that sort of thing. Hopefully, the cottage would prove restorative for Tizzy – although he'd tell her nothing of its supposed benefits, of course. Sam chuckled at the very idea as he went in search of the unclosed window.

Restless after sorting out the spare room for Tizzy, Sam made another coffee and drunk it this time. He ran a hand through his hair. What mess was she about to land him with now? More to the point, his little sis had other big brothers, three of the brutes. Why was it always down to him to pick up the pieces when things went wrong. Sam pulled a wry face. As if he didn't know! His bros were all married, up to their ears in family commitments. They cared and were kind enough, but didn't have time for Tizzy's inability to structure her life. So, it was to Sam that their little sis always turned.

Sam debated ringing one, or all of them to demand that they share the load. Hell, he was in a new job and he had commitments, too. He knew what their answer would be, though. Perhaps he did need to stop being so patient. Then Sam scrolled through his phone to Tizzy's latest revelation and knew it wouldn't be this time.

CHAPTER TWELVE

Poppy's week continued with one difference. Whereas on the Monday her heart had given a little skitter whenever she caught sight of Sam, now she felt relieved not to see him. It meant there was no anxiety around trying to read his mood or decode anything he might say. Although she wanted to believe his story of a friend in need who'd captured every free hour, in reality how plausible was it? She couldn't rid herself of the nagging doubts.

The routine practice meeting on Wednesday made her wavering confidence in Sam dip further. As Andrew Doyle introduced Bramblewood's new GP trainee, Dr Grace Powell, Poppy was struck by how attractive the young doctor was. Grace looked more like a film star than a medic. Slim and blonde, with a ready smile for everyone, she practically simpered when Sam announced he'd be taking her under his wing. Poppy glowered, wondering if it was her imagination or was Sam being overly solicitous?

No matter how much she tried to quell that thought, the worm of jealousy was there. Ridiculous! He was being friendly, that was all, keen to put the trainee at ease. It was his nature. Besides, the other doctors were behaving no differently. The male docs, anyway, Poppy acknowledged with another flash of irritation. What was it with men and blondes?

With an effort she made herself listen as Sam put forward a proposal. He suggested they offer an early morning appointment slot to those patients who found it difficult to take time off work for medical appointments. There were murmurs around the room as those present debated the pros and cons.

"A pilot scheme to begin with." Sam's expression was animated. "Two mornings a week I propose a 07.30hrs. start. Then review in three months. Thoughts, everyone?"

"Fine by me." Andrew Doyle shrugged. "In fact, a good balance as David and Liz already offer a later finish on a Tuesday." He named two of the other Bramblewood GPs.

"You've got my vote." David nodded. "We need to be responsive to patient need, and people often do struggle to arrange time off work for medical appointments. Back in the day, when I joined Bramblewood, didn't we also run an emergency surgery between 09.00hrs and 11.00hrs. on alternate Saturday mornings? Perhaps this is the moment to discuss reintroducing that. I don't recall why we stopped."

"We stopped the Saturday morning clinic when we forged stronger links with Coombe Vale Surgery." Andrew frowned, tapping his pen. "It was decided they would pick this up and generally it works well. The thought among the powers that be was that it only needs one or two surgeries in each area to be able to offer emergency care at the weekend. However, I did say that this would need reviewing at some point. I'm not sure it ever was. Thanks David, a timely reminder to revisit this."

"I'll have input on local need once I have a few A&E sessions under my belt." Sam's dark eyes glinted in the way that Poppy had come to recognise meant he was swiftly calculating something. "First full session coming up this weekend, as it happens. It will be interesting to see who pitches up, from where, needing what intervention – and whether their own GP surgery could have met the need equally well, if open. Pressure off front line services always makes good sense."

"Indeed." Andrew nodded in agreement. "Right, I guess that winds things up for today, folks, unless anyone has a burning issue to raise. No? OK, that's it, then."

Everyone drifted out, the staff meeting disbanded. The remaining hours flew by.

Soon her day was over and Poppy returned home – although she still struggled to think of her flat in that sense. Quickly, she rang Maisie. Best to let her know about the proposed weekend visit in advance. Aside from her concern over Sam, it would be great to see her cousin again and find out at first-hand how her Aunty Bea was doing. After she'd checked the train times, Poppy decided to pack in advance. Hopefully, she could head to the station immediately after work on Friday and reach Exeter before nightfall.

Was it wise to share her doubts about Sam with Maisie? Poppy chewed her lip. Whilst she didn't want her fledgling relationship to come under scrutiny, a different perspective on the matter could prove useful. Especially if it was the opinion of folk she trusted like Maisie and her Aunty Bea. Poppy had to admit that she'd been aware of their antagonism towards her ex-partner, Mark from day one. A pity she hadn't heeded their misgivings; a lot of angst could have been avoided! However, it was easy to be wise with hindsight.

There was another reason why Poppy needed company this weekend. She'd felt low since waking and a glance at the date told her the reason why. The anniversary of her second miscarriage approached, the day when the tiny spark of life inside her had died. Her first miscarriage had been so early on that Poppy had barely been aware of the pregnancy. The second loss had been different. Three months gestation, nausea, the whole gamut. She had begun to make plans, think of baby names. Shakily, she recalled the fateful moment she had been sent home unwell from a night shift ... only to discover her ex naked in bed with a nubile blonde. Bile rose at a memory as vivid as if it had happened yesterday.

Distraught and in pain, Poppy had fled, catching a train, then a taxi - giving the address of the only safe harbour she could think of. Her Aunty Bea hadn't failed her, stoically by her side over the ensuing days as Poppy began to bleed heavily and lose her baby.

The images remained vivid, despite Poppy's attempts to wipe the trauma from her mind. What felt more of a blur was the resulting hospital admission, a matter of urgency to halt the bleeding. Afterwards a deep depression had taken hold. Only the physical symptoms had served to connect her to the world around. Vaguely, she recalled a ward nurse hooking up a third unit of blood, an emergency transfusion to help replace blood that had been lost. As she drifted in and out of consciousness, Poppy hadn't had the energy to care whether she lived or died.

Discharged to her Aunty Bea, full recovery had taken time. Throughout it all Mark, to the best of Poppy's knowledge, had never once attempted to see her. However, she did recall her father's surprise appearance under the guise of needing to come over from Spain on business. He'd been a rock, as well as instrumental in retrieving her possessions from the flat she'd shared with her ex. In his own quiet manner, Peter Lambert had been furious at the treatment meted out to his daughter. She never did discover exactly what had passed between the two men, but strong words had been exchanged. Her father had wrapped her in his arms and promised the situation had been dealt with. He'd claimed there was nothing more for Poppy to worry about – so she wouldn't. Determinedly, she wiped her eyes.

On Thursday evening, Poppy retrieved her overnight bag from the top of the cupboard, and began packing. Although she preferred to travel light the weather had changed. The day had been overcast and blustery, with heavy showers of rain that brought the temperature down. Exeter might be milder but it would be silly not to take a few warm things, plus a nice dress in case of need. As she reached for her favourite, peachy coloured jumper, her gaze alighted on Sam's navy sweatshirt. Poppy sighed. Why had she forgotten to return it? She wondered if it was a Freudian thing.

The sweatshirt belonged to Sam. Maybe, deep down, she didn't want to part with it.

Decisively, she draped the garment over the arm of the sofa where it couldn't fail to catch her eye. No more excuses, she'd return it after her weekend break. Definitely!

On Friday afternoon, hearing that Poppy had a train to catch, Laura insisted her colleague leave early.

"Honestly, Poppy," Laura gave her a swift hug, "just go. Shoo! Enjoy your weekend. Gracious, you've covered for me before. Besides, we've had two patients cancel this afternoon and it wasn't a long list to start with. I'm hardly going to be run off my feet, and Faye's around if there should be any problems."

Inwardly relieved, Poppy grabbed her bag, smiled, and headed for the 'bus stop. Not for the first time she debated saving up for driving lessons and a cheap car. The benefit of her own wheels would be huge. It wasn't the most straightforward of journeys to travel out of Woolacombe if you didn't drive. First, she must go to Barnstaple, then make her way to the North Devon station for the Exeter bound train. However, the evenings were light at this time of year, and she enjoyed the scenic route.

The earlier leave time paid dividends with regards avoiding the usual Friday rush. Soon Poppy strolled onto the North Devon platform ready for the Exeter bound train. She didn't have long to wait. Once on board, she nabbed a window seat, and settled down to enjoy the journey. The scenic route never failed to hold her enthralled.

Maisie met her at Exeter St David's, waving madly as she came through the ticket barrier and pushed her way through the throng. The pleasure Poppy felt at seeing her cousin again made her feel unexpectedly teary.

"Great to see you, too." Maisie gave Poppy a fierce hug, then stepped back, holding her at arm's length. "Let me look at you, Pops. Hmm, it's as Mum and I thought – you're feeling miserable. No need to contradict me, we haven't forgotten what the date is. And we're going to spoil you rotten this weekend, no argument. Mum is in the car, by the way."

Poppy opened her mouth to protest but Maisie was having none of it. Then she gasped, seeing the flash of a diamond on the third finger of her cousin's left hand.

"You dark horse, Maisie Fletcher! When did this happen?" She grabbed Maisie's hand and studied the square cut stone. "Wow, it's gorgeous. Don't tell me you finally said yes to the long-suffering Darren?"

"No, I'm not telling you that." Maisie gave an enigmatic shrug. "Darren and I parted company three, oh gosh, nearly four months ago."

"You've met somebody else!" Poppy gaped. "What happened? And why didn't you say anything? I thought we were besties as well as cousins."

"Listen, you'd applied for your new job, then you were busy relocating to the rural wilds of North Devon." Maisie looked serious for a moment. "You had enough on your plate without me bending your ear, Pops. Anyway, there was no big drama. You know me, I don't do dramas. One day I woke up, realised I liked Darren, but he didn't set my world alight – and maybe I didn't do it for him, either. I think our relationship had been drifting for a while."

"So," Poppy urged her on, "what happened next? You separated and met someone else, someone who does set your world alight?"

Her cousin had always been full of surprises, but this was the biggest to date.

"In a nutshell, yes." Maisie grinned. "Literally two days later. His name is Tim, but I'll share the rest over supper. Hopefully, you'll meet him this weekend. Now I trust you're hungry because there's a huge casserole in the slow cooker."

She glanced at her ring. "You're thinking this is quick, but when it's right, it's right, Pops. You just know."

Did you, though? Poppy frowned; she hadn't known. She followed Maisie towards the parking area in a daze, wishing she had her cousin's confidence.

Poppy's plan to help them out was quickly thwarted. Both Maisie and her aunt insisted she was there to be pampered. She found herself with little more to do than sit chatting with her much-loved Aunty Bea. And she had to admit it felt wonderful! Poppy realised how much she'd been missing family and resolved not to leave it so long before her next visit. People were precious and time slid by quickly. Often the weeks and months drifted by without noticing; good intentions were fine but useless if not acted upon.

All too soon it was Sunday. Poppy helped her cousin prepare a traditional roast lunch and met Tim, who had been invited to join them for the meal. Without fuss or ado, he found the cutlery drawer and began to lay the table. Poppy liked him on sight, thinking his calm steadiness a perfect foil for Maisie's more impulsive nature. Indeed, he fitted into the family seamlessly, making her aunt beam by the proffering of a large bunch of carnations. She hid a smile, seeing her Aunty Bea blush.

"Got to stay on side of the future m-in-law." Tim winked, catching Poppy's eye. "Points to score, you know."

Poppy returned his grin. She helped Maisie to dish out the meal on warmed plates, while Tim was delegated to carve the joint – which he did to perfection.

The kitchen could be described as a mess, as it always was after Maisie had been working in it, but the roast tasted delicious. The four of them talked as they ate, Tim continuing to quietly impress. The hours sped by.

Later, as Maisie dropped her back at St David's Station, she quizzed Poppy on her first impression of Tim. Happy to say how much she'd liked him, Poppy smiled, giving her cousin a big thumbs up sign.

"Really, Pops?" Maisie beamed. "That's great! I do value your opinion, you know."

"Yes, really. He's lovely," Poppy laughed, "but don't be influenced by anything I say, follow your own gut instinct. You know my track record. I'm a useless judge of men."

"Listen, Pops, you made one bad choice." Maisie fixed Poppy with a stern look as she unclipped her seatbelt. "One mistake, that's all. It's time to stop beating yourself up over it. And for what it's worth I think you need to stop fretting and cut Sam some slack."

In the silence that ensued Poppy stared, nonplussed. Had Maisie not listened to a word she'd said about Sam going cool on her? Or was she so loved up herself that she couldn't help but see everything through rose tinted spectacles.

"Didn't Sam stay with you the night Mum had the accident and behave like the perfect gentleman?" Maisie regarded her shrewdly. "How many guys do you know who would do that? Wait, I'll answer - very few!"

"Yes, I know, but ... " Poppy shrugged, unable to explain to this new Maisie her deep fear of trusting someone and being cheated on again.

This was a pain she couldn't survive twice, so best that she didn't chance it. And Sam's current behaviour threw up too many red flags. How could she trust him?

"But nothing." Maisie smiled as the cousins shared a swift hug before parting. "Listen, I'm not saying Sam has to be your forever guy, only that he's a decent bloke who obviously likes you. Isn't that enough for now? Stop analysing and let yourself enjoy life a bit. Live in the moment. You are allowed to have fun for fun's sake, you know, Pops. Anyway, hurry, or you'll miss your train. I'm sure that's it pulling in now."

Fun for fun's sake; this was a new concept. Poppy found she rather liked the idea. Maisie's words ran round her head as she dashed onto the platform. She found herself a window seat and stashed her holdall in the overhead luggage rack before settling down for the return trip to Barnstaple. The guard's whistle blew almost immediately. Any later and she would have missed the train. Poppy glanced at her mobile, checking for any new messages. There were none. She'd rather hoped for one from Sam.

She nibbled her lip. Bar a brief text wishing her a good weekend, his silence was loud. Odd, now she considered it. She scrolled through her stored numbers, debating whether to ring and ask if he was free to collect her at Barnstaple. Then, just as quickly, she let go of the idea. If Sam had wanted to collect her, he'd had ample opportunity to offer. In fact, he hadn't even asked what time her train was due. No, Poppy decided, she was perfectly capable of making her own way back to Woolacombe. She shuffled in her seat, trying to ignore an edge of foreboding. The train gathered speed and she stared out the window, forcing herself to concentrate on the scenic view.

Monday morning dawned bright and clear, despite an ominous weather forecast issuing a storm warning. Poppy itched for a run. She'd woken early and had ample time. Quickly, she slid out of bed and donned her running gear. Her gaze rested on Sam's sweater. She picked it up and sniffed. His male scent still lingered.

It would take only a moment to knock on his door and return the sweater as she passed Rowan Cottage. In fact, it would be daft not to! Poppy banished the little whisper that said 'yes, and wouldn't it be nice to see Sam, too,' and focussed on refolding the garment to slip it into her backpack. Had his unexpected visitor gone? Details had been scant. Poppy had no idea how long the person was staying. But surely a tap on the door as she passed would be acceptable even if his house guest remained.

Outside the air was fresh, ideal for running. She wondered if Sam could be down on the beach already. Poppy began to jog, her hair tugged by a capricious breeze. In a little over ten minutes, she reached the top of Lantern Lane. She spied an unfamiliar car parked on the piece of waste ground beside Sam's vehicle as she looked down the road. It could belong to anyone, she reasoned. Then something else grabbed her attention. She blinked and looked again; yes, it was still there. A large 'Sold' sign erected by the next-door property!

Poppy skidded to a halt, feeling light headed. Did that mean Rowan Cottage was poised to come on the market, too? She had to find out if Sam knew anything. It would be strange if he didn't, especially if this mystery cash buyer was interested in both properties. That would certainly force Sam's hand. While he may have no plans to move on yet, she couldn't imagine him happy to be a long-term tenant. Although, of course, the new buyer might be an investor, not planning to live in either cottage himself. Slowly, Poppy approached the cottage's sturdy, oak front door and lifted the iron knocker. Almost immediately the door was thrown open to reveal a stunning blonde with thick, wavy hair and a questioning look in her tawny eyes. A visibly pregnant young woman. The shock made Poppy reel.

"Hi, I'm Charlotte." The young woman pulled her cream silk bathrobe tighter, and the questioning look intensified. "Can I help you? Sam's not around, I'm afraid."

"Um, I ... ," Poppy thought quickly, reaching into her backpack to fish out the sweater, "just wanted to return this as I passed by. I ... I'm a colleague of Sam's at Bramblewood."

"Ah, I recognise this old thing." With a tinkly laugh, Charlotte took the garment from Poppy's numb fingers. "He's had it for ages. Typical bloke, keeps his clothes for yonks. Left it somewhere, I suppose?"

Poppy mumbled agreement and stepped back. She felt sick now, and desperately needed to put distance between them. "Bye. Sorry to disturb you."

"You didn't, I was up already. Come in and wait if you like." Charlotte's expression was open and friendly. "He's only nipped out for milk and a few groceries. We meant to do that yesterday, but there was so much to talk about, what with the baby and everything." She pulled a wry face and patted her bump. "Poor old Sam, I should have known I could rely on him for support. I kind of landed him with a mess, but things feel more sorted now."

"Oh, um, good." Poppy really didn't want to engage. "Sorry, I must go."

Hastily, she turned away, wishing that her legs hadn't turned to jelly. It was clear now why Sam hadn't wanted her around for a while. His 'friend with a problem' was obviously an ex-girlfriend who had pitched up with a surprise pregnancy. No wonder he hadn't wanted to discuss the situation. By the sound of it, their relationship was back on track. No wonder she hadn't received any texts, Poppy thought furiously. Obviously, he'd had more important things to occupy his mind - like the news he was about to become a father! Exactly when had he been planning to tell her?

She broke into a run, fighting a wave of nausea. Men, they were all the same – at least, the ones she seemed destined to encounter.

Perhaps she was jinxed. Poppy sobbed as she recalled her cousin's advice to cut Sam some slack and concentrate on having fun. Of course, that had been said before the knowledge of a pregnant ex-girlfriend. She gave a humourless laugh. Put a positive spin on that if you can, Maisie Fletcher! Well, she'd had her heart broken once and she was damn sure she wouldn't let it happen again. No guy was worth it.

Poppy scrubbed at her face, wiping away tears that insisted on falling. She refused to cry anymore. Besides, she only had herself to blame. She should have heeded her instinct to avoid men. Every last one of them spelt trouble. How to act around Sam after this debacle was a more pressing dilemma. Inevitably, this made working with him at Bramblewood Surgery awkward – to say the least. Luckily, bar Julia's inkling there might be something between them, no one else had picked up on anything. Certainly no one was aware they had spent a weekend together. She'd be saved the embarrassment of having to give any trite explanations – and the shame of being cast in the role of the other woman once Sam's ex was officially back on the scene. The very thought made Poppy cringe with embarrassment.

Sam's act of omission had forced her into the role of the type of female she detested. Someone who stole another woman's man. Quite obviously, she'd been a stop gap after his relocation. He hadn't been free to start a new relationship with anyone. Poppy concluded there were two options. Take Sam to task and demand an explanation or wait and see what he had to say for himself if and when he contacted her. She chose the latter.

Poppy sighed, wondering why life had to be so complicated and decided it must be fate. She wasn't destined to find her own happy ever after. She reached the main entrance of her apartment and knew it was time to move on – in every respect. First, though, she would visit the letting agent's office and confirm the position with Rowan Cottage. Not today, but soon.

After a quick shower, she must make tracks for Bramblewood. Poppy ran up the stairs, determined to focus solely on her career from now on, no matter how lonely the nights may feel. Trust was important. Some girls just weren't destined to find their soul mate.

She didn't have long to wait before her phone rang and the situation came to a head. Poppy stepped out of the shower, wrapped herself in a bath towel and snatched up her mobile. Sam's name flashed up on the screen. Fired by anger, her tone was terse.

"Hello." She paused, determined not to make it easy for him. "What do you want? Make it snappy, Sam. I'm due at work shortly."

There was silence at the other end. Good, she'd thrown him! Well, let him speak next. Silences were uncomfortable, but she was determined not to be the first to break this one. She stalked through to the kitchenette, still holding her mobile as she rattled drawers in search a teaspoon as she made herself a drink.

"Poppy?" Sam sounded distracted. "Are you there? Hell, this is a dreadful line! Listen, I believe you've met Charlotte. So, I guess you've an idea what I've been dealing with. Bit of a nightmare initially, but everything's been straightened out now. Anyway, we can talk about all that later. She leaves tomorrow."

Every nerve in Poppy's body felt raw. She crashed her mug down on the work surface, unable to trust herself to speak. Her body trembled.

"Poppy, what on earth is that racket?" Sam sounded puzzled. "Anyway, hear me out. There's another PPG Meeting coming up, a special one linked with the garden project. How about you and I grab a bite in the pub afterwards? In fact, why not stay the night at Rowan Cottage – we can always go into work separately the next day if you'd prefer."

There was a pause. "I've missed you like crazy, sweetheart."

Poppy felt her jaw drop. Was he was suggesting that they carry on as if nothing had happened? Really? As if he didn't have a pregnant ex-girlfriend who had shown up on his doorstep – with whom he had 'sorted things,' whatever that meant! This was unbelievable. She experienced a white-hot bolt of fury.

"Quite right, no explanation needed." Poppy managed to keep a hold on her temper; staying cool was usually the best option. "I think we need to chill, Sam, go back to being just work colleagues. We got in too deep too quickly, and I didn't realise that you ... anyway, I don't do relationships with complications."

"Complications?" Sam's voice rose an octave. "I don't follow. You're not making any sense. If you mean Charlotte, I'm sorry I didn't tell you about her and the pregnancy before, but I didn't have the full facts myself. But, as I said, that's all sorted."

"You don't intend to offer any support once the baby is born, then?" Poppy was incredulous. "Or see it? Well, I ... "

"Don't be ridiculous. Of course, I'll see him. Charlotte's having a boy." She detected a testy note in Sam's voice. "Listen, we'll catch up after the PPG Meeting. No argument. We have some talking to do."

She had to make a decision. A talk it would have to be, but Poppy determined to keep it brief. He'd have no opportunity to convince her to see him again, the rat.

"OK, but I won't change my mind, Sam." She kept her voice level. "And I'm going back to my flat afterwards."

He tried to say something but she cut the call.

CHAPTER THIRTEEN

"There's something different about you this week, Poppy." Laura's comment took her by surprise as they met at lunchtime. "Can't quite put my finger on it." She glanced shrewdly at her colleague. "You're not as bouncy or smiley. It's a bloke, isn't it?"

"No, of course not." Poppy made a derisory noise that she hoped didn't sound too fake. "Sorry to disappoint. You're looking at a girl who's been there, done that and got the T-shirt. I promise you I'm well and truly over blokes. I'm a career girl now, a certified spinster."

Too late she noticed the door of the nurses' room was ajar and Sam was striding past. Had he overheard? Poppy hoped that he had. It would pave the way for their talk later, when they had a drink together after the PPG Meeting. She had studiously avoided all but necessary contact, though it made sense to keep her promise to see him in the pub one last time to clarify matters. Despite how attracted to the man she might be – and, annoyingly, she still found Sam very attractive - she refused to sleep with him behind another woman's back. In Poppy's book that was a big no-no. The special PPG Meeting was scheduled for tomorrow. The plan was to gather in the garden itself, since the prime reason was to meet the new gardening volunteers and see how the project was progressing. A brief catchup with Sam afterwards would be painful, but necessary.

"If you say so. "Laura shrugged. "Though me thinks the lady doth protest too much. Anyway, weren't you going to nip out for some fresh air, Poppy? I may do the same, although in my case it'll be a stroll round the corner to sit in that gorgeous walled garden with my sandwiches. Why didn't we ever make use of it before? There are benches there that Sam got someone to donate. He's certainly innovative, isn't he! The place is coming on a treat."

"Hmm, yes, we have had some garden furniture donated." Poppy frowned, trying to recall exactly what items had been offered. "At least you'll have a comfortable perch. 'Bye, Laura, I must dash into town."

To avoid further questions, Poppy didn't mention the reason she wanted to slip out. It wasn't to buy food; she had a snack with her. She'd planned a quick trip to the letting agent's office. Hopefully, there wouldn't be a queue, and she could make her enquiry and leave without undue delay. Swiftly, she grabbed her bag and left.

A few patients were dotted around the waiting room as she walked through, indicating the doctors were still in consulting mode. The morning session had kept both her and Laura on their toes, and – judging by patient bookings - the afternoon promised to be equally hectic. Whilst she loved her profession, Poppy was mindful it wasn't the sort of job where you could risk being late. In a busy GP Practice, snatching an extra ten or fifteen minutes here and there wasn't an option. She left Bramblewood, trying to look nonchalant and returned Faye's cheery greeting as they passed each other.

Once in town Poppy dodged the window shoppers, feeling irritated. She wasn't out for a leisurely stroll! The letting agency hove into view. She didn't recognise the young assistant behind the reception desk today. However, the girl's smile was friendly enough.

"Rowan Cottage you're enquiring after, with regards a purchase. I see … " The girl pursed her glossy lips, tapping her varnished nails on the desk. "I'm sure there's a sale going through already. It's no longer on our books as a rental property."

"No, that's the cottage next door." Poppy felt another spurt of frustration. "That one doesn't have a name, only a number - 5, I think, but I did notice a 'Sold' sign outside."

"Ah yes, the same buyer has offered on both properties." Her expression cleared and the young receptionist gave an emphatic nod. "I'm sure of it. I'm not supposed to tell you this, but I don't see the harm. The buyer is the current tenant. He didn't want a 'Sold' board put up in front of Rowan Cottage – sometimes people don't – which is why there isn't one."

"Oh." Poppy held onto a nearby chairback for support, feeling lightheaded with shock.

"Yes, those cottages fly when they come on our books. In my opinion, there are just as nice properties the other side of town away from the sea, if you don't mind a … "

Poppy mumbled a reply, experiencing a roil of nausea. She fled from the office, declining an invite to wait for someone to be free from the sales department to talk to her in more depth. She had zero interest in what else was on their books that may suit, because nothing else would suit! Not now, maybe not ever. Quite the worst thing was that Sam had done this without a whisper of his intentions. Surely, he knew how much Rowan Cottage meant to her – and he'd completed the purchase behind her back!

After the discovery of Charlotte, it felt like a double betrayal. No doubt Sam intended to join the two properties together and create one, stunning home. In all likelihood, this was forward planning for his future family. A family which didn't include her. His comment about having no desire to move on made perfect sense now. Obviously, he didn't need to go anywhere. Tears threatened. Hurriedly, Poppy brushed them away. She refused to cry again. Taking slow, deep breaths she began to walk, aware she needed to calm down by the time she reached Bramblewood Surgery.

In the event she arrived slightly late. However, she managed to paste on a smile and convince Laura and Faye that she was fine. Her red eyes must be due to hay fever.

Sam saw Poppy come through the main entrance as he stepped towards the waiting room to call in his next patient. He was struck by her expression. Fierce, determined – and something else, too. Something he couldn't read. Hell, she looked sad!

He raised his hand in acknowledgement, but Poppy's expression remained stony. Either she hadn't seen him, or she'd chosen not to respond. He wouldn't be surprised if the snub was deliberate. Her present behaviour was at odds with the Poppy he knew. Something was amiss, that much was obvious; unfortunately, being a mere male, Sam hadn't a clue what it was. Had something happened during her weekend away? Maybe her aunt was unwell.

At least she'd agreed to have a drink with him after tomorrow evening's special PPG meeting, even if she was steadfastly ignoring him in the interim. He'd have to be content with that. All his attempts to ring her had been futile. She didn't pick up his calls and text messages went unanswered. Her barbed comment about not wanting a relationship with complications had left Sam mystified. Very strange! He frowned, noting the rigid way Poppy held her body as she disappeared from view into the practice nurses' office. She reminded him of a twig about to snap.

"Clare Hunter." Sam glanced around the waiting room as he called for his next patient. Despite a few hopeful gazes in his direction, no one moved. He tried again, louder this time, "Claire Hunter, please."

"Oops, that's me." A young woman scrambled to her feet, returning a glossy magazine to the rack. "Sorry, Dr Brocklehurst, I was caught up in the story."

"Then I'm sorry to interrupt." Sam returned her smile. He led his patient through to the consulting room and invited her to take a seat. "So, what brings you here today, Clare?"

"I've had this earache for almost a week." Clare grimaced. "My left ear. It's really painful, stops me from sleeping, especially if I accidentally roll over in the night and lie on it. I've felt poorly, too. And I'm not hearing very well sometimes. Like just now."

"Hmm, hold still. Let's take a peek and see what's going on." Sam reached for an otoscope, and checked both her ears as gently as he could.

He was aware of Clare's wince as the cold steel touched her skin. Her left ear looked markedly red and inflamed, telling him immediately what the problem was – an infection. On examining her throat, Sam saw that was quite red, too. He palpated her cervical glands, unsurprised to find them markedly enlarged.

"No wonder you've been feeling rubbish." He grimaced in sympathy. "You have a rip- roaring ear infection; your throat is affected, too. You'll need a course of antibiotics. Can you take ... ?" He named a first line drug of choice, waiting for Clare to nod before he returned to his computer and printed out a prescription. He grinned reassuringly and handed it to her. "Hopefully, this should sort things out. Make sure you finish the course."

Sam noted his patient's uncertain expression and seeming reluctance to leave, and queried, "Anything else you're concerned about?"

"Only this lump." Clare lifted her arm, indicating a visible swelling in her armpit. "It's been there for months, not sore, or anything. It's probably nothing, but since I'm here anyway I thought I may as well show you."

Sam suppressed a sight. The lipoma, or swelling in layman's terms, was visible even without palpation. True, it might be nothing at all – or it might be everything. As was so often the case, potentially the most important symptom had been left until last.

This was a typical door handle disclosure. He guessed he should be used to them by now, it happened so often. But the fact remained that he never failed to feel frustrated.

There was so much in the media to highlight the benefits of early detection of disease. In Sam's book, there was little excuse for folk not to act promptly.

"Ah, I see it. I need to do a full breast examination." He smiled to allay the panic he saw in her eyes, and stood to swish a mauve curtain round the examination couch in the corner. "If you'd like to go behind that curtain, please Clare. Remove the top half of your clothing and wait for me while I nab one of the nurses to act as chaperone. Back in a jiffy."

Sam stepped outside and approached the first nurse he saw – Poppy. Ideal! Hopefully, she was between patients and free to spare a moment. He explained the situation, relieved to see her nod and turn to follow him into his consulting room.

"Clare, this is Poppy, one of our practice nurses. She's going to be here while I examine you if that's OK." Sam lost no time in doing a meticulous examination of both breasts. Then he stepped back, inviting her to dress. "Remind me how long you've noticed this swelling?"

"Er, I'm not sure, ages ago." Clare blushed, looking nervous as she pulled on her top. "Five, maybe six months? To be honest, I thought it's only a lump, it doesn't hurt, so I didn't pay much attention. Anyway, I wasn't too worried because it's not an actual breast lump."

"In fact, the axilla, the underarm area, is linked to your breast and does have breast tissue." Sam frowned. "We take heed of any changes here, and I'll be referring you to the hospital breast clinic. You should have an appointment within two weeks, inform me if not."

"The Breast Clinic!" Clare paled. "You don't mean there might be something seriously wrong, like c-" she stumbled over the last word, "cancer?"

"That's not what Dr Brocklehurst said." Poppy placed a reassuring hand on Clare's shoulder, holding her frightened gaze. "It's standard procedure for any breast or axillary lump to be checked out, that's all. The hospital has a really good system in place."

"Poppy is quite right." Examination complete, Sam had returned to his desk. "Not so long ago I would have simply referred you for an ultrasound and be led by the results of that with regards a referral. But the system has changed. We refer to the specialists first now." He winked to lighten the mood. "Obviously, the hospital bods don't rate the medical acumen of us mere GPs."

"What do you think it is, Dr Brocklehurst?" Clare looked stricken. "I've heard of the two-week referral process. My Mum had that last year, and it was really scary. It's for fast tracking when a doctor suspects something nasty, isn't it."

Clare's face worked. Sam was aware that she was barely holding herself together. Obviously, the word hospital had thrown her. While the change in protocol with regards the referral process hastened diagnosis, on the negative side it often led to heightened patient anxiety without cause. Yet there was no way round this.

"Your swelling, what we docs term a lipoma, is soft, mobile on palpation and doesn't seem to be attached to the deeper tissues." Sam's tone was measured. He needed to reassure his patient, yet not give false hope. "All positive signs. And both breasts appear normal. But I prefer not to guess. You've had this a while, and it needs exploring. It's a straightforward procedure. You won't even have to wait for the scan report to be sent to you. It's a much better system now. You'll be told the results on the day, plus anything else deemed necessary, like a biopsy, will be done there and then."

"Oh." Clare twisted her fingers.

"For that reason, it's good to take someone along with you if you can." Poppy smiled encouragingly. "Hospitals can be a bit daunting on your own. And don't go home thinking the worst. As Dr Brocklehurst will tell you, the likelihood is that it's not cancer at all." She glanced at him for confirmation. "Breast lumps are funny things. They can be hormonal, or even stress related. Have you experienced more stress than usual lately, Clare? You mentioned your mum's health just now."

Poppy's approach was spot on, Sam had to give her that. Watching her in action with patients was akin to sitting in on a communication skills master class. She had exactly the right touch: professional yet empathic. Instinctively, she had gone straight to the nub of the issue. However, the next instant Clare began to weep uncontrollably. In between sobs, she described how tough the past year had been as her mother battled bowel cancer. Despite a positive surgical outcome, the family had been left rocked and vulnerable.

Sam waited a few moments then, by tacit agreement, he left Poppy to take Clare to a quieter part of the surgery. He knew without asking that Poppy would organise a restorative cup of tea and keep an eye on her until the young woman felt recovered enough to go home. The patient's breakdown didn't concern him unduly. In fact, giving vent to her emotions would have been therapeutic. Hopefully, he was right in sensing the axillary lipoma wasn't malignant – but he never played guessing games.

Sam hoped Poppy wouldn't face too great a patient backlog herself, but that was the thing about medicine. When the unexpected happened, you went with it – saw things through. There wasn't an alternative. It was a key reason why appointments often ran late, although folk seldom understood that.

Sam grimaced as he moved to summon his next patient, an apology at the ready.

The day wore on. If anything, the pace stepped up a few notches. After their earlier interaction, Sam snatched only brief glimpses of Poppy. He'd wanted to acknowledge the calm way she'd handled Clare, but the opportunity didn't arise. Instead, it was heads down for them both, beavering away in their respective consulting rooms. If time permitted, he might drop her an email, a few lines to acknowledge her assistance. His lip curled; faintly ridiculous when they were just down the corridor from each other.

Towards the end of the afternoon Sam spotted Poppy leave. Without her, he sensed the essence of the place subtly change. Sam scowled, pacing restlessly whilst waiting for his computer screen to load. Strange how it felt like Bramblewood was missing something vital when Poppy wasn't around. His glanced at the window, the lure of the beach strong. Not long now until his session finished. Then he could go for a run – the best release for pent up tension in Sam's opinion. With luck he might bump into Poppy down on the sand, too; especially if he didn't text her first to flag up his intention to be there.

Sam stretched and sat down at his desk again. It would be great to send a message to invite her to join him on the run ... except that that would be the surest way to make her avoid him. He scowled; with each passing day the loss of their easy rapport hit harder. What to do about it was the question. Sam scowled. He disliked problems he couldn't resolve.

What thoughts must have gone through Poppy's head when she'd seen the 'Sold' board outside his next-door cottage? Sam felt a stab of guilt. Regardless of best intentions, not mentioning his plan to buy both properties didn't seem very clever now. Instinct told him that she'd already found out about Rowan Cottage, too. Not the way he'd planned on telling her, that was for sure. How could he have been such a prize idiot!

Dammit, if only Poppy would take his calls he could explain, or at least try to. Tell her that he hadn't intended her to find out like that. One thing was for sure; the cosy image he'd had of sharing the news of his purchase over a celebratory meal was fading fast. Sam grimaced. Unfortunately, the sale had been agreed on the very evening she'd left work early to travel to Exeter – and he'd been preoccupied with Tizzy. It hadn't felt right to put information like that in a text message, and the 'Sold' sign had been erected earlier than expected. He realised he should have rung her, but it was easy to be wise with hindsight.

Sam took a moment to grab a coffee before returning to his computer screen. As always, there were routine lab reports, blood tests and hospital letters to wade through, followed by patients to contact. He sighed, wondering why, when he was passionate about medicine, he felt jaded today. However, it didn't take a genius to work out the answer to that one. A grey eyed beauty by the name of Poppy Lambert had blown into his life and sent his ordered world spinning into chaos. And it was a totally new experience.

Hit by a sudden awareness, Sam stilled. He didn't know how it had happened – he certainly hadn't meant it to – but he had fallen deeply and irrevocably in love. Yet there was nothing he could do about it. Poppy continued to hold him at arm's length and he could only pray their fractured relationship was repairable. Or find the right antidote to banish her from his head because he sure as hell didn't know how life had become this complicated!

A buzz indicated Bramblewood's receptionist was on the line. Sam took the call and listened before giving a terse reply. Yes, on this occasion he would see the patient who'd pitched up late without an appointment. The presenting symptoms sounded urgent, although why the chap had sat on them for days was a mystery. He rose to call the man in, suppressing a flash of annoyance. Why couldn't folk act more responsibly!

Yet Sam knew his frustration lay elsewhere. He had been a medic long enough to know there were a variety of reasons why folk led messy lives. While it could be sheer fecklessness, sometimes it was down to circumstances beyond their control. He reminded himself that he was there to dispense medical aid, not set himself up as judge and juror.

"Robert Jenkins, please."

"Thanks for fitting me in, Doc." A gaunt, unkempt young man with red, swollen knuckles pushed himself up from the chair, each movement visibly difficult. He stooped under the weight of a bulging rucksack. "Arthritis playing me up again, an' I've lost me new job. Third time I've been fired this year! Too many days off. I've had to move out of me flat, too. No money coming in to pay me rent, see."

Immediately Sam's focus was all on his patient. He waited courteously for Robert to make his way into the consulting room, each step a painful hobble. This was going to take more than a quick prescription to sort out. First, he scanned Robert's medical notes to determine his patient's exact diagnosis, treatment plan and when he'd last had a hospital review. As expected, there were gaps in Robert's follow up.

"I could issue new medication today, but it would only be a stop gap. I'd like to refer you back to hospital for the specialists to review." Sam held the young man's gaze. "And I want you to attend the appointment, OK, Robert? What happened last time? Apparently, you were a no-show."

He didn't give the young man room for any excuses. Missed appointments and non-compliancy were not helpful to anyone.

"Boss wouldn't give me the time off." Robert shrugged.

"Hmm, I see." Sam saw the sheen of tears that Robert tried to hide. "I'll have a word with the hospital bods and explain. Meanwhile, let's look at the options available. Where are you staying at present?"

"Dossed down in a doorway last night, didn't I! But me mate's back in a couple of days, he'll see me right."

Robert's act of bravado didn't fool Sam for a moment. The lad was desperate. A glance at the screen to check his date of birth confirmed Sam's suspicion. Robert Jenkins was barely twenty years old. And he didn't look like someone who was particularly street wise.

"No family you can go to – parents, uncles and aunts?" Sam's tone was gentler but even as he put the question, he guessed the answer.

"No." Robert glanced away. "I'm on me own. Fostered since I was ten. They put you out when you're eighteen, don't want to know anymore."

Sam gritted his teeth. The odds were not stacked in this young man's favour. In all likelihood they never had been stacked in his favour.

"Listen, Robert - I'd like to check you over. So, if you can manage to get up on there, please." Sam indicated the examination couch. "Let's see what your other joints are like."

As expected, this latest flare of arthritis had taken a toll. The damage was widespread. Swiftly, Sam made a decision. He turned to reach for the telephone.

"I'm going to arrange a hospital admission, Robert. And while you're in there someone will help you sort out new accommodation – and benefits you're entitled to. OK?"

Robert's shoulders sagged, whether from relief or defeat, Sam couldn't tell.

CHAPTER FOURTEEN

"Like I said, we need to cool it, Sam." Poppy toyed with the stem of her glass, fixing him with her beautiful grey eyes. Eyes which, right now, were decidedly stormy. "Go back to how things were, just colleagues. That relationship is salvageable, we work well together. Anyway," she cleared her throat, "I don't want any deep analysis. We moved too fast before we really got to know each other."

Sam took a gulp of lager and gazed into the swirling, amber liquid for a moment. Nothing he heard Poppy say made any sense. He did not understand any of it.

"Are you saying you want us to take things slower, sweetheart?" He spoke quietly. "Because I can do that. You set the pace, and we'll take it as slow as you like. I had no idea you were feeling rushed."

"No, that's not what I'm saying!" An angry flush stained her pale cheeks. "Please hear me, Sam. It's not about taking it slow. I don't want any sort of relationship with you, apart from a working one."

He saw her arresting grey eyes shimmer with tears and frowned. Surely there was a disconnect here. Why would Poppy be sad if this was really what she wanted. It made no sense, not to Sam, at least. Had he understood her, or was he simply being obtuse? After all, as Tizzy had levelled at him, he was just a guy. A guy who, somewhere along the line, had managed to get things spectacularly wrong.

"Then tonight is about saying goodbye," Sam studied her, "is that it? I'm missing something here, Poppy. You keep saying you don't do complicated. Then explain what you mean because you've lost me. I thought we had a good thing going. A great thing, in fact."

"We did have a good thing, Sam." A lone tear slid down her cheek. Sam watched her swipe it furiously away. "Then Charlotte came along, and ... obviously, her situation puts a different light on things. I'm amazed you don't get that!"

Now she had totally lost him. It was the end of a long day Rob Jenkins was still on his mind and he was tired. Sam began to feel irritated. He didn't need riddles.

"Charlotte? What on earth does she have to do with anything?" He knew his voice had risen, but he was beyond caring now. This was absurd. "Listen, Poppy, I can understand you being annoyed about Rowan Cottage. But believe me when I say that I gave specific instructions for a Sale board not to be put up yet. I fully intended to ... "

"No explanations, Sam" Poppy raised her hand to silence him. "I'm not interested. I said that at the beginning, remember! You won't change my mind and I've nothing else to say, so it's best if I go now. Please don't follow me."

Her drink unfinished, Poppy snatched her bag and stood. Sam resisted trying to stop her but it was hell to watch her leave. The evening stretched bleakly in front of him. He downed his drink in a couple of gulps, and debated ordering another. Hell, why not stay in this quiet corner of the pub until closing time; returning to Rowan Cottage had lost its appeal.

A few others from the PPG Meeting had wandered into the pub now, Sam noticed. He experienced a flash of irritation, hoping they hadn't spotted him. Hastily, he swung round again. Making polite small talk, tonight of all nights, held about as much appeal as trapping his hand in a vice. What did appeal was getting blind drunk, until he was too out of his head to feel anything. Indeed, if it wasn't for the fact that he was on duty tomorrow, this was exactly what he'd do, Sam thought grimly. He'd have one more drink, though.

"Hi, Doc, thought I recognised you!"

A familiar voice forced him to look up. An eager hand was thrust into his. Sam had no option but to take it, stretching his mouth into what he hoped passed as a cheery grin. He nodded to acknowledge the little group. After all, none of this mess was their fault. They didn't know this was the night the love of his life had given him the heave-ho. Their world hadn't stopped, even if his little bit of it had juddered to a halt. Also, he had spearheaded the Garden Project, hadn't he! How churlish would it be, then, not to give this eager bunch of volunteers a warm welcome. With luck, all he had to do was get in the drinks and exchange pleasantries before he sloped off into the dark night. Poets of old waxed lyrical about such heartache. Sam was no poet, and the only remedy he knew was distraction to blot out the pain, or at least blur the edges.

"Right, guys, my round. No argument." He rose to go to the bar. "What's everyone tipple?"

The gathering dusk wrapped round her like a velvet blanket. Poppy wept as she walked back to her flat, thankful the streets were empty. Had she stayed a moment longer, she'd have launched herself at him, pummelling Sam's chest. How could he think for a moment the position he'd put her in was acceptable? Correction, the position he wanted to put her in

– a girlfriend on the shadowy side-lines. While he took up with his old flame, Charlotte, keeping Poppy as a mistress with all the connotations that held. Well, she refused to collude with his plans. She had misjudged Dr Sam Brocklehurst. Poppy's lip curled; badly misjudged. Proof positive that she was useless at reading men. From now on she'd avoid them. This was a good reminder that she was better off single.

Poppy sighed; loving Sam had been an aberration. A brief fever she would recover from, given time. How much time was the question. Sadly, she knew this would be a protracted healing, and relapses were certain. She hoped she had enough stamina to pull through the painful part. Poppy closed her eyes and pictured her beloved gran. The old lady seemed to be looking at her sternly. She fancied she could hear her gran's voice encouraging her on. 'Come on, my girl, chin up! You'll get through this.'

Another thought struck, and Poppy wanted to weep anew. Whilst they could work together without it interfering with their professionalism, long term how realistic was it? To see Sam on a regular basis would be akin to picking a scab before the wound had healed, a constant trigger for pain. Especially once he and Charlotte had set up home together in Rowan Cottage, or whatever name they decided to call the conjoined property. Poppy imagined how it would feel to catch glimpses of their baby son down on the beach, or as she passed by Rowan Cottage on a run. No, it would be too difficult. She couldn't do it.

The solution was obvious, although the very idea brought a lump to her throat. She hadn't been at Bramblewood for long, but that couldn't be helped. It was time to hunt for a new post – starting right now. Miserably, Poppy pulled out her laptop and logged on. The search had begun.

Her mobile phone rang, disturbing her job search. However, she'd noted a few possibilities already, and the further away from North Devon, the better. She had even toyed with the idea of an overseas post. The ringing stopped only to start again a few moments later. Irritated, Poppy glanced at the screen for caller ID: Maisie. It was the second time her cousin had rung. Maybe the third, she'd lost track. Poppy ignored it, not in the mood for talking. Not even Maisie could put a positive spin on things tonight.

It was midnight before Poppy rose to draw the curtains. She wondered how the same silver moon that shone when she was happy could still shine so brightly when she was sad. Ditto, the myriad stars twinkling against a backdrop of dusky sky. Poppy sighed; why look to the heavens when they appeared so unmoved by her distress.

After a fitful sleep she awoke determined to focus solely on the future. As for Sam, he was yesterday's news. Kicked into the long grass, as Maisie would say. Dr Sam who? Perhaps another weekend in Exeter was in order. Poppy felt weary to the bone. She bit her lip, and recalled her consultant saying that stress wasn't good for autoimmune conditions. How to avoid it was the question when stress seemed to be everywhere she turned.

Aware of the dark circles under her eyes, Poppy dismissed her colleagues' concern, stating only that she hadn't slept well. Given the circumstances, this was true. Vaguely, she alluded to culprit being a dog barking intermittently throughout the night. Only partly a fib, as there had been a dog barking somewhere in the vicinity, although nothing that would have disturbed her normally. Both Laura and Faye looked sceptical.

"Hmm, if you say so." Laura eyed her uncertainly as they stood together in the treatment room. "Changing the subject – and I do hope you'll say yes, Poppy - if you're free on Sunday, fancy joining me and the kids on the Tarka Trail? We watched the film, 'Ring of Bright Water' recently, and they're mad keen to walk it. But hubby's working again and I'd like a bit of adult company. Faye hopes to come along with Jack, her eight-year-old. He gets on brilliantly with my two monkeys. No pressure if you've got other plans, but it would be great to have you with us."

Poppy hesitated. She didn't have any other plans, but the Tarka Trail was the trip she'd planned to do with Sam. The walk would be bitter-sweet.

However, that trip wasn't going to happen now – or, indeed, any other trip with Sam. She was a single girl now. Poppy felt a wash of sadness. Did she want to spend Sunday on her own? Laura was good fun, ditto Faye. They got on well as colleagues; it would be nice to spend time together outside the confines of work. Besides, what would she be doing if she didn't join Laura? Mope around her flat, that's what – and she really must stop doing that. It wasn't healthy. Besides, it would be nice to take away good memories when she left.

"Thank you," Poppy summoned a smile, hoping her delayed response hadn't been misread. "I'd love to. Where shall we meet?"

"Oh, that's great!" Laura beamed. "Listen, I know you don't drive so, why don't you walk over to Bramblewood, and I'll swing by and pick you up from the car park here." She adjusted her navy tunic top. "Right, duty calls. We'd better crack on before ... "

The insistent sound of an alarm cut her off in mid-sentence.

"Cardiac arrest, Consulting Room 3," Faye burst in, "quick, oxygen and the defib!"

Poppy blinked. Consulting Room 3, wasn't that Sam's room? Wasting no time, she grabbed the portable oxygen cylinder stored in the corner of the nurses' room and tore after Laura who already had the defib. A middle-aged man lay collapsed on the floor. His ashen complexion had a bluish tinge, and Sam was already on his knees doing rhythmic chest compressions. Poppy opened up the oxygen, attaching the tubing to a face mask and ambu-bag to assist with resuscitation. Faye deftly set up the defib machine and stepped aside as two other doctors rushed into the room to assist. A visibly distraught woman hovering by the collapsed patient was ushered out by Laura.

The next ten minutes were tense as they fought for the man's life.

Miraculously, although still unconscious with a worrying cardiac tracing, Sam had him breathing on his own again. At last, away in the distance, came the welcome sound of an ambulance siren, shriller with each passing second as the vehicle made its swift approach. Poppy shared the collective relief as flashing blue lights hove into view outside the window. A rapid transfer to hospital underway, Sam elected to travel in the back of the ambulance with the patient. With his recent A&E experience it made sense to have him onboard.

Laura popped her head round the door to update them on the patient's partner, Alison Rathbone. A family friend had been contacted who was able to collect her from Bramblewood and follow the ambulance to the main hospital. Thankfully, Mrs Rathbone accepted she was too shocked to be safe behind the wheel herself. All that was left to be done was record actions taken, tidy the consulting room and restock the emergency equipment.

The buzz of activity died down and the surgery returned to normal. By tacit agreement, Sam's more urgent booked appointments were shared between the remaining GPs. Poppy glanced at her fob watch, surprised to note that not as much time had elapsed as she'd thought. Yet it had been time enough for someone's life to hang in the balance. She wondered how Mr Rathbone would fare. How fortunate his cardiac arrest had happened in a medical setting. Staff had been quick to instigate resuscitation measures to elicit the best outcome possible. Every second counted when someone's heart stopped beating.

Mood sombre, Poppy continued her session. By the look on Laura's face, her colleague was feeling equally subdued. Even the normally cool and calm Faye had a pensive expression. If you worked in an acute setting like a hospital, such dramas were par for the course. You ran on adrenaline, half anticipating them.

Yet somehow it felt different when such an event happened in the middle of a routine doctor's surgery in a tranquil settling like Woolacombe, Poppy thought.

A few hours later she spotted Sam stroll in through the main entrance. He grinned, giving them the thumbs up sign to indicate it was a positive outcome for their patient. Dr Sam Brocklehurst was back and there were smiles all round. Suddenly the place felt lighter again. Despite her resolve, Poppy's heart leapt, too. In a while there was a peremptory knock and Sam put his head round the office door, catching the practice nurses as they were finishing up for the afternoon.

"Great stuff earlier, guys." He nodded approvingly. "Thank you, that was smooth teamwork. Ian Rathbone's condition remains stable. He's in the Coronary Care Unit, awaiting transfer to a specialist unit in Plymouth where he'll undergo a triple bypass. Apparently, he'd had no cardiac symptoms leading up to today's event. His appointment this morning was for something totally unconnected. Jack, the A&E consultant confirmed it was Ian's lucky day to arrest in a GP surgery. Our prompt action saved his life."

Did she imagine it or did his gaze rest fractionally longer on her than the others? Poppy looked down, feeling her cheeks glow. Furious with her reaction, despite Sam's track record as a player, she determined to apply for another job at the earliest opportunity. Heavens, it had to be her priority! She rose to pick up her bag, attempting to act normally. Her session was over, time for home. She had post in the flat waiting to be sorted. Her life didn't revolve around Dr Sam Brocklehurst's good opinion.

"Have a pleasant evening, everyone. See you all back here tomorrow." Sam disappeared into his consulting room as the nurses dispersed.

"He is rather gorgeous, isn't he." Laura sighed. "The best doc we've had here for ages. I wonder what he's doing this weekend?"

"If by best you mean sexiest, please remember you're meant to be a staid married woman, Laura." Faye laughed. "Afraid you'll have to put up with me and Poppy for the Tarka Trail on Sunday. Great you're able to come along, by the way." She smiled at Poppy.

"Hmm, I suppose, but a gal can still look." Laura giggled, waggling an eyebrow. "Even staid old married ones, like me. Anyhow, the way Sam's eyes follow Poppy around no one else has a chance. Denials unnecessary, Nurse Lambert, I know what I see."

Faye grinned as Laura gave a saucy wink.

"And I think it's cute. I don't know why you two don't put yourselves out of your misery and just go for it."

"Oh, what nonsense!" Flustered, Poppy made a dismissive gesture. "Bye, folks."

She ignored the giggles of her colleagues, left Bramblewood and set off for her flat. Still tense, she ached to go for a run on by the sea, yearning for the wide, open space. The fresh sea air and soft sand beneath her feet never failed to be a tonic, but recently she'd avoided the beach for fear of encountering Sam. Ridiculous! Poppy decided this was a knee jerk reaction she needed to overcome. She mustn't let what happened mar her enjoyment of something so therapeutic, especially as she might be leaving the area soon.

Not might be, she corrected herself quickly, would be leaving the area soon! A pity, either way. She had come to Woolacombe with such high hopes. Sometimes life plans didn't work out, that was all there was to it. Poppy took a deep breath and resolved to go running on the beach, regardless of Sam.

The mail lay on the table where she'd left it that morning. Poppy sifted through the assorted envelopes. Nothing to get excited about, bills mostly. Then she took a sharp intake of breath, spying a neat white envelope with Maisie's handwriting on the front. Hurriedly, she slit it open and pulled out a card – a wedding invitation, no less! Her eyes misted. She grabbed her 'phone and tapped in Maisie's number immediately, feeling a stab of guilt. No wonder her cousin had been trying to contact her so insistently. She really should have returned her call – calls in the plural – before now.

"Poppy, thank goodness!" Maisie sounded relieved. "Why have you been ignoring me? And don't say because you've been busy 'cos I'm not buying it."

"Maisie, I'm sorry. Listen, I ... " Poppy found herself interrupted.

"I was worried, Pops." Her cousin's tone was accusatory. "If you hadn't rung tonight, I planned to come to Woolacombe and find out what's going on myself. OK, spill. I want to know everything. And I mean everything!"

"Nothing is going on, Maisie. Honestly, I have been busy, scouts honour – or should that be guides honour." Poppy swiftly changed tack and mentally crossed her fingers, remembering her cousin's inbuilt radar when it came to sussing out problems. "So, you're going ahead with it, then? The wedding to Tim. I've just found my invite."

"Of course, why wouldn't I! No reason to hang around." Ever practical, Maisie continued. "Like I said before, when you know, you know. We don't want a flashy do; just small and intimate, with only the people there that count. And I'd love you to be my bridesmaid, Pops. Will you?"

"Wow, you bet! I'd be thrilled to." Thrown, Poppy blinked back tears.

"Oh no, where's my tissue? Ooh, how exciting! We'll have to meet up for girly shopping trips, Maise, and ... " she hiccoughed, "and everything. The full works."

"Don't start blubbing, or you'll set me off." Maisie laughed. "OK, who's the lucky chap you'll drag along as your plus one? The dashing Dr Brocklehurst, per chance? I bet he scrubs up well. In fact, I can picture him now, tall, dark, and dashing in a suit and tux. And ... "

"No, not Sam." Poppy cut in before Maisie could go on. "Things didn't work out. We're not seeing each other anymore. It's a long story."

"I'm not in any rush." Her cousin's tone changed. "Tell me – now, Pops, or I swear I will be pitching up on your doorstep. I knew there was something wrong."

Poppy sighed, and regaled the news about Charlotte, the pregnancy, and the unexpected sale of Rowan Cottage. After she finished there was silence.

"Maisie?" For a moment, Poppy wondered if the connection had been lost. Then,

"I think you should have heard Sam out, Pops. Talked to him properly that evening. I admit it looks bad on the surface, but ... "

"But nothing!" Poppy could hardly believe the stance her cousin was taking. "He's a player, Maisie, end of. Anyway, speak later, if that's all right. It's been one of those days, and I'm off for a run on the beach. I need to clear my head. Listen, text me a few dates that fit for you, I'll check my work rota and let's meet up for that girly shop."

Thankful to have halted Maisie's interrogation, Poppy donned her running gear. It was a little later than she would normally set off, but the days were long and light at this time of the year. Besides, there was bound to be other folk around – not that she sought company. She had grown used to running alone.

Poppy avoided Lantern Lane and took a different route to the beach – less direct, but it meant she didn't have to pass Rowan Cottage. Once down on the flat sands, she let her feet find the rhythm and, face to the wind, simply ran. The salty air, cooler now, fanned her cheeks. It was an ebb tide, the water smooth and calm tonight. She kept close to the shoreline and revelled in the wide expanse of sea and sky. Out here there was no need to think. Poppy emptied her mind and concentrated on the run. A few other joggers were out, but no one she recognised. It didn't matter. She existed in her own little bubble.

The sun sank low on the horizon, leaving a ribbon of gold in its wake. Poppy felt her heart swell. She loved Woolacombe Bay. Without doubt, it would be a wrench to leave. Yet leave she must if she was ever going to forget Sam and start over without his presence to haunt her. There would be other places, other beaches to run on.

'I'm sorry, Gran.' Poppy whispered. 'I tried, but nothing's gone right for me here.' Not quite true, she acknowledged. She loved her post at Bramblewood Surgery. If it wasn't for Dr Sam Brocklehurst she wouldn't be about to hand in her notice. Sam, Sam – why must everything revolve around Sam! Poppy gulped, and wiped away a tear.

Only one more day and it would be the weekend, she realised. Inevitably, Saturday would be filled with chores, plus a food shop to include items for the picnic lunch on Sunday. Walking the Tarka Trail would be bitter-sweet without Sam, but it would be a milestone: proof she could make new friends and survive on her own again. Although this particular set of new friends she would have to leave soon. Determinedly, Poppy tried to refocus as a wave of sadness engulfed her. Gracious, people changed jobs and moved to other areas all the time, especially young people. Sometimes things didn't work out as planned, and that's all there was to it. She must be grown up about it all.

She'd been running for well over an hour. It was time to circle and head back. Poppy slowed, realising she had gone further than intended. A crescent moon was visible, and the first star twinkled in the heavens. She marvelled how the evenings were never completely dark in the summer. She loved the dusky half-light that wrapped itself round the earth like a fleecy blanket. Further up the beach, she noticed a group of lads having a barbecue. The sense of camaraderie made her feel momentarily wistful. A warm summer night and folk out on the beach having fun. She wasn't part of it, though. The knowledge triggered a pang of loneliness.

As she drew near, Poppy noticed several empty beer cans abandoned on the sand and saw that the group had become quite rowdy. Several of the lads stared insolently in her direction, one giving a cheeky wave which she did her best to ignore. Poppy increased her pace as she attempted to pass them. For the first time she felt vulnerable.

"Hey, babe, want to join us?" Another lad stepped out from the group and planted himself in front of her. "There's plenty of grub. And booze." He held up a bottle. "Come on."

The smell of sausages cooking wafted across the sands, making Poppy feel hungry. Not that she'd be able to eat any, of course. The odds were low that they'd be gluten free.

"Thanks for the offer," her unease intensified, "but not tonight."

Older than she'd first thought, she could smell alcohol on the youth's breath, and he didn't seem to be too steady on his feet. Although that should make it easier to out-run him if she had to, Poppy thought. However, he was young and muscular and she was tiring now. If he didn't step aside, she would be forced to dodge round him. Hopefully, she had enough energy left to put on a spurt if he did try to reach out and grab her.

"Why not?" She heard an antagonistic note in youth's voice. "What's wrong with tonight? Tonight's the night, babe. I said come on over and join us."

"Leave it, Jake." The first lad drawled as he took a swig from his own beer bottle. "You're pissed. The girl doesn't want to, you heard. Let her go."

"Not stopping her, am I?" The other lad lurched forward, swaying. "Give us a kiss, darlin' an' I'll let you pass. Can't say fairer than that. Otherwise, well … "

Poppy trembled. In all likelihood he was harmless enough, but it wasn't a pleasant confrontation. She glanced at the rest of the group, some of whom were watching idly, others disinterested. Would any of them come to her aid if necessary? She wouldn't count on it. She was on her own. Then a familiar voice cut in behind her.

"Sorry, mate, you're out of luck. She only kisses me." As if by magic, Sam appeared by her side. He slipped an arm casually across her shoulder. "So, if you boys will excuse us."

"Apologies." The youth gave a mock bow and stepped back to give them way. "Didn't know she was spoken for. No harm done, eh?"

"Indeed. Let's go, sweetheart." Sam nodded as he steered Poppy on.

She was only too happy to follow Sam's lead. He exuded confidence. Also, it helped that he towered over her tormentor who, Poppy noted with satisfaction, had retreated hastily. Sam caught her hand and broke into a jog, obviously keen to put distance between them and the group.

"Thanks for coming to my rescue." Poppy gasped, trying to keep up with him. She risked a sideways glance. "I owe you, Sam. I admit I was beginning to feel spooked back there."

How had she missed him? Dressed in running gear, he must have left the surgery not long after she had, with the same intention in mind. Although she had scanned the joggers who had passed by, she'd not picked him out – easy to miss on such a wide expanse of beach, of course. A thin sheen of sweat on Sam's brow indicated that he'd been running a while and ramping up the pace to boot.

"No problem." Sam threw her a wink. "And no, for the record you don't owe me. I doubt you were in any real danger even if I hadn't pitched up when I did. Not with the rest of the group around. That chap is what my sister would call 'all mouth and no trousers.' Intimidating, I grant you."

His sister - families. This wasn't what Poppy wanted to think about. She turned her attention to the fact that Sam seemed in no hurry to let go of her hand. It made her feel safe. For a few moments she let herself enjoy the gentle pressure of his fingers. Then, despite the comfort of his grip, she knew she must break it. For both their sakes. Besides, there was no way she intended to go past Rowan Cottage, the route he would surely take.

Right now, the sight of the sale board would make her blub again, not to mention weaken her resolve if Sam happened to invite her in. On the assumption his ex-girlfriend hadn't moved in already, of course. Poppy certainly wasn't into threesomes. Oh dear, what a mess she'd landed herself in! She really couldn't handle it; didn't want to handle it, she corrected herself.

"Sam, you go on." Abruptly, she pulled away. "I'll go back via the cliff path." She pointed across the beach. "It's the way I came. Honestly, I'll be fine on my own from here."

She pre-empted his offer to accompany her.

"You want to take the long route back by yourself after what just happened?" Sam's eyebrows shot up in surprise. "I'm not about to pressure you into anything, Poppy, if that's what you're afraid of."

"I know." Poppy felt awkward. How could she explain that spending time alone with him spelt a different kind of danger. "Maybe it's myself I don't trust. Goodnight, Sam."

The words slipped out before she could censor them. Yet it was true. Alone with Sam the attraction remained powerful. Despite his betrayal, betrayals in the plural, his proximity still sent a tingle down her spine. Well, a drop-dead gorgeous guy like Dr Sam Brocklehurst was hard to resist! Nothing more than hormones, Poppy reasoned – but her defences were low. He stood on the beach, expression unfathomable, as she fled.

It was odd. How could she still feel drawn to a man who had let her down so badly? Poppy felt angry with herself. Yet drawn she was. It didn't make sense and she felt too tired to wrestle with the problem. As she jogged to her flat in the dimly lit alley, she recalled the last job advert she'd seen: inviting applications from qualified nurses keen to work abroad. Suddenly this felt like the solution, and Canada beckoned.

The only way to get Sam out of her head was to put distance between them. A distance of thousands of miles! Poppy pulled a face. There must be a flaw in her DNA. She was attracted to the wrong type of guy.

Friday passed uneventfully. Mercifully, Sam didn't approach her, and Poppy was able to lose herself in the familiar routine of Bramblewood. If her colleagues found her quieter than usual, no one commented. Saturday, as predicted, was taken up with chores. And before she knew it a soft, rose-pink dawn was breaking on what promised to be a glorious Sunday.

Poppy rose early. She showered and breakfasted, lingering over her first mug of tea. Then it was time to dig out her trusty rucksack and find a small cool box. She opened the 'fridge door and fished out her picnic lunch, prepared the night before. She was almost ready. Poppy shrugged off her dressing gown and shimmied into a pair of cream, linen shorts, and a white cotton vest top. The weather looked set fair, with the shimmer of a heat haze. She decided to pin up her hair in a loose top knot, but didn't forget to grab a jumper, too, in case of need. Her gran used to drum into her the speed at which the weather could change in North Devon. Many an unwary holiday maker had been caught out.

Poppy studied her reflection in the tall mirror. An additional something was needed to pretty things up. Yet what? She thought a moment, then added a pair of neat, pearl earrings, plus a chunky amethyst stone strung on an intricate silver chain. Much better! Now to decide on footwear; trainers or sandals? She pushed her feet into an old pair of sturdy trainers, ideal for tramps, and quietly let herself out of the flat.

The early morning air was balmy, caressing her skin like a kiss as she set off for Bramblewood. Aware of the streets becoming busier, Poppy enjoyed the luxury of strolling to her place of work without any sense of hurry. A robin caught her attention, perched on a nearby gatepost and looking at her inquisitively. Head on one side, its bright, beady eyes regarded her boldly. Poppy found herself smiling at the little creature. She'd always loved robins, with their jolly red breasts. There was something about this one.

She paused, watching as it flew down to land on the pavement in front of her. Legend had it that robins were a sign someone was paying you a visit from beyond the grave, a person you had loved and lost. The notion didn't feel in the slightest bit spooky; instead, it gave her a warm feeling.

It was nice to imagine that someone from the past might be looking out for her. Poppy bit her lip as her gran sprang to mind. A wise old lady, what would she make of things now? Hopefully, she would understand the turn of events that had her granddaughter making active plans to leave Woolacombe. Or would she be saying 'don't be silly, girl, stay and see things through. Running away isn't the answer.' It was impossible to tell. Poppy suspected she was meant to work things out for herself. However, at this moment she would give anything to be able to tap into her gran's wisdom. And have one of her reassuring hugs.

'Where are you from, little Robin Red Breast?' Poppy whispered as the bird hopped closer, staring at her with its beady, bright eyes. Tentatively, she stooped and held out her hand, wondering if she could cajole it to settle on her palm. This proved a step too far. The next second it bird took flight and was gone, essentially a wild creature. Yet Poppy felt honoured by its brief visit.

Soon she reached the surgery car park. Laura and Faye were already there, waiting in their respective vehicles. Poppy waved; surely, they must be early! It seemed everyone was eager to make the most of this glorious, sunshiny Sunday. Laura gave a cheery wave back, and Poppy did a double take. She skidded to a halt, her heart thudding as her face grew hot. Swiftly, she blinked and looked again, but it was no illusion.

There was an extra person in Laura's car. Someone whose presence would have made her think twice about coming on the trip at all. In fact, she'd have flatly refused.

There In the passenger seat, gazing straight at her, sat Dr Sam Brocklehurst. Surely, he hadn't been invited along, too! Yet why else would he be here? Inwardly, Poppy groaned, aware it was too late to back out now.

CHAPTER FIFTEEN

Sam had had serious misgivings when he'd been invited to join the Tarka Trail excursion. At first, he'd wanted to refuse ... except that he didn't have any other commitments, and a day out in the company of kids sounded fun. He missed his nephews and nieces. But his reservations were reinforced by Poppy's startled expression on spotting him in Laura's sturdy Volvo. Her colleagues obviously hadn't briefed her. Why not, he didn't have a clue. However, her shock was apparent and Sam felt like a heel. Her amazing grey eyes had widened and he'd seen the exact moment she'd wanted to turn tail and flee.

Except that she hadn't fled. Now here she was climbing into Laura's car, positioning herself gingerly in the space between the children's car seats. Sam let out a breath.

"Morning, Laura – Sam." She smiled at the boy and girl on either side of her. "Hi, you two guys."

"Meet Riley and Mia," Laura indicated her children, "my two terrors. They're six going on sixteen. Faye's boy is called Jack, he's eight. A lovely lad. And Sam needs no introduction, of course."

"Hi, Poppy." Sam cleared his throat and nodded to her. "I've had my arm twisted to join you all. Hope that's OK."

"Don't be daft, Sam. Why wouldn't Poppy be OK with it." Laura tutted. "Sorry about putting you in the back, though, Poppy. Afraid Sam didn't fit. He did try, but legs too long." She giggled. "I suppose you'd have been better off travelling with Faye, really Sam. Only I got here first, and she only drives a Mini Cooper which is always packed to the gunnels with stuff. Right, if we're all buckled up, let's go! Faye will follow us."

Laura explained they were making for Fremington Quay first. If early enough, ample parking could be found there after which they would join the Tarka Trail.

"It's actually thirty-two miles long," Laura released the handbrake and glanced over her shoulder, "but, obviously, we'll be doing a fraction of that. The Trail starts and finishes in Barnstaple. It goes in a sort of figure of eight loop. People can walk a section along the South West Coastal Path, or head inland along the banks of the rivers Taw and Torridge, like we'll be doing. It's great fun. We follow an old, disused railway line."

Initially, conversation between the adults was stilted. Sam thanked heaven for the children's chatter, guessing that Poppy did, too. If Laura noticed anything amiss, she didn't comment. Thankfully, once they reached their destination and prepared to set off on the Tarka Trail, awkward moments became less. Largely, Sam acknowledged, due to the bubbly presence of the three children. Faye pulled up beside them in her smart Mini Cooper, and gave a cheery thumbs up before opening the door for her son, Jack to jump out. Interaction between the kids proved an excellent distraction as they set off on their walk.

Careful to maintain a distance, Sam kept the conversation light, paying no more attention to Poppy than he did to the other two women. At least, that's what he aimed to do. Observing her without making it apparent, Sam was relieved to see Poppy visibly relax and her smiles become less strained. Out in the open air, the hours sped by. All three children were eager to hear the Tarka story retold, plus any snippets of Exmoor legend the grown-ups cared to add in.

After they'd walked for a while, at a pace to accommodate the little ones, a decision was made to stop for an early lunch. A suitable spot was picked, and Faye reached into a copious bag to bring out a red tartan rug. She spread it on the ground.

Lunch was a shared affair, with the exception of Poppy, who was careful to keep to her own food box.

"Sorry, folks." She grimaced. "It all looks delicious, but I'm afraid I can't take anything of yours. My stuff has to be gluten free. I'm a Coeliac."

"What a bummer." Faye pulled a face. "Hey, though! We have fresh strawberries straight from the garden, picked yesterday. They've been packed separately, so you'll be fine with those, no cross contamination. Help yourself."

"Thanks, I will."

Sam had to look away as, reaching for a plump strawberry, Poppy bit into the luscious fruit. A thin trail of juice rain down her chin. She laughed, wiping it away with a tissue.

Sam cleared his throat and focussed on Faye and Laura.

"This is a veritable feast, ladies. I must say it's turning into a grand day."

"Ha, we knew you would enjoy it!" Laura grinned, catching her son's hand as he reached for yet another strawberry. "No, Riley, you've eaten enough, don't be greedy. Remember those are for everyone, not only you."

After a short rest to allow their food to digest, the little group strolled on.

"Look, Mum, an otter!" Jack's excited shout had them staring at an expanse of gently rippling water at the far side of the river. "Wow."

"Isn't that Tarka?" Mia's face alighted with joy as she watched the small creature play, its dark head bobbing up and down. "I hoped we'd see him."

"Not the original Tarka, sweetheart." Laura smiled fondly at her daughter.

"Could be from the same family, though." Faye smiled. "After all, this was where Henry Williamson wrote the story. There are still otters living here along the river bank."

"Wow." Riley repeated in hushed tones.

The day was certainly a hit with the children, Sam noted, amused. They were nice kids, too – fun to be around. Unfortunately, he was no closer to repairing the rift with Poppy. A pity because, if honest, this had been part of his agenda when he'd agreed to join them all today. Careful to school her features into a neutral expression in front of Laura and Faye, he noted the frosty look in Poppy's eyes when she thought they weren't watching. Ah well, Sam thought ruefully, a fun day out wasn't the right setting for any deep heart to hearts.

"Hey guys." He snapped his fingers to grab the children's attention. "Let's mosey on. How about a spot of bird watching? Let's see how many different kinds of birds we can spot out here. I bet there are loads."

"Animals, too?" Jack asked hopefully.

"OK, animals, too." Sam grinned, ruffling the lad's hair. "Come on, let's pretend we're trackers on safari, hunting for trails."

He led the way, going a little ahead of the other adults. Soon he had the three children engrossed in a quest for wildlife. They circled him, hanging on his every word as he regaled them with information about the countryside. Sam grinned to himself. All those forages into woods and nature trails he and his brothers had enjoyed as youngsters were paying dividends now. He had gathered a wealth of experience via his own rural upbringing. This was an opportunity to share some of it as they navigated the last lap of their walk before a return to Fremington Quay.

The women fell back and chatted amongst themselves, content to let him take charge of the children. Glad to feel useful, Sam was happy to oblige. A distance ensued.

The afternoon sped by. All too soon the little group was homeward bound, the children happy but weary. No one needed much persuasion to stop by for a teatime snack at a café close to the car park. Faye bagged them a long, wooden table situated in the window. In the end a proper meal was ordered, the walk having given them all a healthy appetite.

"Wow, this day has been such fun!" Laura beamed, sounding like her children as she wriggled in her seat. "I vote we do it again before summer is over. Thanks, Sam, and Poppy for joining us."

"Yes, it's been marvellous," Faye sighed, "but, ooh, it's good to sit down! I really don't want to, but I'm afraid we must head back after this cuppa. Jack's grandparents are due this evening. Poppy, I meant to ask, how do you like being buried here in North Devon? Not missing the bright city lights too much?"

Sam saw Poppy hesitate, a myriad expressions crossing her face.

"I've always loved this part of Devon. I came here lots as a child." She paused as if searching for the right words. "And I love my job at Bramblewood, working with you guys. But it's true, I do feel a bit cut off, especially not driving. Actually, this might be the right moment to say that I plan to go abroad for a spell. The idea hit me, and I've applied already. Nurses gain such a wealth of experience if they work overseas."

There was a collective gasp. Amid the cries of dismay, Sam felt like he'd received a punch to the solar plexus; Poppy leaving Bramblewood was unexpected news indeed!

"But ... but you just said you love working at Bramblewood." Laura looked horrified.

"You can't leave us now. We've only just got to know you. Anyway, didn't you say your gran used to live in Lantern Lane and that's why you'd always wanted to come back?"

"And now you are back," Faye studied her, "maybe it's not like you thought it'd be."

Everyone waited for Poppy's response in the shocked silence that ensued.

"Hmm, yes." She toyed with her teacup. "True. It's not always easy returning to a place you loved in the past. Inevitably, so many changes and ... well, anyway, I don't have any ties. I spotted a recruitment ad for nursing overseas and thought why not be adventurous, spread my wings a bit while I can."

"Don't do anything in a hurry, Poppy, that's my advice." Faye rose, grabbing her son's hand. "Right, washroom, monkey. Let's wipe those sticky fingers before you get in the car and make everything messy."

"I'd better do likewise with my little monkeys." Laura followed suit. She glanced over her shoulder as she marshalled her own two children. "I hope you know you'll be hugely missed if you do leave. You're an excellent nurse and great to work with – and my friend."

Sam had to glance away as Poppy's eyes filled at Laura's accolade. The silence was loud after the others had gone. Poppy seemed ill at ease again now that they were alone together. However, they wouldn't be alone for long. Sam had one burning question and directness was needed. This wasn't the moment to prevaricate.

"Don't go because of me, Poppy. I'm not fooled for an instant. You do love it here." Sam gave her a searching look. "Listen, you've met Charlotte. Can I ask who you thought she was?" He frowned at her sharp retort. "No, don't say not now, not here. This is important. Please answer."

"Charlotte is your ex-girlfriend, the mother of your baby." Her beautiful grey eyes stormy, Poppy glared. "How you could ever in a million years even dream that I'd ..."

"No, you've got it all wrong, sweetheart. Charlotte is my sister." Sam ran a hand through his hair. "Hell's bells, Poppy."

He bit back a few more choice words. Why had it taken him this long to realise what was behind the abrupt change in her behaviour. Typical bloke, he had been too dense to see the blindingly obvious. It all made sense now, though.

"Look, I didn't realise you hadn't twigged the connection." He sighed. "She had a spot of man trouble and needed a bolt hole. Oh, and pregnant, to boot! Long story, sorted now, and I think they'll be fine. For once in her life, Tizzy seems to have picked a decent bloke. It turns out the main problem was that past history meant she didn't trust her instincts."

Tizzy? Poppy gaped.

Sam frowned again. "Let me get this straight. You thought I'd taken up with my ex for the baby's sake. A baby I'd only just discovered I'd fathered ... and I was trying to keep you warm on the back burner, too?"

"Hmm, something like that." Poppy flushed crimson. "What else was I to think? And I didn't know your sister is really called Charlotte. Tizzy doesn't sound anything like that."

"Tizzy is a family nickname, dates from way back. Actually, she hates it. Anyway," Sam felt irritated, "you could have asked me straight out what was going on. Or didn't that occur to you? Listen, we've things to discuss but my turn to say not here."

She murmured something which may or may not have been an agreement, but Sam knew he had to leave things where they were for the moment.

It hurt to know she'd thought of him in that light, an opportunist out to get her into bed, regardless. A player - the type of guy he had no time for. The knowledge threw up questions of his own. Sam left his tea and rose to pay the bill as the others appeared.

"My shout, ladies." He mustered a grin. "Call it a thank you for today's invite. I've had a grand time." Faye made to remonstrate, but he raised his hand to quiet her. "No, I insist.

Anyway, you ladies were kind enough to share the treats from your picnic baskets with me. In my book that makes us quits."

"Then thanks Sam, but you really don't have to." Faye bit her lip. "Or get our teas and cake if you insist. The kids have all had sausage, chips, beans and ice cream."

"It won't break the bank." Sam shrugged, throwing the assembled children a wink. "Besides, kids make the day. It's been great spending time with yours."

"You wouldn't say that if you had them 24/7." Laura laughed. "My two, at least."

"I'd cope." He chuckled, thinking again of his array of lively nieces and nephews.

The return drive felt sombre. Laura concentrated on the road, the children dozed and Poppy stared fixedly out of the car window. The bomb shell she'd dropped wasn't mentioned but it hung in the air. Certainly, the news went round and round Sam's head: Poppy planning to leave! How far along was she with those plans? Hell, he had no idea if putting her straight on Charlotte's real identity had been enough to change her mind. Somehow, he must make her see sense. Quite simply, she had to stay – because he had fallen in love with her. Hell, he wished he hadn't, though! Right now, she made him furious.

Sam was so deep in thought that he failed to notice as they neared Bramblewood Surgery. Laura pulled up by the kerb instead of entering the car park.

"This do for you, folks?" She smiled in response to Poppy's nod. "Great. 'Bye guys, see you both on Monday."

Sam unclipped his seatbelt and jumped out with alacrity. He stood waiting impatiently for Poppy. It took her longer to extricate herself, wedged between the two children in the rear of the car. Faye's vehicle was nowhere in sight. Sam vaguely recalled a toot of farewell as she turned off the main road a couple of miles back. Where had she said she lived? It eluded him. Amid the slamming of car doors and shouted goodbyes, he and Poppy stood alone together on the pavement.

"Let's walk." Sam made a swift decision his voice terse. "Listen, I'm not going to harass you, Poppy, or pressure you to pick up where we left off – although that's what I'd like to happen. If it's not what you'd like, then I'll respect that. But no more talk about leaving North Devon, OK?"

Expression troubled, she didn't answer, simply fell into step beside him. They walked on in silence for a few minutes. Then Sam reached for Poppy's hand and squeezed it. She didn't resist but when he glanced at her he saw that her face was pinched. They needed a final clearing of the air after which he'd have to let the cards fall as they would.

"Poppy, about Rowan Cottage." Sam heaved a sigh. "I made enquiries regarding a purchase only a day, or two after I moved in. Buying next-door, too."

"Then why not tell me?" He could feel her tension. "Instead of letting me rabbit on like a fool about my hopes to buy the place! Not to mention all that wasted effort trying to raise a mortgage."

Her cheeks burned bright as she snatched her hand away.

"Oh, and the humiliation of being told by some snotty letting agent that I couldn't afford Rowan Cottage, there was already an interested buyer who was prepared to pay over the asking price. I never dreamt the buyer was you, Sam! Can you imagine how that felt?"

It was a fair point, Sam conceded, although he hadn't realised that she had pursued the cottage quite so vigorously. Then again, why wouldn't she have done when it held such happy memories of her childhood. All in all, he had to admit he'd been a fool.

"My offer took a while to be accepted." Sam tried to explain. "Apparently, the owner was overseas and hard to contact. There was a query about when, or even if he wanted to sell. There didn't seem to be any point in telling you until the sale was definite. With hindsight, a mistake, I see that now. But it certainly wasn't a deliberate intention to deceive you."

Sam noted her set expression. Words were not enough to convince her.

"The sale came together only recently." He continued. "You were away for the weekend. A text didn't seem right, and I didn't want to disturb you with a call. I had some hare-brained notion of surprising you with a candlelit dinner and announcing my purchase over the meal, and ... anyway, that scenario didn't happen. You saw the 'Sold' sign before I had a chance to say anything. Not the way I'd intended you to find out, I promise."

Poppy remained silent, giving Sam no indication of her thoughts. Her flat was in sight. Soon he'd be heading off to Rowan Cottage alone. It felt wrong to part with things still unresolved between them, yet he had little choice. He wasn't going to force the issue. That wasn't his style. Sam took Poppy gently by the shoulders, and turned her to face him. Tonight, time was against him. He'd agreed to a late evening session at the hospital.

"I've said my bit." Sam gazed into her grey eyes. The shimmer of tears nearly undid him, but the next move had to be hers. "It's your call now. Think about what I've said. If you'd like us to try again, meet me at Ben's Plaice around seven-thirty next Friday evening. If I don't see you there, I'll take that as your answer. And, if it's no, so be it. I won't hassle you, Poppy. Just don't leave Woolacombe on my account."

He stepped away. It was hard to let her go but he saw no alternative.

Once inside Rowan Cottage, Sam donned running gear and headed for the beach, in need of a blast of salty sea air. He grimaced, relishing the physical release that running always brought. He missed Poppy, yet deep inside there was a smouldering core of anger. True, they hadn't known each other for long, but surely time was relative. After everything they had shared together, how could she have thought the worst of him. She had, though, and the knowledge stung. Maybe one of them should leave Woolacombe.

A fresh thought niggled. Did he really want a relationship with complications, no matter how deep his feelings ran? Maybe, as Poppy said, they were better off as friends. The romance that had blossomed so swiftly had been nipped in the bud; sometimes these things happened for the best. She professed to be a career girl. He wasn't ready to settle down, either, not when he really thought about it. And not if it meant a continual roller coaster of emotions. Things had become too intense for Sam's liking.

He had enjoyed the children's company today, though. They'd been so easy and comfortable to be around. Sam thought about the last time he'd been around young folk –

his nieces and nephews – and resolved to visit them more often. Hell, he could be cast in the role of favourite uncle, the one without kids himself, who always spoilt them rotten. Sam stilled; maybe a move was on the cards for him. A return to his own roots.

CHAPTER SIXTEEN

Unusually, the front door to the building stood open. One of the other tenants must have popped out briefly to buy milk, or something. Pleased she didn't need to fumble with an often-stubborn latch, Poppy hardly glanced at Sam as she slipped inside. Aware he was walking away, part of her hoped he would turn and try to follow her – while another part desperately hoped he wouldn't. She needed space. How had life become so complicated?

With shaky fingers, Poppy slid the key into the lock of her flat. Then sank down onto the small sofa that dominated her main room and reached for her mobile.

"Maisie, is that you?" She gripped the 'phone, suddenly desperate for the sound of her cousin's cheerful voice.

"The very same! You dialled my number, didn't you!" There was a laugh at the other end of the 'phone. "OK, what gives, Pops?"

"Nothing, I … " Poppy gulped, wiping away a tear. "Oh, just about everything! Listen, if I take a couple of days off mid-week, say Wednesday and Thursday, is it OK if I come over? Then I'll tell you. Actually, I've got Wednesday off, anyway, and I'm sure I can wrangle Thursday, too. Let's have a nice girly time and shop for your wedding."

Poppy held her breath waiting for Maisie's answer.

"Yep, that works for me. Sorry Pops, I just had to check my diary, but there's nothing I can't delegate. Perks of being the boss. Now, let's chat. How has your day been?"

At the end of the call Poppy's spirits felt lighter. If she could cope with the next couple of days, soon she would be meeting up with Maisie. Her cousin had a good listening ear, although heaven knows what she'd make of this latest debacle.

Poppy felt restless, despite having been outdoors all day. For the sake of something to do, she spent the evening spring cleaning her flat. Not that it needed a clean, but the other alternative was to go running and she dare not do that for fear of bumping into Sam. Instinct told her it was likely he'd head for the beach, too. It was his preferred way of dealing with things, turning mental energy into physical. Unless he wasn't free, of course. Too late she recalled his mention of an A&E stint that night.

Poppy sighed; it was an opportunity lost. Too late to go out running now. Suddenly Woolacombe felt too small for them both. Despite what Sam had said earlier, if their relationship was irreparable, Poppy knew that she couldn't remain in the area. Miserably, she opened her laptop, aware that a decision had to be reached – and soon.

Monday morning dawned all too swiftly and Poppy was back at Bramblewood Surgery, trying to avoid Sam. Also, she had to catch the Practice Manager, Julia to request an extra day off. Neither challenge went as smoothly as hoped.

"Sorry it's a late request. I plan to visit relatives in Exeter," Poppy cleared her throat, "and it would be easier to have an extra day. My cousin is getting married. She only told me recently and I need to catch up with her before the big day." She added, "I'm going to be a bridesmaid, you see."

"Hmm, it is rather short notice, Poppy." Julia's brow furrowed. "Let me check what Thursday looks like and have a quick word with Faye before promising anything. It may be possible, but I'll need to get back to you."

In the event, Poppy didn't have the extra day off confirmed until Tuesday afternoon, half an hour before her session finished.

"Hey, Thursday is fine." Faye put her head around the door as Poppy was updating her patient notes. She winked. "Julia was a bit huffy, but we've rearranged things and it's OK. Enjoy your extra day off, Poppy."

"Thanks so much." Poppy smiled with relief. "I really thought it was going to be a no."

"Well, Julia does prefer time off booked in advance," Faye said, "but she realises that things do crop up. Listen, I don't want to see you hanging around here today. Make sure you finish on time. Laura and I will sort out any remaining patients if needs be."

Poppy nodded, and turned back to the computer screen. Anticipating her request would be granted, she had packed a small overnight bag in readiness. All she needed to do once back at the flat was retrieve it and head for the train station. Immediately she felt some of her anxiety dissipate. There were too many thoughts buzzing around her head, too many decisions to make that left her weary. A couple of days in Maisie's company was exactly the tonic she needed to repair her broken spirits.

"Yep, that's the one!" Maisie clapped her hands in delight as Poppy twirled in front of the full-length store mirror. The soft peach material swished gently around her hips, a perfect complement for Maisie's ivory wedding dress. "If you're sure you're happy with it?"

"Totally." Poppy smiled as she slipped back into her own clothes. "It's gorgeous! Anyway, it's your day, not mine."

"Sorry that everything's a bit of a rush, Pops." Maisie pulled a face. "To be honest, if you hadn't said you were coming over today, I planned to ring and ask if you were free at the weekend."

"Well, here I am," Poppy shrugged, "so, it's fine."

"I know we said we wanted things to be low key," Maisie continued, "and we do, but it's surprising how much there is to organise even for a small do. Maybe Tim and I should elope instead."

"You'll do no such thing, Maisie Fletcher." Poppy wagged a stern finger at her cousin. "I'll have you know I intend to wear this glam frock. It's nothing but pre-wedding jitters. Right, let's purchase our wares and find a nice coffee shop somewhere."

Maisie was obviously in need of a de-stress. For once Poppy felt like she was the leader of the duo. It was a new experience. She led Maisie towards the till, then frowned, casting her cousin a sidelong glance. Hopefully, she was correct in her assessment of the situation, and it was only pre-wedding jitters. At least the day had been jam-packed, leaving no time to fret about Sam. They still had shoes to purchase, but anything else could wait for another day. Even Poppy found herself wistfully contemplating a latte in place of her usual tea.

Twenty minutes later they were sitting in the window seat of a café in Gandy Street overlooking a newly opened, upmarket shoe shop.

"I reckon we try there first." Maisie pointed across the narrow road as she sipped her cappuccino. "I'm thinking cream, or beige, strappy, with a heel."

"Hmm, sounds good." Poppy nodded, glad to see her cousin perk up. "By the way, what do you plan to do about hair and make-up on the day?"

"Didn't I tell you?" Maisie scooped up the froth from her drink with a long-handled spoon. "Remember my best friend from school, Georgia? Well, she's a qualified make-up artiste now, or whatever they call it. She's offered her services for free, bless her."

"Wow, that's great!" Poppy blinked. "I didn't realise you and Georgia still kept in touch."

"We never lost touch, but she moved away for a time after she got married. Anyway, she is back now. And says it will be her wedding present – she'll do you, too, of course, Pops. She's going to be my flower girl. I did ask her to be another bridesmaid, but she says she feels a bit too matronly for that, what with only recently giving birth to her second."

"A flower girl?" Poppy wasn't sure exactly what duties that involved.

"Yes, a rather old-fashioned term." Maisie puckered her brow. "To be honest, I'm not sure quite what the role entails. Something to do with flowers, no doubt. Anyway, Georgia suggested it herself when she turned down the bridesmaid role."

"What about her dress?" Poppy sat up straight. "Shouldn't she be with us today?"

"Oh, I told her the colour scheme I had in mind. She knows I'll be wearing cream – and she's chosen her dress already. Look!" Maisie laughed, whipping out her 'phone to show Poppy a photo. "Don't forget Georgia is a professional make-up artiste."

Poppy found herself staring at a stylish fall of tangerine froth that not only set off Georgia's dark colouring and porcelain skin to perfection but blended beautifully with the dresses they'd bought. She sucked in a breath. It was stunning.

"I thought flower headbands for you both." Maisie warmed to her theme. "Georgia can be in charge of that. And charcoal grey suits with plain white shirts and black dicky bow ties for the men."

"Very smart." Poppy nodded approval. "Right, we'd better drink up and hit the High Street again for our last bit of shopping. Shoe shops, beware, here come the girls!"

It wasn't until breakfast the next morning Poppy realised that she hadn't mentioned the dilemma over her job. Or said anything much about Sam. As if picking up on her thoughts, Maisie fixed her with a sharp look as she buttered a slice of toast.

"OK, Pops, it's been all about me so far. Tell me what gives with you and that delicious Doc? Come on, spill."

Hesitantly, Poppy tried to explain what had happened, ending with her reluctance to remain at Bramblewood if she and Sam were not an item. To see Sam every day would be intolerable. Yet had she made her feelings clear; indeed, did she even know them herself? Usually one to favour quick responses, her cousin looked pensive. She topped up her mug of tea before answering. She reached for the marmalade, eyeing Poppy thoughtfully.

"There are no guarantees in life, Pops. Oh, I know I don't need to tell you that, but I think you need to stop analysing things so much. You're tying yourself up in knots. Just go with what your heart tells you."

Poppy stared. This wasn't the advice she'd been expecting. Heavens, it wasn't even helpful. Maisie was wrong. Hadn't she gone with her heart before, or thought she had, only for disastrous results to follow! She wouldn't, couldn't, risk a repeat performance.

"Listen, Pops." Maisie stilled, putting aside her toast. "All I can tell you is that your eyes light up when you say Sam's name. You come alive, even when you're furious with him. It's like he's the dynamite, you're the touch paper. Can you trust him? Long term, I honestly don't know. But you can't always play it safe. I think you'd regret not giving him another chance. He doesn't even have to be the one, if you decide you don't want him to be. Be a bit wild for once, enjoy a smoking hot romance."

Maisie winked. "Something to tell your grandkids about. The one that got away – or didn't, depending on how the story ends."

There was a moment's silence during which Poppy wondered if her loved-up cousin had lost the ability to be rational. It certainly seemed like it. She sighed and pushed away her own plate.

"Listen, I've an application ready to send off to an organisation supplying British nurses to a Canadian hospital. I thought of Australia first, but … anyway, the scenery is stunning. You and Tim can come out to visit, see for yourselves. It's near Lake Louise in the Rockies, and the experience I'd gain would be … "

"Phooey," Maisie made a rude noise, "you no more want to go to Canada than I want to fly to the moon, or anywhere else, for that matter! North Devon is where you're meant to be, Pops. You're happy there."

"Was happy, you mean." Poppy felt her eyes prick with tears. "Past tense."

"Stop thinking of Sam as the one, Pops." Maisie frowned. "Rewind the tape. Think of him as a great guy you could have fun with over the summer. Even career girls are allowed to have fun in their spare time, you know." She chuckled. "Honestly, if I hadn't met Tim, I'd be tempted. No, no, don't worry," she held up her hands, "joke, Pops! Anyway, I have met Tim, so that's that. He's the guy for me."

"And Rowan Cottage?" Poppy choked on a sob.

"Don't they say that's what's meant for you won't pass you by?" Maisie smiled. "Sam may change his mind about the purchase. Who knows? But you're still in Woolacombe."

Poppy knew her cousin was right. Suddenly things didn't look so gloomy anymore.

CHAPTER SEVENTEEN

The week passed by torturously slowly. Thankful for the demands of medicine, Sam relished his busy schedule. Yet he paced restlessly, unable to focus on anything constructive when he was at Rowan Cottage. The plans he'd made regarding changes to the property seemed unimportant now. He should put things in motion, arrange quotes from builders, etc., but the truth was he'd lost heart. The purchase felt soured. In the dark small hours when he couldn't sleep, Sam contemplated signing over the deeds to Poppy once the property was officially his – if she'd accept, of course, and not throw the gesture back in his face. Hell, he'd gladly move out and let her do as she pleased with the place, no strings attached. It was only bricks and mortar. If Rowan Cottage would fulfil her dreams, then fine. He'd find some other place to lay his hat.

Sam wondered how Poppy was faring. From a distance she looked OK, the epitome of professional calm. It might be a front, of course. Head down in his consulting room, he'd only caught glimpses of her as she moved briskly between the nurses' clinical room and patients' waiting area. Had she reached a decision, and if so, what was it. The question gnawed at him. Patience wasn't his strong suit, but he always kept his word. He'd given her until Friday for an answer. Sam guessed he'd have to kick his heels and wait.

The week wore on until at last it was Friday. Grateful for a busy surgery, Sam counted down the hours until the arranged meeting time at Ben's Plaice. Against the odds, he managed to finish work on schedule. A quiet word with Andrew had his colleague readily agreeing to stay on and see the few patients who still lingered. Poppy had left already, Sam noted as he strode out of Bramblewood's main entrance. A glance at the time had him heading for the clifftop venue without going home first.

The sea looked rough Sam saw as he walked the cliff path. Gulls swooped and soared as foamy, white topped waves rolled into shore, making a familiar shush-shush sound before breaking on the sand. A few hardy surfers were out on their boards, wet suits gleaming in the sharp light. Despite the choppiness, Sam guessed the water was safe enough for seasoned swimmers. It was an in-coming tide, each breaker reaching higher up the beach than the last.

He strode on, his eyes trained on the way ahead. And suddenly there it was, the swinging sign that said in bold black lettering, 'Ben's Plaice.' Sam pushed open the door, hardly daring to hope. As usual on a Friday evening it was chock full of customers. It took him a moment to look past them to the seated area behind.

If Sam had been worried that Poppy wouldn't show, his fears proved groundless – because there she was waiting for him at the very same table that they'd occupied the first time. Her body language told him that she felt equally nervous. She sat by the window, her gaze on the ever-changing sea. Sam paused a moment, drinking her in. Yes, she was there, but what exactly did her presence mean. It was too early to raise his hopes. An awareness hit him that she could be about to say anything. Spine ramrod straight, head turned away,

Poppy sat still as a statue. Sam stepped forward and, voice husky, uttered her name.

Poppy's head snapped round. A shy smile played around her mouth as she stood, poised to greet him. They moved towards each other at the exact same moment. Stiffly, at first, then all at once she was launching herself into his arms.

Sam held her, burying his face in her fine, silky hair. Words weren't necessary, he realised. They shared an implicit understanding. At length, laughing, they both spoke at once.

"You came."

It was, of course, inconceivable that either of them would not have come tonight.

"Fancy a fish and chip supper?" Sam held her away from him and gave a quizzical lift of his eyebrow. "Before going back to Rowan Cottage – if I promise not to jump your bones, beautiful lady. We've a lot of talking to do and this is a bit too public."

Poppy nodded, her lovely grey eyes shimmering with tears. Sam took her face in his hands and kissed her long and hard, then went to the counter to order their supper. All right, she hadn't given him an answer yet. However, his gut feeling was positive.

What changes there'd been, Poppy reflected, standing under the cascade of warm water as she finished her shower. She tipped back her head and rinsed off the last of the shampoo before working in a generous dollop of conditioner. She had another date with Sam lined up, her seventh – plus, they met to run on the beach together whenever possible. Less than two months ago she'd been contemplating a new job, even relocation overseas. Today the very idea shocked her. Poppy grimaced. True, she and Sam had agreed to take things slowly this time round. It was difficult when even a day spent apart felt unbearably long. Another weekend had snuck up. Sam had proposed another outing on the Sea Nymph to make the most of the latest spell of good weather. She could hardly wait.

Poppy dressed quickly after her shower, and donned a rather daring black, polka dot bikini. With the accent on comfort and coolness, she teamed it with a fresh, cream coloured cotton top and a pair of faded denim, cut-off jeans. Then, after twisting her hair into a neat French pleat, she grabbed a sun hat. She was as ready as she'd ever be!

On cue came the toot of a car horn, the sound floating up from the street below. Sam! She raced downstairs and found him parked by the kerb, engine idling as he waited for her. Handsome dude, Poppy thought, feeling her face heat as she waved. Whatever the future held, she was determined to enjoy a wonderful summer. Her cousin was right about one thing. Sometimes you had to live in the moment and not overly fixate on the future.

Sam reached to open the car door on the passenger side. His warm brown eyes twinkled as he threw her the sexy grin that made her spine tingle. Poppy felt a thrill of desire as her stomach gave a little flip. He'd been busy this past week, putting in extra sessions at the hospital as well as his regular hours at the Practice. No surprise, then, that his five o'clock shadow spoke of late nights and no time to shave this morning.

"Suits you, Dr Brocklehurst." She slid into the seat beside him and pointed to the faint beard growth. "I like a bit of designer stubble on my men."

"You do, do you?" Sam gave a throaty chuckle. "Thought the shave could wait. Instead, I saved time by collecting our picnic before picking you up. Everything is stowed in the boot, so buckle up, sweetheart, relax and enjoy the ride."

"I did offer to sort the picnic." Poppy said. "Save you the bother."

"No bother." Sam shrugged. "Anyway, it's not as if I put it together myself. The lady who runs that little bistro near Bramblewood did it for me, according to my instructions. No need to worry, sweetheart; everything is gluten free. All I had to do was swing by and collect the hamper. It's a lazy guy's picnic. OK, let's go."

He winked and she giggled, aware that Sam was far from a lazy guy. On the click of her seatbelt being fastened, Sam indicated, stepped on the accelerator and pulled away.

The warm sun had given him a tan which only added to his rakish appeal, Poppy thought. She stole a glance at his strong profile, left hand resting confidently on the gear stick as the car gathered speed. And decided to do just that – relax and enjoy the ride. Sam navigated the Saturday traffic and soon they'd left Woolacombe Bay behind. She sighed with pleasure, watching the countryside drift past under a cloudless, azure blue sky.

Things had been going well between them, very well, Poppy felt. Yet she had no idea if Sam's thoughts ran to the long term, or if dating her was just a pleasant interlude. However, if this summer was all they ended up having, she resolved to cherish every moment. Quite a sea change from the way she used to view life, Poppy acknowledged. The route to Sam's Instow mooring had become familiar now. She gazed at the rugged coastline as they neared their destination, aware that no place would ever hold her heart like North Devon.

On arrival at their destination, Sam set about launching the dingy. Once aboard, he rowed them across the smooth river waters to where his precious boat, the Sea Nymph was moored. The cabin cruiser rocked gently with the swell. With his swarthy looks, Sam put Poppy in mind of a devil-may-dare pirate. Clad in a navy rugby top, and torn shorts, she thought all that was needed to complete the picture was a jaunty, red bandana – and maybe a flag depicting the traditional skull and crossbones. His grip was firm as she caught his hand to help her climb on deck.

"Sit and relax, sweetheart, while I weigh anchor. How about we sail for a bit, then drop anchor again down river where we've swum before, and have a dip, if you fancy it."

"Aye, aye, Captain." Poppy did he bade, giving a mock salute. "You're in charge."

He made her feel utterly safe. When Sam said relax, she did so without question.

A heat haze shimmered off the water. They whiled away next few hours with a delicious mix of sailing, swimming, and sunbathing. Stretched out on her towel to dry off after their last swim, Poppy dozed. She was vaguely aware of Sam moving about on deck but took little notice, too comfortable to roll over and find out what he was doing. Lulled by the warmth of the sun, she drifted into a proper sleep. He would wake her if he needed to was her last conscious thought.

The next time Poppy opened her eyes she saw their picnic had been laid out neatly on a portable table, complete with disposable plates and cutlery, plus gaily coloured napkins. Her breath caught on seeing a single red rose in a makeshift vase, plus two plastic champagne flutes. She blinked; Sam had gone to more trouble than he'd led her to believe.

"Hungry?" Sam noticed her move and lifted an eyebrow. "I wondered when you planned to wake up." He threw her a wink. "I was beginning to fear I might have to eat all this grub myself. Not that I wouldn't give it a go, I'm famished! Right, let's dig in."

Poppy scrambled to a sitting position and felt her heart thud. She felt like she was missing something here but what? However, Sam said nothing else, so maybe she was imagining things, and this was no more than a romantic gesture on a hot summer's day. Poppy smiled, taking the plate he held out, suddenly aware that she was ravenous, too.

The meal, comprised of sandwiches, small sausage rolls, quiches, and salads, was a welcome interlude. There was even melon and a dish of plump, sweet strawberries to share for pudding. Poppy ate hungrily, her appetite sharpened by all the fresh air and swimming. However, she couldn't fail to notice the way Sam glanced at her every so often. He seemed edgy, as if poised to say something that was difficult to articulate. What was the hidden agenda? She sensed there was one.

Cold fingers of fear clutched at Poppy's heart. Was Sam poised to break things off - tell her that it had been amazing, she was amazing, but now it was over? Stranger things had happened. Suddenly, instead of feeling hungry, Poppy felt sick. She blinked; aware he was speaking and she hadn't heard. She swallowed. This was it, the bombshell.

"Poppy Lambert," Voice gruff, Sam cleared his throat, "I love you and - -. Hell, I've been wrestling with how to do this properly for ages, so I'm just going to spit it out." He reached for her hand. "You're gorgeous, I adore you, and please will you marry me?"

Stunned, Poppy could only cry tears of happiness as he pushed a small box towards her, a jeweller's box. Inside, on a bed of sapphire coloured satin, lay the most exquisite pink diamond engagement ring. She gasped as he slid it onto her finger. A perfect fit.

"Oh Sam, it's beautiful!" Ecstatic, she leapt up and threw her arms round his neck. "I love you, too. And yes, of course I'll marry you."

His grin spoke volumes as in one easy movement Sam lifted her off her feet. River and sky tilted as Poppy gave herself up to the longest, sweetest kiss she'd ever had.

Sometime later, lying beside him on the cabin's narrow bunk, Poppy woke to watch the slanting sunlight play across Sam's bare chest. One arm still slung round her waist, his breathing was deep and rhythmic, the sweep of his sinfully long, sooty eyelashes indicating sleep. She continued to watch but he didn't stir. Slowly, she ran her hands across his toned torso, stroking gently, letting her fingers tangle in the dark whorls of hair. She revelled in his low growl of satisfaction, smiling as his brown eyes opened.

"You are insatiable, Nurse Lambert." With a sexy grin, Sam flipped Poppy onto her back, and started a slow exploration of his own.

"And a very bad influence for a staid medical chap. I think the sooner we get you hitched and settled down, the better."

"I totally agree, Dr Brocklehurst, one hundred percent." Poppy gave herself up to the blissful sensations rippling through her body as Sam caressed her. Her breath came out on a blissful sigh. She felt like she was touching heaven. "Let's not wait. Let's get married soon."

"Fine by me. Didn't you say your father plans to visit the UK this autumn?" Sam paused thoughtfully. "October?"

"Hmm, yes." Poppy nibbled her lip.

"How about we sort the venue and do it then, after Maisie's do? Short notice, but if you're happy to go further afield, I have an uncle who is a vicar in Wiltshire. He'll fit us in. We can live in Rowan Cottage for a bit – until we need to vacate for the main structural alterations to be done when the two cottages are knocked into one, of course. But if that's not what you want tell me, Poppy. Your choice. We'll marry and live wherever you want."

Her answer was a long, lingering kiss that served to accelerate what had already been started.

"An autumn wedding sounds wonderful." She whispered between kisses. "No fuss, just family and close friends to help us celebrate."

"If we must." Sam growled. "I'd happily elope with you tomorrow, sweetheart."

The next few hours flew by as they made heady, passionate love. After a brief respite, another swim followed, Poppy careful to remove her engagement ring before she dived in the cool water. Carried on the breeze from the riverbank she thought she heard the faint call of a sandpiper. She listened to the sound she'd come to associate with home.

At length, with the tide on their side, Sam weighed anchor and turned the ketch, taking them out of the estuary. They were out into the open sea now, hugging the coastline. The water quickly became choppier. Sam glanced at Poppy to check if she was all right, but she found the increased pitch and toss of the boat exhilarating. Every so often a larger wave would break over the prow. It threw up frothy white spray, making her yell and Sam laugh. After a while he steered the Sea Nymph into a calm inlet and dropped anchor again.

They finished off what was left of their picnic in the mellow evening sun. Here in the open sea Poppy was conscious of the lift and sway of the boat in the water. A neap tide today, Sam explained, occurring after the first and third quarters of the moon when tidal variations were less marked. He reassured her that sailing conditions were good for the moment, but added that they'd need to head upriver before the current grew any stronger.

"Would you believe it, I nearly forgot!" Sam smacked his head and reached inside the cool box. "To hell with that juice. Grab those champagne flutes, sweetheart, and let's toast the occasion properly with Prosecco."

There was a satisfying pop as he uncorked the bottle, followed by a glug as he poured.

"Cheers." Poppy raised her pink tinted flute, giggling as the bubbles tickled her nose. She felt like staying aboard the Sea Nymph forever and never going ashore. "To us."

"To us." Sam held her gaze and raised his own glass. "Thank you for saying yes, Poppy Lambert, and making me the luckiest bloke on the planet."

"Ditto, for asking me." Poppy's voice was a whisper as they clinked glasses in a toast.

Behind them the sun had sunk low on the horizon, washing the evening sky in vivid shades of red. The sea shimmered with reflected colour as the day finally drew to a close.

It was later in the season now. The moon, a pale-yellow orb, was already riding high in the dusky summer night, with the evening star plainly visible below it. Venus, the Roman goddess of love.

Her heart full, Poppy wished she could frame this moment and hold it forever.